COWARDS

DIE MANY

TIMES

Peter Hey

Cowards die many times before their deaths.
The valiant never taste of death but once.

William Shakespeare, Julius Caesar

Also by Peter Hey

When Beggars Dye: A Jane Madden genealogical mystery

A forest with no trees

Once again, a mention for the boxer George Foreman. Remember, he doesn't get too hung up on names, nor need you.

'I named all my sons George Edward Foreman. And I tell people, "If you're going to get hit as many times as I've been hit by Muhammad Ali, Joe Frazier, Ken Norton, Evander Holyfield – you're not going to remember many names."'

I wouldn't stress too much about dates either.

Prologue

A hint, a snapshot, a clue. Sometimes they're all we have. And from those traces we elaborate and build. A vast edifice grows to tower over us. We live in its shadow. But the shallowest of foundations merely prick into sand. And then a wind blows and the earth rocks.

You're not the man I thought you were. You're fake news, a cautionary tale, a fiction, a blot. You're a ghost. I can't let you haunt me anymore.

The churchyard

It was cold, the damp, clinging cold of his youth. It conspired with his memories and his guilt to make his eyes run with tears.

The gravestone was more a marker than a memorial. Barely four inches high and wide, it carried no sentimental verses of love and loss, not even a name, just a pair of initials whose significance would eventually fade, no matter how durable the local gritstone in which they were cut.

'Please forgive me, Lord.'

He spoke the words out loud as he struggled to restrain his sobs. It was a name he had not called upon for years and had left his lips involuntarily. He looked up at the sky and realised he was alone, his soul lost to eternity. He mouthed a final farewell and turned his back.

The churchyard sat on a small, flat hummock to one side of the valley bottom. Dark hills climbed all around and filtered into a sky hung heavy with dense grey cloud blackened by coal smoke. His destination lay across the stream and up a narrow lane that followed the course of a tributary, tiny but fast-flowing in all but the driest months. The village lay between, a long ribbon of two-up two-down terraces, a few shops and the imposing bulk of Graver's Hall. Graver's would be throbbing with activity, its walls vibrating to the tune of the engines within, but there would still be people on the streets who might recognise him. He raised the black fur collar of his heavy woollen coat and pulled his hat down low. He knew he had aged more than his decade of exile and hoped that would prove an effective disguise. In truth, the alien expense of his clothing distracted from the man beneath. He would be dismissed as a visiting industrialist, perhaps a manufacturer of tools and machinery. Local lads did not make good, certainly not the likes of him.

The school was new to him. Much larger than the old building, its stonework still stood out buff and gold amongst the soot-stained buildings all around. Children were playing in the yard, running, jumping and clapping against the chill. The schoolmistress was by the gate, a heavy brass bell in her hand ready to signal the end of their freedom. He did not know her, and her charges were all too young to know him, so he allowed himself to pause as he walked past.

The man's eyes were immediately drawn to one boy leaning quietly against a wall. He looked taller, older than the rest. He seemed to be watching the others as if in some position of delegated authority. His blond hair and handsome features were also incongruous amongst the darker, plainer uniformity of the others. The man breathed deeply, sucking icy air into his lungs. The last time he had seen that face it had been cruelly scolded and burnt.

And dead.

He moved closer and addressed the schoolmistress. She answered his question without suspicion and confirmed what he already knew. The boy's name matched the initials on the grave. It was the name of the body that lay beneath.

The man's mind entertained no thoughts of ghostly reincarnation. He simply nodded his gratitude and checked the boy's address. Again the teacher was forthcoming. The man doffed his hat and continued on his way.

The crystal sea

It was hot, the unrelenting, draining hot of the region undersold as the Warm Coast. Despite being mid-May everything was already baked dry, everything but his skin, which constantly glistened with sweat. He wasn't a young man and his claim on middle-age was becoming increasingly thin. His imposing bulk was going to fat, and on days like these he sometimes thought of returning to the more temperate climate of home. The people he had run from would surely be past caring, but what did he have to return to? It was years since his last visit and even then he had felt like a foreigner in his own country. He had changed but it had changed more. This was his home now, so he simply turned up the air conditioning and tried to avoid the midday sun. And had another drink, the curse of living life as a permanent vacation.

He sat on the terrace of his villa, under the shade of a scarlet bougainvillea that had been coaxed around the open rafters of a wide veranda. Ahead of him, a flat expanse of dusty orange clay dotted with arid scrub sloped down to the water's edge. The lagoon barely rippled. There were days when he rued the lack of waves and surf, but today it was at its most serene and beautiful, reflecting the sky like a vast sheet of glass. The distant edge of the mirror was a seemingly unending horizon of high-rise hotels and apartments. The Strip ran along a narrow sandspit that millennia of prevailing tides had dragged northwards until it stretched some 13 miles. In summer it swarmed with holidaymakers drawn by the contrast between the open ocean to one side and the calm inland sea behind. By night, it glittered like a wall of fairy lights, but its noise and bustle were too far away to disturb the sleepy quiet of this inner shoreline.

He took in the view and wondered how he could ever consider leaving it. He placed his empty glass on the marble-topped table and checked his watch. He yawned. The heat made him lethargic, but that was not the reason for his lateness. He was not new to this game and he knew how to play.

'Terri! I'm going out now. Shouldn't be too long,' he shouted. He waited but there was no reply. She was either asleep or ignoring him. It didn't matter. She wasn't there for her conversation.

He reached for the white panama hat he would once have considered an affectation. He still wore his hair long but it was thinning at the crown. He also needed to protect the surgeon's work on his face. The normally subdued scars shouted their presence if he allowed them to burn.

The villa stood alone on a beak of land projecting into the bay. The town ended abruptly 100 yards away. Development had ceased during the last recession and the sellers of holiday homes still outnumbered the buyers. Whilst isolation suited him, it meant there was nothing but an unmade track leading to the end of the first road. In the winter rains, the deep, claggy clay could be almost impassable, but now it was iron hard and rutted.

He walked past his nearest neighbour, known by everyone as the Shack. The owners had extended it over the years, including a modern kitchen and plumbing, but had managed to maintain its character as a ramshackle beach bar. Back in England he would have called it his local and as a regular customer he preferred to do business elsewhere.

The seafront promenade was half a mile long and lined with tall palms, spaced to offer regular shade. It was early afternoon so there were only a few people on the sandy beach with a handful in the sea. He saw no faces he knew and kept walking till he reached the sailing club at the far end. He didn't sail and didn't like those who did. He was pretty certain they wouldn't like him. It was here he chose to have his more difficult meetings.

He recognised the convertible Mercedes parked alongside a high wall. The top was down and the black leather seats were coming into the full glare of the sun. He suspected the car had been there some time and the shadows had shifted. He allowed himself a smile and continued to the terrace at the rear of the building, where it overlooked a modern concrete harbour lined with boats.

'I'm sorry I'm late,' he lied, his face betraying the true extent of his remorse. 'Been here long?'

A man in his early thirties was sitting at a café table under a large umbrella advertising a brand of vodka. He was wearing sunglasses, white linen trousers and a loose short-sleeved shirt in a subtle peachy pink. That he looked casually handsome was more down to expensive grooming and hours in the gym rather than fine features and bone structure. In front of him was a glass of colourless liquid that could have been mineral water or something stronger.

'No, no, just got here myself,' replied the younger man, before adding an almost immediate correction, 'Well, I was here on time, obviously, but I've been enjoying the view. Very pleasant.'

He adjusted his Ray-Bans nervously.

The larger, older man pulled back a chair and lowered himself down. Even seated he looked menacingly big. 'It's what drew me to the place. I started out on the Strip, made some contacts,' he said. 'Then I found this place.'

'Maybe a bit on the quiet side for me…' The younger man made an apologetic gesture with his hands. 'Just personal preference, obviously.'

'Oh, I like quiet, Adam. You know, a nice quiet life, minimum of fuss. It's too hot to lose your cool, don't you think?'

'Yes. I agree.' The man identified as Adam was avoiding eye contact and stroking the condensation down the side of his glass.

'It really pisses me off when things disturb the... What's the word?' The older man stared across the table but was met by a blank face. 'Equilibrium. That'll do,' he finished.

Adam turned towards the marina and tried to steer the conversation onto a different course. 'There are some lovely boats moored here.'

'You a sailor, Adam? You look like a sailor to me.'

'Well, when I was a boy my dad and I had a dinghy on the Thames. There was a yacht club in Teddington where we lived. One day I hope to have a decent-sized cruiser like the blue one over there. One day, obviously.'

'Obviously,' nodded the older man with only a hint of mockery. 'Nice part of London, Teddington. Expensive. We didn't do a lot of sailing where I grew up.'

'Where was that? Where's your home turf?'

'I'm not sure that's any of your business.'

The evenness of the response somehow underlined its rudeness and Adam's face flushed.

'Talking of business,' continued the older man, 'let's get on with it. How's that fancy bar of yours doing? Cash rolling in now?'

'Look, we haven't hit the high season yet. I'm still confident in the concept. Upmarket surroundings attract a better class of clientele. People who are prepared to pay top dollar. And I'm a good front man. I know how to relate to these people, create a good atmosphere. They want to party, I'll give them a party.' Adam was aware he had started to gabble and breathed deeply. 'I just need a little more time.'

The older man maintained his steady tone. 'Against my better judgement, I gave you more time. I told you it was your last chance and now I want my money.'

'Look, I just don't have it yet. As you said yourself, this is business. There are risks. Investors don't always get the returns they hoped for, certainly not in the short term. But I'm confident we'll get the overall plan back on track.'

'The banks refused to lend you the money so you came to me. I do my business differently. You may be a wet, middle-class kid from Teddington, but you knew who you were dealing with.'

The younger man pressed his palms together as if in an act of prayer. 'I don't have the money. I can't give it to you. Not yet. It's as simple as that.'

'There's only one thing that's simple round here. And it's not me.' The older man wiped his forehead and let his fingers trace the vestigial scarring above his right eye. 'Let me explain things to you, Adam. Simply. I grew up in shit street, shit town. Now I've got a villa on the beach, a flash motor and a bird young enough to be my daughter. She's not with me for my looks, is she now?' He paused though not in expectation of a reply. 'Do you think I'm a charity? Look at this face. Does it look like the face of a kind man, or a total, irredeemable bastard? Sell your car; sell your apartment; sell your wife for all I care. Get me my money or I'll introduce your overprivileged arse to the world I come from.'

The older man laid two massive forearms on the table. Crude, long-faded tattoos darkened the tanned leather of his skin like elaborate bruises. The younger man looked down at his own arms, cosmetically muscled in the gym. He kept his eyes lowered but visualised the large face whose unsettlingly dead-eyed stare was glaring into him. He saw cracks and lines and a sagging jawline. He saw hair more grey than black. He saw tiredness. But did he see doubt?

As the older man walked back beneath the palm trees, the adrenaline dissipated and he began to notice the heat again. His feeling of success seemed to drain like the sweat from his pores. He could still intimidate, but there had been a palpable hesitation. Even posh pretty boys thought they could argue the toss now, for a while at least.

There was a solitary bench in the shade and he sat down and placed his panama hat alongside him. He ran his fingers through his lank hair until he found the bare patch at the back. It felt as if it were glowing.

The faintest of breezes was creating a gentle swell on the surface of the sea. In the middle distance, a lonely, conical island rose from the waters. In this light it looked completely devoid of vegetation. It was a uniform, dull brown. Not for the first time, it reminded him of the slag heaps that had blighted much of Britain's industrial landscape during his childhood. In the intervening decades they had been flattened, grassed over, disguised. In that moment he saw that there was no hiding the ugliness that continued to dominate his own life. Material success and status earned through greed, selfishness and violence. He was a man who had abandoned those he loved and exploited everyone else. Perhaps it was time he thought about a different lifestyle. Perhaps the car and the girl would have to go. He wasn't sure he'd miss them and he couldn't keep doing this forever.

Another favour

'Hello, Janey. This is a pleasant surprise.'

'Hi, Dave. Is it a convenient time? I can always call back later.'

'No, now's good. I was thinking about…' There was a hesitation on the line. 'Well, what can I do for you? Or are you just ringing up for a chat?'

'Do embittered ex-wives normally phone their two-timing former husbands for a chat?'

'Ouch, Janey. That was a bit strong.'

He sounded genuinely hurt, uncharacteristically so: he wasn't the sensitive sort. Jane felt obliged to backpedal, a little at least.

'Sorry, only kidding. You know I've forgiven you for being a two-timing bastard. Well I haven't really, but I'm going to pretend because I need to ask you another favour.'

He seemed happy with the explanation. 'Ha, ha. I love you too. Go on then, ask away.'

It was her turn to be taken off-guard. 'Just like that? I expected you to put up more of a fight. The last time I asked for your help you said it was precisely that, the last time.'

'You're always going to get round me in the end.'

'But I'd got my arguments prepared and everything.' She was suddenly wary of sounding flirtatious and her manner became more businesslike. 'Look, Dave, it's a personal matter this time. It's about my father.'

'Your father? What's come up?'

'I went to see my mother, like you suggested. God, you should see her house! It's near Bournemouth, right on Poole Harbour. There are ferries and yachts, just at the bottom of the garden. It's stunning.'

'You and she got on okay?' he asked cautiously.

'Yeh, pretty much. We didn't hug and kiss, but she's not the huggy, kissy type and I'm the mad, resentful type, of course. But given that, it could have gone much worse.'

'That's great, Jane. It's got to help with some of those demons in your head.'

'But it's what she told me about my father that's thrown everything up in the air.'

'Go on,' he prompted.

'All my life I've blamed her for driving him away. It turns out that childhood memory of him getting on a ship, well, it never actually happened. It's haunted me over the years, but it isn't real. They told me he'd sailed to South Africa to spare my feelings. The bastard had just left my mother for another woman. And left me... because he wanted to make a fresh start and just didn't care.'

'Bloody hell, Jane! That's heavy. Are you okay? Maybe you do need to see the doc again and get back on the pills.'

She shook her head. It was a gesture unseen down the phone line, but it helped her reinforce the negative response in her own mind. 'No. I'm good. Goodish. All my life, I've been looking for him around every corner. But it turns out I was looking for someone else. Someone who loved me. And he didn't.'

There was a few seconds' silence as Dave struggled for an adequate reply. He couldn't find one. 'You said you wanted a favour. What can I do?'

'My mother said the bastard only moved to London, initially at least. Subsequently went abroad. The thing is, she reckoned he was a bit of a villain. I'm not sure what records the Met might have on him from back then, but I need you to look for me. The stupid thing is, if I'd have known all this when I was in the force, I could have checked myself.'

'You sure you still want to find him, Jane?'

'Yes.' There was a hardness to her voice. 'It's just that I'm not going to have stars in my eyes anymore.'

'Did your mother give you any more clues?'

'No, it's all very vague. Though I do now have a photo of him. I can email it to you.'

Dave's eyebrows lifted. 'That would be interesting. You've described him to me so many times. Does he look like you remember?'

'It's him.'

'Full name Stephen Jones. No middle names? Nothing helpful like Stephen Rupert Bridlington Jones?' asked Dave, hopefully.

'Just Stephen Jones. Stephen with a '"ph". That's what's on my birth certificate anyway. It's part of the reason I've never been able to track him down. My mother wasn't even sure where he was born. He travelled around a lot he reckoned.'

'Okay. I'll look. I'll probably find a few customers called Stephen Jones, but I'll do my best.' Dave paused while he thought through how to deliver on his offer. 'Trouble is, I'm on a residential course at the moment. I won't be back in the station for a week. I can't really phone up and ask one of my guys to misuse police resources on my behalf. Not with the prat of a sergeant I've got at the moment.'

Jane felt a surge of disappointment but pushed it aside. 'I've waited all my life – a couple of weeks won't make much difference. My father doesn't have the same hold on me as he used to,' she said, willing herself to believe it was true. 'So where are you? Anywhere nice?'

'Hutton. You know Lancashire Constabulary's headquarters up near Preston.'

'Okay, not necessarily my first choice of holiday location. What's the course about?' The ex-policewoman in her meant she was only partly feigning interest.

'It's for inspectors looking to make superintendent. Lots of political stuff about equal opportunities and diversity, the changing face of Britain. I'm currently writing a presentation called, "Are the poor getting poorer?" would you believe.'

'Doesn't sound like your kind of thing.'

It was Dave's turn to shake his head unseen. 'My boss has been trying to get me on it for a while. I'd been resisting, but then… I had to get out of the flat for a while.'

'Things okay with you and Bridget?' The concern in Jane's voice was sincere.

'We've decided to split up. Well, she's decided and I can't change her mind.'

'Can I ask why?'

'I've not got another woman, if that's what you think,' he replied defensively. 'I know I've got form, but it's not who I am. I know I did it to you with Bridget, but…' He exhaled deeply as if he were too tired to explain.

'I know. I know,' said Jane. 'Let's not go over old ground. I was a nightmare at the time and, well, what happened happened. So, if not that, what's gone wrong?'

'We've not been getting on that well for a while. I can be too domineering, apparently, and I'm unbearably untidy.'

'She's got the untidiness right. I don't remember you being domineering, but maybe I didn't let you. Oh, Dave, I'm sorry, honestly I am. I only let myself hate you 25% of the time these days and even then I don't particularly want you to be unhappy.'

His tone stiffened. 'We both know I'm big enough and ugly enough to get over it.'

'Probably too ugly to find someone else,' she teased.

'Probably. Look, Jane. Maybe we could have a drink together sometime? There aren't many people I can talk to and… who knows? Maybe, and I'm talking in the long term obviously, you and I could be properly reconciled.'

He winced as the words came out and he realised he'd gone too far.

'I don't think that would be a good idea,' said Jane, her firmness cut with a vague suggestion of apology.

'No, you're right,' Dave returned quickly. 'Sorry, I guess this Bridget thing is messing me up more than I want to admit. Look, I'll be in touch when I've dug around for your father. Now I'd better get back to this presentation. I'm staring at a page headed, "Can the police have a role in the childhood obesity crisis?" Seems obvious to me, but I've got to get with the programme.'

Jane was only half listening as he spoke, an unwelcome question nagging in her mind. Could she, should she, ask Dave to that weekend's event? Tommy really, really didn't want to go. It might be kind, but it was surely stupid. Dave stopped talking and the silence forced a decision.

'Okay, I'll wait to hear from you. And thanks again. Love you. Bye.'

The last sentiment slipped out. It was no more than an automatic, historic echo. She felt sure Dave would recognise it as such and she didn't correct herself. She hung up.

The fire truck

'Sold! Sold to the distinguished-looking gentleman with the black moustache!'

The auctioneer brought down his gavel with an elaborate flourish and the room erupted into applause punctuated by enthusiastic whoops and cheers. It wasn't the most expensive lot of the night, but it was the most entertaining. Only one person seemed to miss the joke.

Sarah had her head in her hands. She swivelled her eyes and gave her husband a look of bemused resentment. 'It's an old fire engine, Duff. You've bought a stupid bloody fire engine!'

As well as the black moustache, Duff's face wore a pink glow generated partly by the excitement of his triumph but also by a rather fine vintage port. Though he'd been passing it round the table, it had largely kept going and back to his own glass.

'I know, my love,' he beamed. 'Isn't it magnificent?'

'What are we going to do with a bloody fire engine? Have you seen the size of the thing? You're probably not even licensed to drive it.' Sarah was beginning to calculate practicalities and it was not improving her mood.

'We'll find someone to drive it. I can use it for promoting the business. We can take it to local fetes and parades, raise a bit of dosh for good causes. And my little ginger love…' A playfully naughty glint appeared in Duff's eyes. '…the best thing is – it even matches your hair!'

Jane and Tommy glanced at each other, not quite sure how Sarah was going to react. They'd been laughing but both were suddenly wary of a potential explosion. It didn't come. Sarah just sank back in her chair.

'For the millionth time, you stupid old duffer, my hair is a rich, dark auburn. It's not, and never has been, ginger. And it's certainly not fire-engine red!' Despite herself, a smile was beginning to creep onto her lips. She shook her head in resignation. 'Oh, pass me some of that port,' she sighed. 'What am I going to do with you, Duff?'

They were at a charity auction organised in aid of research into childhood leukaemia. The great and the good, and the wealthy, of the East Midlands had paid thousands of pounds per table to attend. Some had donated lots to be auctioned, others were happily bidding over the odds to buy them. One property developer, who owned large swathes of Leicester, gave a Harley Davidson motorcycle he'd had customised and bought it straight back again. The auctioneer and master of ceremonies was a young American comedian now based in the UK and a regular on British TV panel shows. He was raunchier in the flesh but managed to work his audience into something of a competitive frenzy. Men and women, but mostly men, keen to prove they were rich and successful enough to spend money like it didn't matter.

Duff was largely immune to such drives, but he had dreamed of being a fireman as a boy and the boxy red engine with its wheeled ladder just seemed irresistible. Despite his period of anglicisation, the American comedian insisted on calling it a fire truck and cajoled another like-minded, middle-aged man into driving up the price.

'Are you seriously going to let Tom Selleck over there go home with your fire truck?'

'Okay, Tom. Now it's your call. He doesn't seem to realise this is your fire truck, man. You know you and that moustache just belong behind that wheel.'

Jane and Tommy kept their hands firmly down throughout all the bidding. They were out of their league but were enjoying the fun. They were Duff and Sarah's guests and had been politely told not to ask or worry about the cost of the tickets. Sarah had offered to find a plus-one for her oldest friend, but Jane had resisted the attempt at matchmaking. She also thought it would be an opportunity to thank Tommy for his help on her first case as a professional genealogist. She was relieved he seemed to be enjoying himself. He'd been less than enthusiastic when she'd invited him and she worried she'd browbeaten him into coming. She knew he found social situations difficult but convinced herself it would be good for him. When they'd arrived and he'd sat at the table, looking awkward and uncomfortable amongst the loud and confident people that surrounded him, she'd felt guilty for her arrogance. But Duff and Sarah had taken him under their wings, keeping him involved in the conversation, and he had gradually relaxed.

Tommy had caught the train up to Nottingham that morning, and Jane had taken him straight out shopping to buy a new bow tie. It was to accompany an inherited black dinner suit that was of uncertain vintage, the sheer weight of the material suggesting it was far from new when his father had acquired it. On close inspection the jacket appeared to have been modified at some stage in its long life to be given a shawl collar. In style it seemed reminiscent of Elvis's famous gold lamé suit of the late 1950s and Jane wondered if the alteration could possibly date back that far. Fortunately, it still hung well and fitted Tommy's slim frame like a glove. It later drew an appreciative, 'Cool tux, dude,' from the stage when Tommy tried to slip past unnoticed on his way to the toilets. If the wheel of fashion favoured the suit, the same could not be said of the tie it came with, which was deep-purple velvet and as big as a giant butterfly. Jane refused to let Tommy wear it and selected a slim, elegant model in black silk from one of the few remaining gentleman's outfitters in the city. Tommy was horrified that it required tying by hand – its purple kinsman having a conveniently elasticated strap – but Jane said it had instructions and they'd cope.

Having sorted out his clothing, Jane then turned her attention to Tommy's grooming. His rich caramel complexion was still marred by the dark bags beneath his eyes that were testament to his nocturnal, insomniac lifestyle, but there was little she could do about that. His Afro was starting to look a little wild and unkempt, so the next stop was the hairdresser. Tommy tried to object – the reason he'd let his hair grow was because of his aversion to barbers – but Jane overruled. She took him to a shop that specialised in Afro-Caribbean hair and told the stylist to simply tidy it up, taking as little off as she could.

Back at home and having finally conquered the bow tie, Jane stepped back and admired her handiwork.

'Tommy, you look really, really sharp. You'll be turning heads tonight. If we weren't mates I could fancy you myself... But for God's sake don't touch the tie!'

Tommy had been reaching towards the unaccustomed restriction around his neck. He briefly looked into Jane's face and then his gaze dropped habitually towards the floor.

'You look really good too,' he said. 'I've never seen you in an evening dress before. You've got... Well, you look good in it.'

'Thank you. It's my one and only grown-up frock and it doesn't come out very often. The colour's a bit muted for me, but Dave always liked me in it. We'll probably be the poorest people there tonight, but we won't be the shabbiest.'

Several hours later, the last auction lot had been sold, and the American comedian thanked the attendees for their generosity and made a joke about being a cross between Jesse James and Robin Hood, robbing from the 21st-century rich of Nottingham. A five-piece band made their way onto the stage and started playing covers that would have gone down well at any wedding. Sarah was trying not to think about the fire engine and Duff still had a huge smile on his face. Jane had been avoiding the port, but one too many glasses of sauvignon blanc were pushing her to the dizzier side of tipsy. She was relaxed and happy and life felt good.

'The band are really brilliant! Like really tight,' said Jane. They were far enough back from the stage that she didn't have to raise her voice too much. 'A bit like me, I guess.' She grinned at her own pun. 'But I think it's definitely time to dance.' She turned towards Tommy and gave him a nudge.

Sarah tapped Jane on the arm to attract her attention and bent towards her. 'You dance with Duff. I'm not talking to the old fool. I'll dance with Tommy.'

Jane shrugged her indifference and leant across to Duff. 'Duff, darling, your wife says you've got to dance with me.'

Duff tweaked his moustache. 'I had thought my dancing days were behind me, but how can I refuse such an attractive offer?'

Duff led Jane onto the now crowded dance floor leaving Sarah alone with Tommy.

'Sorry, Tommy, you probably wanted to dance with Jane,' said Sarah, bringing her mouth closer to his ear.

Tommy shook his head. 'No. I'm not much of a dancer anyway and... it might not be a good idea.'

Sarah's tongue was suitably oiled and she probed further than she would have considered polite had she been sober. 'Jane's always been a bit blinkered. She doesn't realise how attractive she is. Maybe you should tell her you're in love with her.'

Tommy looked horrified. 'I'm not—'

'You can see it in the way you talk about her, the way you look at her,' interjected Sarah, softly squeezing Tommy's shoulder.

'Look, we're just friends,' he countered. 'And that's for the best. It works well for both of us. I'm not exactly her type. I'm not exactly a macho man like Dave am I?'

'That might be a good thing,' offered Sarah.

'No. It wouldn't work. I'm sure you can see it wouldn't work. This way we talk online, meet up occasionally. I kind of have her even though I don't. It… It gets me through the night. I don't know if you can understand.' Tommy picked up his glass but put it straight down again. 'Sorry, I must be drunk. Blurting all this out. You probably think I'm a total weirdo. There was a girl where I used to work who certainly did.'

Sarah put her hand on his. 'You've hardly touched a drop and I don't think you're a weirdo. And maybe you're right. I suspect Jane is holding out for another Dave'. Sarah stared accusingly at her own glass. 'Sorry, you probably think I'm a nosey old bitch, putting you on the spot like this. We've all had crushes, of one sort or another.'

Tommy had been reduced to embarrassed silence, so Sarah found herself expanding. 'When I was at college, there was this guy who all the girls fancied. I danced with him once. Just once. Got too close and it broke my heart. That's why I didn't think it was a good idea when Jane asked you. She wouldn't realise…'

Tommy smiled his thanks.

The conversation faltered and they both looked towards the dance floor. Duff and Jane were dancing an impressive jive. On closer inspection, Duff's portly frame was largely immobile and he contrived to spin Jane around him with an apparent minimum of effort, little flicks of his hands sending her turning one way then the other. Their expressions showed they were both having great fun.

Sarah tapped Tommy's hand again. 'Come on. You're not in love with me. Let's show them how it's done.'

Tommy still looked unsure, but Sarah's expression told him refusal was not an option.

Jane woke the next morning around 10:00 am. She immediately wished she hadn't as her head pulsed like there was something hard and sharp piercing her temple. She reached for the glass of water she always took to bed, but it wasn't there. She wondered if having a guest had changed her routine and made her forget, but then realised she had no recollection of getting home so simple intoxication was a more likely explanation.

She closed her eyes and tried to will herself back to sleep but it was quickly apparent it was a lost cause. Dave had always sworn on taking a dose of paracetamol before crashing out after a heavy night, but Jane never seemed to remember. She lifted herself out of bed, checked her pyjamas were respectable and wandered downstairs to the kitchen in search of hydration and medication.

There was a mug freshly washed on the draining board and a note on the kitchen table. Jane realised she had never seen Tommy's handwriting before and was taken by how neat it was. She would have expected a geeky scrawl, but this was beautifully formed, almost artistic. That impression was reinforced by the accompanying doodle depicting its author, complete with Afro hair, waving good morning.

Tommy had borrowed a key from the hook on the wall and gone out to the shops. Snippets of the previous evening were beginning to creep back into Jane's mind and she vaguely recalled trying to make a cup of tea when they got home and spilling most of the milk on the floor. There was no tell-tale stickiness underfoot, so she assumed Tommy had cleaned it up. Guiltily, she poured herself a large glass of water and rummaged around her pills drawer for something to deaden the pain in her head and neck.

The drugs were just starting to take effect when she heard the front door open. Tommy walked in with the happy expression of someone not being punished for the excesses of the night before.

'Tommy, why don't you look like I feel?' was Jane's greeting.

'I slept really well, for once. Alcohol doesn't normally agree with me, but maybe a couple of glasses of wine every now and again is a good idea,' he replied cheerfully.

'God, I'm never going to drink again,' moaned Jane.

'You hung over?'

Jane's only reply was raised eyebrows.

Tommy read the gesture and tried to sound sympathetic. 'You were a bit drunk last night. You wanted to go on clubbing, but we managed to get you in the cab. It was good night, though, wasn't it?'

Jane briefly forgot her self-pity. 'Did you enjoy it Tommy? I felt I bullied you into going. I know it's not really your thing, but we had a good time, didn't we?'

Tommy grinned his agreement and placed a plastic milk bottle on the worktop before switching on the kettle. 'Tea or coffee? And I bought us a couple of bacon rolls from the café across the street.'

'That sounds nice. I think I'll be able to hold one down. And coffee, please.' Jane suddenly registered they were in her kitchen, not his. 'Tommy, sit down, I should be doing all that.'

Tommy waved her back into her chair. 'It's okay. Your need is greater than mine. I was going to offer to cook breakfast if the café hadn't been open. I can do domesticated you know.'

Jane tilted her head to one side. 'Is there anything you can't do? I've discovered this morning you have beautiful handwriting and you can draw. I just assumed you'd be all maths and science at school, not arty too.'

'I wasn't exactly top of the class in sports, and I guess, well, from a social point of view...' Tommy left the sentence hanging and turned back towards the kettle.

Jane thought about probing more into his schooldays, but decided it might be kinder not to. Her focus returned to her own, self-inflicted suffering.

She was feeling slightly better after eating and they took refills of coffee into the extension her grandfather had built at the back of the house. Jane opened the French windows to let in light and air from the small walled garden beyond. They sat at the dining table and Jane, still in her pyjamas, began to laugh as more of the previous evening began to emerge from the fog.

'Duff really did buy a fire engine, didn't he?'

Tommy caught the giggles and they interspersed his reply like hiccups. 'I suspect he might be regretting it this morning!'

'But he's a really good dancer. I never knew. You weren't bad yourself, Tommy. Though Sarah seemed to be monopolising you, I noticed.'

'She's lovely, isn't she?' said Tommy, with a distant warmth in his eyes.

'She is lovely,' agreed Jane. 'But I hope you're not falling for her, Thompson Ferdinand. She's my oldest friend, not to mention a married woman with an errant husband to look after.'

'An errant husband and a fire engine,' added Tommy.

A broad grin broke across Jane's face and the aches and pains of overindulgence were temporarily eclipsed. 'I wonder if she's emailed me this morning yet. We girls love a post mortem.'

Jane reached across the table for her laptop.

'How old is that thing?' asked Tommy with a degree of concern.

'I've had it a while,' admitted Jane. 'Still works. A bit slowly sometimes, I guess, but I'm not a hard-core gamer or anything. It's fine for what I need – just browsing the

Web and when I have to do a bit of typing. I use my phone a lot of the time.'

'I doubt if the operating system is still supported,' said Tommy, continuing to sound worried.

'I'm not sure I know what that means and if it really matters. You know, so long as the thing still works,' replied Jane.

'It means it's not getting software updates. Any security flaws won't get plugged and it could be vulnerable to hacking. I hope you've got a decent antivirus on there.'

Jane didn't feel up to a technology discussion. 'Okay, okay. I hear you. You're the expert, but let's see if we've got an update on the fire engine situation.'

She logged in and opened her mail. Apart from a spammy marketing circular, there was only one new message. It wasn't from Sarah.

'Tommy, listen to this,' said Jane excitedly. 'I've got an email from a Dr Guy Ramsbottom. One of his patients is our previous client, Margaret Stothard. She's recommended me, well us, to help with his family history research. It looks like we've got another commission!'

Tommy's face was still serious. 'Jane, I was meaning to talk to you about that. Maybe you should go on a few more training courses. I know they're running some at the Society of Genealogists right now.'

Jane nodded dismissively. 'Absolutely. I'm sure you're right. But I still think there's no substitute for learning on the job. And…' Her tone became more sheepish. '…you can always bale me out if I get stuck? You did build one of the world's leading genealogy websites, after all. There can't be many of those society types who know as much as you.'

'I'm not sure about that,' said Tommy, partly from modesty but also from the self-doubt that was inherent to who he was. 'And I'm not sure how much time I'll have. I told you last night – I'm starting a new contract. Still working from home, but programming again.'

'Tommy, of course! That's brilliant news.' Jane leant over and clasped his hand. 'It's great that you're feeling up to it. Okay, I promise only to bother you if I really, really need to…'

The trident

Jane arranged to meet Guy Ramsbottom at his home in the countryside some 20 miles north of Nottingham. To get some background, she googled his name and discovered he was a consultant ophthalmologist at the city's main hospital. Jane also couldn't resist trying to see his house using the online street-level images, but it was set back from the road and obscured by trees.

Jane was grateful she'd looked at the map in advance as the isolated rural lane was long and the few irregularly spaced houses all had names and no numbers. Nonetheless, the entrance drive caught her unawares as she came round a blind corner, and she had to turn the Mazda at the next junction and come back from the opposite direction.

The wooden five-bar gate carrying a sign for 'Laynston' was propped open and a short, winding track led through thick hedgerows to an open gravel area next to a small black barn that seemed in the process of renovation. There was space for several cars, but only one was parked, on the side furthest from the barn. Jane pulled in opposite it.

At police college, some emphasis had been placed on vehicle recognition. A good officer should be able to record make, model, colour and registration plate of any car or van involved in an accident or behaving suspiciously. It was something for which her male colleagues seemed naturally equipped, one response in particular lodging in Jane's mind: 'The suspect was seen driving away in a dark-red metallic Vauxhall Astra Mark 5 diesel estate. Smoking a bit from the exhaust, so probably high mileage.' Jane, in comparison, had always struggled. Registration numbers were okay: that just took concentration. Colours were obviously fine too, but that was the limit of her natural discernment. There were silver cars – a boring predominance thereof in Jane's view – red cars and blue cars, but Jane had never really differentiated beyond that. A silvery-grey Jaguar looked much like a silvery-grey Volvo to her. Jane knew her car blindness was largely due to disinterest but made a deliberate effort to learn the insignia of the different manufacturers. Some, like Ford, Fiat and Kia, helpfully designed their badges around their names. Others, including most of the Japanese, opted for stylised symbols. A few even went for obscure mythical beasts like the griffin, whatever that was supposed to be.

This parked car was big and black. Briefly, Jane's mindset was back in her previous life and she felt compelled to try harder. It looked very sleek, almost like a sports car, but had four doors and a boot. There was a deep shine to its paintwork which suggested it had been cleaned and polished very recently and very thoroughly. The personalised number plate gave no clues to its age. The large emblem on the grille had Jane flummoxed. It was some kind of barbed, three-pointed fork. She thought it bore resemblance to a letter W and began racking her brain for a make of car beginning with W. A name popped into her head from somewhere.

She was about to look closer when she heard a voice from over her shoulder.

'Admiring the Quattroporte? Beautiful isn't she?'

Jane turned and saw a short, balding man in his mid fifties. He was dressed in pale blue chinos and a black polo shirt. It was a simple, casual look but somehow it conveyed expensive quality.

'Quattroporte,' she repeated. 'It's not a Wartburg then?'

The man's face slumped into a look of horror. 'It's a Maserati! Quattroporte is the model name. It means four doors in Italian.'

Jane smiled, 'Of course.'

'It's a Maserati,' he repeated, dolefully.

Suddenly reading the man's expression, Jane responded with embarrassment. 'Sorry, Maseratis are good aren't they? I don't know what a Wartburg is, but I'm sure they're nothing like this. I'm not a car person. I didn't mean to offend you.'

The man still looked crestfallen. 'A Wartburg was a horrible, ugly thing built in communist East Germany. It had a 2-stroke engine that literally used to stink. You drive an MX-5. It's a good little soft top, the modern-day Lotus Elan.'

Jane didn't know what a Lotus Elan was either, but felt on safer ground with her own car. 'My husband, well ex-husband, chose it. I chose the colour.'

The man appeared to be slowly thawing. 'You don't see many in green.'

Jane decided to change the subject before she dug any more holes. 'Are you Guy? I'm Jane, Jane Madden.'

'Yes, I'm Guy. Nice to meet you, Jane,' he said, trying hard to sound more positive. 'Thanks for being on time.'

Guy led her up a short flight of steps and a building emerged from behind the screen of trees. It was built of warm red brick and had a steeply sloped slate roof. It contrived to look ancient, yet had an air of newly restored perfection. Its frontal aspect had two impressive gables and a wooden-railed gallery ran around some of the first floor. A wide stone terrace extended from one side and was partly shaded by a long pergola draped in roses.

'Wow!' said Jane. 'Nice house!'

'We've spent a fair amount of time doing it up. Its core is Jacobean, but it's been extended over the years. We've knocked a few rooms into one, but we've still got seven bedrooms,' said Guy matter-of-factly.

They walked towards the terrace, round the corner and then went inside through some open bi-fold doors. Again, Jane's jaw dropped slightly. More than a few walls had been removed to make a space this big. They were standing in a kitchen with a vast central island and units fronted in gleaming opaque glass. There was a magnificent beamed dining room to one side, complete with huge stone fireplace, and a sunken living area with three of the largest sofas Jane had ever seen, formed into a U-shape. Everything looked hi-tech and minimalist, except for the dining area whose decoration and furniture offered a sharply antique contrast.

Jane was about to say, 'Wow! Nice house!' again, but managed to stop herself. She had already made herself look stupid over the car.

'Coffee?' asked Guy. 'Cappuccino, latte, espresso?' He was standing in front a complicated-looking machine, all chrome pipes and valves, that would not have been out of place in a fancy high street café.

Jane normally drank instant, but suspected the chances of finding it in this kitchen would be the same as there being a Wartburg in the drive. 'Erm... An Americano, please. With a tiny bit of milk?'

Guy seemed reasonably happy with the reply and busied himself at the controls. After some hissing and bubbling he prepared two cups and they took their drinks out to a Victorian garden table under the terrace pergola. From there they looked out over a perfectly striped lawn as big as a football pitch and surrounded by high hedges and flowering shrubs.

'Beautiful garden,' said Jane, judging the comment slightly less inane than 'Nice house'.

'Thank God for gardeners,' answered Guy, taking a sip from his cappuccino. 'Always get the professionals in. That's my mantra. Stick to what you're good at. Which leads us very nicely to your own area of expertise.'

Jane blinked at the word expertise, but pushed any doubts away. 'So, your email said you had a specific family mystery to solve?'

'Indeed. Margaret Stothard's one of my private patients. She said she gave you a similar challenge and you did a fantastic job. I must confess I did have a go myself – the TV ads make it sound so easy – but ended up with more questions than answers.'

Jane leant forward. 'You've already done some research online?'

'Yes. And at first it did seem very straightforward. I found the Ramsbottom family tree, but it just wasn't what I expected.'

Jane looked confused. 'The tree was already there? You didn't have to step your way back through the generations?' Her eyebrows lifted as the penny dropped. 'You mean someone else had already done the work and made it public? A relative of yours?'

'A cousin. We've lost touch with that side of the family.' Guy gently stroked the back of his hand as if feeling for the right words. 'My father's youngest brother went off the rails. They had different mothers, you know how it is.'

Jane wasn't quite sure how it was, but decided to let it go. 'Have you been in touch with your cousin? To talk about your family history?'

'No, I'd rather not, if I'm honest. Not directly anyway. We won't have anything in common after all these years. You're welcome to contact her, obviously. If it helps.'

'Okay. Thank you. So what's wrong with the family tree your cousin's put together? You said it wasn't what you expected.'

Guy's eyes swept over his garden and his house. 'As you can see, I'm a successful surgeon. I come from a line of doctors stretching back three generations. I'm aware of the privilege inherent in my… genealogy. I inherited the intellect, of course, but it also takes money to fund all those years of medical training. Even more so the further back you go. There would be no grants or student loans in my great-grandfather's day.'

'I'm sure you're right,' said Jane, wondering where the story might be going.

'But that's the problem,' continued Guy. 'My great-grandfather appears to have had an impoverished background. His father was a coal miner who died very young. His mother was a charwoman of some sort. And yet my great-grandfather ends up in general practice. Where did the money come from? It doesn't make sense. If I'm honest, I had thought I'd be descended from landed gentry, that kind of thing. There was that cockney TV soap actor whose lineage was traced back to royalty, for goodness sake.'

Jane lifted her coffee cup from the table and then, after a thoughtful pause, put it down again. 'It's possible your cousin's made a mistake in her research. A lot of the trees you find online are flaky to say the least. People take the first hint of evidence they find and don't cross-check it.'

Guy looked encouraged. 'I was hoping you might say that.'

The conversation was interrupted by the loud clatter of gravel which sounded like someone had swung into the parking area at some speed. A large engine was revved and then silenced.

Guy smiled. 'That'll be Polly back in the Range Rover. She's one of life's more aggressive drivers. And she does like to make an entrance.'

Seconds later, a tall woman with short black hair and glasses strode up the steps and onto the terrace. She was wearing riding boots and breeches and a sullen expression. She ignored Jane and addressed Guy in an indeterminate European accent.

'I've had enough. That silly little stable girl doesn't treat me with any respect. Doesn't she know who we are?' Her words suggested anger but her tone of voice was blandly emotionless, the monotonic moan of someone who endured a constant battle with the rest of the world.

Guy raised his right hand as if asking for permission to speak. 'Polly, let's talk about that later. This is Jane.'

Polly scanned Jane disapprovingly. 'It's your old car parked in my space, I suppose. Horrible colour.'

Jane was taken aback by the unexpected and unnecessary candour. She knew green wasn't to everyone's taste, but she was also wearing a shirt in a similar shade. And she felt hurt having her car described as old: she'd had it a few years now, but it was hardly ready for the scrapheap.

Had she been prepared Jane would have dismissed the comments as trivial, spoilt bitchiness, but she was caught unawares and raw emotion kicked in. Surprise avalanched into indignation. Somewhere within a vulnerable child screamed, 'Who does she think she's talking to?' Jane felt her face flush and her hands tighten into fists. For a brief moment she thought she might lash out in response. She began breathing slowly and deliberately in an effort to regain control and reign in her anger.

As Jane struggled to maintain her composure, Guy intervened. 'Don't mind my wife, Jane. She's Dutch. They speak their mind.' It was more well-rehearsed justification than apology.

Jane wasn't convinced barefaced rudeness was a national trait but managed to force a limp smile.

Polly didn't reciprocate and turned back to her husband. 'She's the one you'll be paying to trace back the Ramsbottoms, I suppose. I told you, it's a common peasant's name. If English isn't your first language you translate it literally – male sheep's arse. Thank God I kept Van der Bijl.'

'As I've explained before,' said Guy patiently, 'there's a town called Ramsbottom in the north of England. And when, and if, I get my knighthood for services to medicine, you'll happily call yourself Lady Ramsbottom. Silly little stable girls will always know who you are then.'

As the couple bickered, Jane felt justified in mentally dissecting Polly's appearance. She was at least ten years younger than Guy, three inches taller and looked like she might once have been willowy and, perhaps, beautiful. Now she was noticeably broad about the hips and wore glasses that were unattractively functional. Jane got the impression that she would have let herself go as an act of deliberate spite.

When Polly had left them and marched off into the house, Jane was sufficiently calm to resume quizzing Guy about what he knew of his family background. He brought out a laptop and they looked through the information he had so far unearthed. He took a pragmatic attitude when Jane explained she couldn't guarantee to find the financial source of his great-grandfather's medical training but would check the accuracy of his family tree and take it back as far as she could.

Jane climbed back into her car feeling optimistic and excited. The commission was interesting and, hopefully, well within her capabilities. Her mood dropped slightly when she realised she was boxed in by a very large white 4X4. It took some very careful manoeuvring to effect her escape. She didn't think Guy would forgive her if she dented his Maserati. And Polly would probably demand a new one if the Range Rover got scratched. Jane was tempted nonetheless.

The minister's wife

In London it had just been announced that Queen Victoria had given birth again. Far away in the northern county of Lancashire, the industrial revolution was driving a dramatic rise in population, and the dioceses were subdividing parishes and building new churches to accommodate the growing number of souls potentially lost to secularism or dissent. Some funding was provided by a Westminster parliament who saw the moral guidance of the established church as a bulwark against the bloody revolts that had occurred on the other side of the channel. In more remote areas, the Anglicans had also responded to competition from the non-conformists who had built their own houses of God closer to the new communities serving the mills, quarries and mines in the moorland hills. Accordingly, St Michael's had been constructed above the narrow, winding road that had once led through isolated farmsteads, but was now lined with industrial sheds and cramped housing. In the early Norman style with a squat square tower adorned by circular turret housing the stairwell, its fresh stonework betrayed its lack of age, but it would soon darken and take on the appearance of timeworn permanence. The living was not generous and could not attract a university-educated clergyman. The vicar was therefore not from the southern gentry but a schoolmaster's son raised in the city of Manchester. Reverend Ralph Kershaw was slightly built and softly spoken, and sought gravitas through long side whiskers that some of the less respectful villagers likened to spaniel's ears hanging besides his otherwise clean-shaven face. One of his main challenges was to prevent further attrition to the nearby Baptist chapel which had stood for nearly 50 years and was already straining at the seams of its more prosaic architecture. Despite his youthful enthusiasm, he was having only limited success. Often he would be obliged to carry out the legal formalities of marriage, but the newly wedded couples would not return to his pews or bring their children to be christened at his font.

Harry Richards was an altogether more dignified-looking man, straight backed, tall and greying at the temples. To northern ears his Somerset accent sounded commanding and aristocratic, but his own humble origins were betrayed by the occasional rural note. His father had once been a garden labourer before establishing a successful business bottling ale and liquor. The profits funded a modest schooling for the young Harry, but his later conversion to teetotalism meant it was not something he chose to relate. Finding work as an apprentice bookbinder, his dedication to his local church led to his being recommended for a place at the Bristol Baptist College, where the aim was to supply 'a succession of able and evangelical ministers' for 'destitute' congregations. His studies included Hebrew, Latin, Greek and mathematics, as his tutors sought to transform enthusiastic and committed preachers into scholars on a par with their brethren in other denominations. After four years, Harry was deemed ready to be sent out and was allocated a church in the wilds of the Pennine hills. It was not a mission he intended to take alone. He had already found a wife, the daughter of a well-to-do farmer who owned land on the outskirts of the city. She was devout, literate and with a great love of music and the arts. That she was plain was of little consequence. And her headstrong nature was something he thought he could tame.

Unlike his Anglican counterpart, Harry Richards did not enjoy a spacious vicarage next to his church, but was accommodated in a terraced cottage overlooking the small river that flowed through the village. The house was only slightly larger than the average, but he and his wife were able to employ a general servant who lived in.

After ten years of marriage, Elizabeth Richards remained childless but devoted her energies to her husband's ministry, in particular to the Sunday school that provided the only education available to most local children. It was a source of great pride to the couple and had helped attract many parents to the Baptist congregation.

'I think it's going to be a fine day. I may do some sketching later. Do you think my little apprentice will be able to come?' shouted Elizabeth as she gazed out of the window onto the moors beyond.

Her husband did not respond initially, but waited until he had joined her in the front parlour. 'Elizabeth, my dear, his father will need him to work. You know that.'

'But he's such a gifted boy. He shouldn't be pushing tubs of coal around, or whatever it is that dreadful man will have him doing. He's got such fine, elegant hands—'

'Elizabeth. Listen to yourself. His father is a simple man trying to keep a roof over his family's head.'

'But the boy's so young!'

Harry Richards softly placed his hands on his wife's shoulders. 'Please, my love. These people are among the poorest of Christ's flock. Toil is their lot in life. Their reward awaits them in paradise.'

'But when I was his age—'

'When you were his age, your father indulged you. You were the apple of his eye.' Harry squeezed her shoulders with an affection that was, in itself, largely paternal. 'He wanted you to be a fine young lady, to play piano, to read poetry, to sew. He saw you had a talent for painting and drawing and encouraged it. He could afford to, and to him, it was a source of pride and pleasure. The people who live in these hills have little time for pleasure. And they must take their pride in their work and in their devotion to the Lord. They must know their place in His great scheme.'

Elizabeth had been staring into her husband's face, but now dropped her gaze. 'You're sermonising again,' she said, somewhat sullenly.

He placed two fingers under her chin and raised it gently. 'That's my lot in life,' he replied.

Elizabeth slipped her head away and returned her focus to the window. 'The stream's looking wild. I hear it broke its banks down in the valley. Flooded the track of the new railway.'

A threatening storm seemed to have passed and Harry smiled. 'We've suffered some heavy rain these last weeks. The cotton likes it wet, of course, and the sheep don't seem to mind. Though when it's coming at you sideways on the wind, it's as if you're immersed in Noah's flood itself,' he laughed.

Elizabeth watched a distant hawk hovering in the sky before it darted down into the hillside. 'Do you think we'll ever be able to move back home?' she mused. 'It gets so bleak here. And I could be a great help to my mother now she's on her own.'

'Again, you know the answer to that, my love. We go where we are needed. And that, for now, is here. It is these good people that we must help.'

Elizabeth turned back sharply towards her husband, her earlier notion swamping her thoughts again and causing her emotions to flare. 'But the boy can do so much more than digging out stupid rocks, or tending to those infernal mechanisms in the mill!' She raised a hand apologetically but persisted in a quieter, pleading voice. 'He reads and writes so beautifully. Numbers came so easily to him. And he draws like an angel. He'll just end up married to an ugly local girl and grind himself to death providing for a houseful of children. He deserves more.'

Harry sighed. 'Why is he singled out and not the rest of the young lads in your schoolroom? Be truthful now. In your heart of hearts, is it not because his handsome features have won you over and hold your affections as if he were your own son?'

'That's not fair!' burst out Elizabeth, as tears began to well in her eyes. 'Please do not hold my own barrenness against me, husband. I have tried to be a true and proper wife—'

'You have been a fine wife,' confirmed Harry quickly. 'And if the good Lord has chosen not to bless us with child, ours is not to question His wisdom.'

'Why do we bother teaching them to read and write if they are just going to labour like their fathers?' Elizabeth snapped, her hurt seeking deflection.

'Come now,' said Harry evenly. 'We have discussed this often enough. It is so they can study the scriptures, and gain enlightenment and comfort from the word of the Lord.'

'But in this case, given his God-given gifts, could we not seek to intervene, to help him find a better life. The other boys bully him because he is different anyway.'

Harry's eyes looked up at the ceiling as if seeking divine guidance. 'You are making him soft in a world where he needs to be hard.'

'That stupid Hargreaves girl has set her eyes on him. Her father is a nasty, brute of a man. Is that the kind of hard you had in mind?' responded Elizabeth defiantly.

Harry's patience had expired. 'Enough!' he shouted, before lowering his voice if not his temper. 'I forbid you to interfere with the Ramsbottom boy any further. You are giving him false hopes. Expectations that will be dashed and cause him nothing but pain. Let him be bullied! It will make a man of him. Let him marry an ignorant, ugly girl! She, at least, might be obedient. Let him work himself to death! It will take him sooner to paradise.' Harry paused and then spoke his final words slowly and forcibly. 'Let him be.'

'Excuse me, sir,' interrupted another voice nervously.

Reverend Harry Richards turned his head to see a thin young woman standing by the parlour door. 'What is it, child?' he said calmly.

'Apologies, sir, but it's gone two o'clock. You asked me to remind you of the burial this afternoon.'

'Indeed. Thank you. You may leave us now.'

The maidservant obediently made her way back towards the scullery, and Harry addressed his wife once more. 'I trust you will be attending the service, my love?'

Elizabeth faintly shook her head. 'Forgive me if I don't. I'm not sure if I can bear the funeral of yet another poor infant. I might not be able to retain my composure. I know you wouldn't want that.'

'Quite so. I will make your apologies. This time at least.'

Harry thought about taking his wife's hand as a gesture of comfort and consolation, but decided distance was the better policy. He left the room.

The boy who was born twice

Back home in Nottingham, Jane was going through the small mountain of post that had built up over just a couple of days. As she suspected, there was nothing of any great interest. Her shredder had packed up, and she was reduced to tearing her personal details out of any correspondence not addressed to 'The Householder' or 'The Occupant' before dumping it in her recycling. She vaguely recalled someone on TV once promising that technology would deliver a paperless society. Somehow the information revolution seemed to have had the opposite effect.

Admin completed, she opened her laptop and turned her thoughts to Guy Ramsbottom's family background.

Guy had known his paternal grandfather and recalled many details of his life, including his date and place of birth. Guy's personal knowledge of his great-grandfather was limited to his name, George Ramsbottom, and the fact that he had been a GP with a practice based in Manchester. Guy had one photograph of George, depicting a successful, confident man in late middle age, dressed like an Edwardian gentleman complete with fine moustache. He was markedly more handsome than his great-grandson, though the gene for a receding hairline was starting to make an appearance. There was nothing in his face or demeanour that suggested he'd had to battle his way up from the lower orders.

Jane found the online family tree that had been created by Guy's cousin. It included over 2,000 people, branching out widely and reaching back into the 17th century. It had evidently been worked on over a number of years. Jane homed in on the Ramsbottoms and found George being born in 1872 and dying in 1945. On the 1911 census, he was established as a doctor of medicine with a young family and two servants. His then home still stood and Internet images showed it to be an imposing Victorian villa now slightly run down and divided into flats.

George's earliest appearance on the ten-yearly census records was in 1881. He was an eight-year-old scholar with five older siblings, most of whom had occupations Jane recognised as being associated with the cotton industry. George's youngest brother was listed as an 11-year-old 'doffer'. That was new to Jane, but a quick search established it involved changing the bobbins on a spinning frame, presumably the lowest unskilled work in a mill. Head of the household was mother, Sarah Ramsbottom, a widow aged 48.

Along with others, they were living in a property called Father Richard Barn. Jane found an online copy of a contemporaneous Ordnance Survey 25 inch map which provided sufficient detail to identify its specific location. It was on a narrow lane outside the village of Blackwell Holme in the Lancashire moors. On the hillside above the so-called barn was a small coal mine and almost directly below was a cotton mill. Switching to a modern satellite image, there was still some kind of building on the site of the Ramsbottoms' home, but the mine and mill were long gone, leaving ghostly traces on the landscape that could only be interpreted through reference to the old map.

When Jane looked back ten years to the 1871 census, she found the family already living in the same place. The head then was given as Thomas Ramsbottom, age 35, an 'Eng. Ast. (Cotton Mill)', a title she struggled to interpret. One glaring anomaly was the re-appearance of George Ramsbottom, somehow aged 14. Guy's great-grandfather wasn't even supposed to be born in 1871. Could his birth date be wrong? Could he really have been much older than he later claimed?

Jane checked the records and the confusion was quickly resolved. There turned out to have been two brothers called George. The elder had died early in 1872. When another boy was born later the same year, his grieving parents chose the same name for their youngest and final offspring. It was something that might be considered rather inappropriate today, but Jane had seen the practice before with Victorian families. It was a time when high childhood mortality forced different sensibilities on the remembrance of those who had been lost.

Loss was something Sarah Ramsbottom was to become familiar with. Having buried her eldest son in 1872, her husband followed the year after. Oddly, Thomas Ramsbottom's death had been registered in a town some eight miles distant. Jane wondered why he had been away from home, but there were several possible explanations from work to hospitalisation and she let it go for the time being. Another slight inconsistency with Thomas was a switch in his career. On earlier censuses his occupation was given as coal miner, not the mysterious Eng. Ast. of a cotton mill.

At first sight, the records corroborated the story Guy had related to Jane. His great-grandfather, George, had been born into a poor family where children were obliged to do low-paying work from the age of 11, if not before. George's father, Thomas, had been a miner turned millworker who died at 37, leaving behind a widow, Sarah, with six children including a young baby. In 1881 George was described as a 'scholar', but Jane knew that was just the standard census term for a school-age child. Moving forward ten years to 1891, Sarah was still an unmarried widow living at the same address, the intriguingly named Father Richard Barn, but George was not with his mother by then, certainly not on the night of the census. He re-emerged in 1901 as a young doctor residing in the home of a more senior colleague. So how had his transformation been financed? There appeared to be no money anywhere in his wider family. He came from a background of manual labourers, miners and mill workers, all earning a subsistence living in the harsh, unforgiving world of 19th-century industrialised England. There was no evidence of social mobility in the later occupations of his siblings. Jane could see nothing to say George's mother had ever been a charwoman as suggested by Guy, but she was described as a housekeeper on the last census before her death. Sarah Ramsbottom had lived to her mid-sixties, probably long enough to see her son qualify as a doctor, but not to enjoy any share in his success.

Jane had not found any immediately obvious errors in Guy's cousin's research, but there did appear to be an absence of detailed birth, marriage and death certificates to back up some of the assumptions. Jane busied herself ordering the key documents and then dug deeper into the tree looking for branches that had been missed or didn't quite link up.

The old DS

Jane was sitting at her dining table, looking out over her back garden. Her laptop was open and next to it was the morning's fourth cup of coffee. It was empty and she was trying to decide whether to make another. She knew it had a tendency to make her jumpy, but its comforting warmth also helped her concentrate. Or perhaps it didn't. Perhaps she should avoid getting up and going to the kitchen, and make a decision on one of Guy Ramsbottom's antecedents instead. Jane was back in the late 18th century, a time before nationwide civil registration, and the parish registers were inconclusive. The family had obviously moved from one part of Lancashire to another, but there were at least two possible places they could have come from. Guy's cousin had seemingly just opted for the nearest, but at times she did seem more interested in the numbers game, building as large a tree as possible, even when the evidence was weak. There was another instance where she'd continued three further generations behind a supposed ancestor whom Jane had found to have died at the age of six.

Jane had just typed a note summarising her questions when her phone rang. Dave's picture appeared on the screen.

'Hi Dave. You back home now?'

'Yeh. Mind you, the place looks ransacked now that Bridget's moved out.'

'How are you coping with that?'

'I'm coping,' said Dave unconvincingly. 'Look, I've got somewhere with your dad.'

'Really?' Jane's voice rose in anticipation.

'There was a vague sniff in the records and the investigating officer was an old DS who was my skipper when I first became a detective. You probably don't remember Bill Cropper? "Cropper the copper" we used to call him.'

'That's the kind of sophisticated humour a girl would remember, but no, he doesn't ring any bells.'

'Well, he's long been retired, but there's nothing an ex-plod likes more than to talk about old times. Back when he had a bit of clout. It'll be me in a few years. Anyway, I phoned him up and we went for a beer in the Black Dog in Hammersmith. It's a bit poncy now, but it was a boozer we used to frequent back in the day.'

The in-vogue expression 'back in the day' somehow always grated on Jane, but she ignored it. 'He knew my dad?'

'He knew a villain called Steve Jones. We're going back a while, but he could picture a huge bloke with an eye patch. That kind of narrows it down.'

Jane's excitement was cut with disappointment. 'So he was a proper villain then?'

'Well, yeh, though we could never pin anything on him. He had some unpleasant friends and was involved in shady business deals. The sort where people end up in hospital, you know the kind of thing.'

'What happened to him?'

'Cropper reckons he might have stood on the toes of a bigger, nastier player and had to move abroad. The point is, Cropper remembers his sister more.'

Jane knew nothing of her father's family, but found herself genuinely surprised. 'My dad had a sister?'

'Stacy Jones. Convictions for criminal damage and assaulting a police officer. And the rest. Cropper reckons he dealt with some real hard men in his time but she was up there with the scariest. I think he was only half-joking.'

'Do you know where she is now?'

'Still living in west London. One of the dodgier estates out near the airport. I've got her address.'

'That's sorted,' Jane said decisively. 'I'm going to see her. She must know if he's still alive and how to contact him.'

Dave's enthusiasm was becoming muted as his ex-wife's climbed. 'Maybe I should come with you,' he suggested tentatively.

'Why?'

'Because she may not welcome a visit from her brother's…' Dave searched for a euphemism. '...long-lost daughter.'

'Dave, she's my aunt. And I can look after myself. I'm an ex-policewoman and I'm not going to be intimidated because someone's a bit rough. Maybe I won't get a great welcome but I'll cope.'

'We could—'

'No. Thank you, but no. If I turn up with a six-foot-four-inch copper she really will slam the door in my face. Now, please, I really am grateful for everything you've done, but please may I have that address?'

'I'm worried you'll make yourself ill again, Janey. You know you don't always react well to things. At least if I'm there—'

'Dave, thanks for caring, but I'm not your problem anymore, And I'll be fine. I explained – my dad doesn't have the same hold on me anymore. Now, give me the address and stop fretting...'

Family reunion

Jane thought about writing to the woman who was likely her aunt but quickly discounted the idea. It was too easy to throw letters in the bin or file them under 'Not sure. I might think about it later.' Jane was too impatient to wait and turning up on someone's doorstep meant they couldn't simply ignore you. They could swear at you and tell you to get lost, and Stacy Jones sounded like the type who might, but at least Jane would have seen her face-to-face. Jane felt she might recognise something of her father and then she could have confidence she was on the right track.

Jane pulled up in her car around 9:30 am. She had woken very early, but delayed her departure so as to miss the worst of London's rush hour. There seemed little point spending an hour sitting in traffic on the M25 when you don't know the person you're visiting will be in, the obvious disadvantage of arriving unannounced. If necessary, Jane would talk to the neighbours and was prepared to hang around to the evening unless she was told Stacy Jones was away.

The house faced onto a large and irregularly shaped playing field. There were a few mature trees on its edges and it had been recently mown, but it still seemed scruffy and poorly maintained. A football pitch had once been marked out, but one of goals was now twisted and leaning and the other had gone completely. A dilapidated wooden fence ran down two sides and had been extensively tagged by local youths, only interested in marking their territory rather than aspiring to be Banksy. The open space had once been the site of an old jam factory and stood at the centre of a sprawling estate that dated from the 1950s, with additions and refurbishments in the '80s and '90s. The buildings were mostly low rise with a few narrow blocks of four-storey flats standing in regimented, parallel line. Along their ends was a parade of shop fronts, but over half had no signage and their shutters were down. Grassy areas were dotted everywhere and Jane imagined it would have come across as a garden city on the architect's drawing board. Now, years of neglect by council and residents alike gave it an air of run-down sadness, and the sort of place you wouldn't dare leave a soft-top car parked overnight.

Jane made sure the Mazda was locked and walked up the short path to the front door. It was a modern white PVC design and identical to that on the adjoining houses. She pressed the bell; nothing seemed to happen so she gave a sharp tap, tap with the door knocker. After a short delay a blurred figure appeared behind the arch of frosted glass panels. The door opened.

'Yes?' It was an accusation rather than a greeting.

Jane hesitated as she studied the woman in front of her. She looked to be in her early sixties, but her age could have been a good five years either side. She had short hair dyed an unnatural shade of chestnut, and the harsh red tinge emphasised the lined greyness of her skin. Her pallor said heavy smoker, an assessment confirmed by the stench of cigarettes that hung in the air around her. She was tall, though not as tall as Jane, and solidly built more than fat. Her face had large, almost masculine features that Jane recognised. They were her own. It was as if she were looking into a fairground mirror that distorted your reflection and showed what awaited you should you lead a hard life.

'Look, what do you want?' The woman's tone had softened as if she too had seen something familiar in the stranger on her doorstep.

'My name's Jane Madden. I think...' The words she had rehearsed in the car escaped her. '...I think you might be my father's sister. I lost touch with him as a child. Sorry, I should have asked – are you Stacy Jones?'

'That's me.' Jane's aunt leant forward and looked both ways down the street, searching for accomplices or prying eyes. 'I always wondered if you'd turn up one day,' she mumbled thoughtfully. 'I suppose you'd better come in.'

Jane was shown into the hallway and found herself looking for a staircase to the upper level. It seemed to be missing though there was the sound of a television coming through the ceiling.

Jane looked upwards. 'Is someone else in?'

'No, that's Terry in the maisonette above. Deaf as a post, the old git. His door's hidden down the side. They wanted these to look like proper houses but they're not. Does me though – now I'm on my own.' There was now an audible wheeze in the older woman's voice.

'Do you have children?' asked Jane.

'Why exactly are you here? I mean, what do you want?' returned her aunt, clearly uninterested in small talk.

By now they were in a cramped sitting room with a scuffed grey-leather three piece suite and a bulky, old-fashioned TV that looked like it would take two people to lift it. A half-full ashtray sat on an ugly side table pretending to be mahogany. Jane's aunt pointed to the sofa and lowered herself into the chair.

Jane sat down herself before replying. 'I know almost nothing about my father. I don't even know if he's still alive. I've tried looking, but there must be thousands of men called Stephen Jones. I just want to get in touch, I guess. Assuming he's willing. And alive.'

The older woman's expression still maintained its sternness. 'The bastard pissed off and left you. Getting even's a family trait. And with a past like his you could easily stitch him up with something. You're a policewoman, aren't you?'

'No, not anymore.' Jane felt wrong-footed and confused. 'How did you know that?'

'Not anymore?' probed her aunt.

'No. The police force and I had a… a falling out.' Jane's discomfort was in danger of making her reveal more than she wanted. She stopped herself before she went any further. 'I do family-history research these days. I'm a genealogist who knows virtually nothing about her own father. Look, how did you know I was a policewoman?'

'They have a smell about them, don't they? Something about the way they stand on your doorstep. Had a good few round my place over the years. The women are the worst. Gave one a good slap once. Hate to give you one too.'

Jane returned the cold stare. 'I warn you, I slap back. Hard. Sometimes too hard.'

Stacy Jones sank back into her chair and the first hint of warmth cracked her face. 'Well, maybe I've met my match. You're a big strong girl. Your father's daughter in more ways than one. He'd be proud of you. If he gave a shit that is.'

'So he is alive?'

'Last I heard. Buggered off abroad years ago. My brother's not the type to exchange Christmas cards.'

'Where abroad?'

'Spain. That's all I know. Costa del Sol or Costa Brava, one of them Costas anyway. Where you sun yourself by the pool all day and drink yourself stupid. He'd be good at that.'

Jane suspected she wasn't getting the full story and decided to try a different approach in the hope her aunt might soften and become more trusting. 'What can you tell me about my father's family? Your family. Our family. I know absolutely nothing.'

Stacy huffed contemptuously. 'Bastards the lot of them. In both senses of the word. Our dad was in the army. Private, sometimes Corporal, Billy Jones. We moved around a lot when we were kids. Until he got kicked out for pilfering. We became too much of a burden so he just buggered off. Your grandmother pretty much went on the game. Is this the sort of family history a nice middle-class girl like you wants to know?'

Jane shrugged. 'I'm not sure I'm middle class. I'm certainly not sure I'm nice.'

Stacy looked unconvinced. 'There's some of your mother in you. She was all airs and graces and full of herself.'

'I didn't know you'd met my mother. She hasn't mentioned it.'

Stacy's eyes flicked to the window as if it were a gateway to the past. 'Just once when you were a baby. She's either forgotten or chosen to. We didn't get on. Stuck-up cow.'

'You remember me as a baby?'

'Yes. And what an ugly lump you were. It was obvious you were your dad's. I did have my doubts.' Stacy slowly put her face in her hands and sighed. When she looked up her demeanour had changed. 'Jane, I don't want to seem a hard-nosed bitch, but I've got enough trouble with my own kids. I'm not taking on my brother's cast-offs as well. I'm sorry if that sounds blunt. I don't think I've got anything I can give you.'

'I'm just looking for clues that will help me find him, or at least understand him better.'

Stacy laughed and shook her head. 'My brother is easy to understand. He's a sod and always was a sod. You're better off without him. Just like I was better off without my own waste-of-space father.'

'But—'

Stacy's face hardened again. 'I'm pretty certain Private Billy bastard Jones is long dead. But if my dad walked through that door now, it wouldn't be all hugs and tears – I'd want to hurt him. And I'd find a way, I promise you. For what he did to us, selfish...' She looked at Jane intently. 'They're not worth it. Let it go, love. Let it go…'

Guy's cousin

Jane was heading westwards on the M62 as it traversed the Pennines, the range of mountains and hills that form the spine of northern England. The carriageways had just diverged to form a narrow island of land on which sat a solitary farmhouse. The farmer had reputedly defied the bulldozers, but in reality the engineers had been forced to split the roadway because of an underlying geological fault. The building's 18th-century windows now looked past streams of constant traffic to an otherwise remote landscape. Despite the bleak beauty of this section of the journey, Jane's preferred route would have been to cut across the Peak District, but motorway driving required less concentration and she wanted to focus at least some of her mind on the meeting that lay at her destination. Instead, her thoughts kept returning to that west London council estate and how little her aunt had actually revealed. There were a few snippets of family history, a brief outline of her brother's childhood and upbringing. Jane had left her contact details, but doubted Stacy Jones would have a change of heart and be more forthcoming. Maybe she really didn't have more to tell. Her indifference was convincing and Jane thought she'd meet the same brick wall if she pushed again. There was one thing that nagged. Did she really still come across as a policewoman?

As the road descended down into Greater Manchester, the traffic briefly ground to a halt as drivers rubbernecked a nasty accident between vehicles travelling in the opposite direction. Nonetheless, Jane arrived a few minutes early and was able to gather her thoughts before leaving her car and climbing the short flight of steps that led to Prospect Villas, a short terrace set on a steep main road to the north of Rochdale. It was of the ubiquitous two-up two-down, stone-built design that characterised all the Victorian working-class houses of the area, but these properties had presumably been elevated to the status of villas by the addition of bay windows. The prospect was an outlook over a wooded hillside, now largely obscured by later red-brick semis on the other side of the street.

The door was answered by a plumpish woman with red cheeks and slightly frizzy shoulder-length hair. She smiled warmly and bubbled a greeting. 'Jane! I'm Betty. It's lovely to meet you! Thanks for coming all this way. Isn't this exciting?'

Jane was shown into a small front room. It would once have enjoyed the panoramic view and had a certain unused feeling that suggested it was normally kept for visitors and special occasions. Its stillness was disturbed by the plastic figurine of a cat which sat in the window, a solar-powered paw clicking up and down in an incessant wave meant to bring good luck. Jane accepted the offer of tea, and began setting up her laptop. Her host soon returned with a pot and a pair of bone china cups and saucers.

'They're pretty,' said Jane.

'I'm so sorry I haven't got any biscuits. I'm trying to avoid the temptation, but I should have gone out to get some,' replied Betty anxiously.

'Don't worry. I'm probably better off abstaining as well.'

'I don't think you need to worry with a figure like yours, Jane. And can I say, I love your taste in clothes. Not many people can carry off orange like that.'

Jane smiled self-consciously and took a sip of tea before guiding the conversation onto more substantial ground. 'It's good of you to see me, Betty. Your cousin Guy suggested you and he were, I don't know, no longer in contact?'

Betty grimaced like a child admitting an act of naughtiness of which they're secretly proud. 'I've only met him once, when we were kids at our grandfather's funeral. It's a long story, but suffice to say my dad didn't live up to the family's expectations. They're all doctors, aren't they? He was more of a free spirit, like me, like his mother. They had different mothers, you know. The relationship was rocky and then there was a huge row at the funeral. They never spoke again. I don't bear any grudges, obviously. Not in my nature.'

Jane smiled again, this time from gratitude. 'All the same, some people would be nervous of having a stranger come round, particularly in this day and age.'

Betty leant over and tapped Jane's hand. 'I trust my intuitions. And like you said, it's much better chatting face-to-face than sending emails backwards and forwards. And it's very exciting for an amateur like me to meet a professional genealogist. Someone who's working on my own tree!'

Jane felt the flush of embarrassment returning but pushed it aside. 'There was one particular area I wanted to focus on. Your and Guy's great-great-grandfather, Thomas Ramsbottom. You have him down as dying in 1874.'

Betty nodded. 'I haven't really looked at him for quite a while. I'm spending my time on my mother's side these days. I started off with the Ramsbottoms, what with it being my own surname, but then I thought, that's just patriarchal nonsense. My genes, my DNA come just as much from my female line. And given that men have done precious little child rearing in the past, what makes me who I am is down to all those women. And what women they were! Some of them raised huge families in houses as small as this one. On so little money. And half of them died in childbirth. Well, not half, but you know what I mean.'

'I know what you mean,' said Jane, grateful for the opportunity to interrupt Betty's enthusiastic flow. 'It was a very different world. But going back to Thomas Ramsbottom—'

'Yes,' responded Betty, her head nodding rapidly. 'I went back and refreshed my memory this morning. He was the coal miner who passed away when he was only 37.'

Jane had been cradling her teacup and placed it carefully on its saucer. 'I don't think he did.'

Betty raised her eyebrows. 'Really? That's interesting. I'm sure I found a death record for him.'

'You found an index entry for a Thomas Ramsbottom who died in the adjacent registration district. His age was right, so I guess you assumed it was the one you were looking for.'

Betty lifted a finger in a gesture of recollection. 'That's right. And there were no others where the age matched up, so it had to be him. By a logical process of elimination. He was just staying a few miles away for some reason.'

Jane reached into a bright-red satchel and pulled out some papers. 'Trouble is, there was another Thomas Ramsbottom born in the same year. You might have missed him because he spent the first part of his life in Yorkshire.'

'So how can we be sure which one died?' asked Betty, slightly deflated.

'I ordered a death certificate. It arrived yesterday and confirmed what I suspected.' Jane handed over the document. 'His father is named as the informant and he's called Levi. There are no Levis in your family. Also, the place of death ties in with where the other Thomas was living on the census just three years earlier. There's a slight confusion because he was a lodger and his landlord got his details a bit wrong – that's not uncommon – but nonetheless the evidence is pretty conclusive.'

Betty studied the certificate and then looked up. 'But our Thomas had to die about that time. By 1881 his wife is listed as a widow and his last child, my great-grandfather, was born in 1872. It's a relatively small window. Why can't we find his death? Or have you?'

Jane shook her head. 'No, I can't find any record of it. I wanted to ask if you had any family mementos, old letters... Anything that might give us a pointer?'

Betty leant sideways and lifted a cardboard filing box that had been tucked beside her chair. She sat it on her knee and expanded it like a concertina. She flicked through the pockets and pulled out two pieces of A4 paper, one of which was a handwritten page of notes.

'This will interest you,' she said, handing over one of the sheets. 'I was sent it by a distant cousin who was also researching the Ramsbottoms. He copied it for me on the understanding I wouldn't put it online. It's Thomas Ramsbottom, our Thomas Ramsbottom. With his wife and children.'

Jane's eyes opened wide. It was a scan of an old photograph that was somewhat chewed at the edges and had the name of a photographic studio printed across the bottom. It was partly faded and water stained but depicted a seated couple surrounded by five standing children with another infant on the mother's lap. No doubt in keeping with the then-current convention, the expressions were all stern and unsmiling. There was a noticeable contrast in the appearances of the husband and wife. He was blond, youthful and attractive. She looked older, decidedly plain and somewhat overweight. The children were a mixture of their parents apart from the oldest boy, in his mid teens, who strongly resembled his father. Written in blue biro across the top was the text, 'Early cabinet card showing Thomas and Sarah Ramsbottom. Circa 1871'.

Jane spoke without raising her gaze from the image in front of her. 'It would be good to see the original. It might hold some more clues.'

'I lost touch with the man who sent it me,' replied Betty. 'He stopped replying to emails and I've a horrible feeling he's no longer with us. But I've just been reading the notes I made at the time. He'd heard a family story that Thomas was a nasty piece of work who left his wife and all those kids. It was even suggested he sailed off to America. I seem to remember looking at his picture and finding it hard to believe. He looks so lovely. Then I found what I thought was his death. I suppose I reasoned that even if he had walked out on his family, he wouldn't have moved much further than the next town. Daddy's gone abroad is a story you tell kiddies, isn't it?'

Jane didn't reply. The last casual remark resonated hurtfully, and she had to turn her face away, towards the window and the plastic cat still clicking and waving at no-one and everyone. On every beat of its paw, Jane found her thoughts towards blond, handsome Thomas Ramsbottom darkening. He was elevated from a name on a few dusty historic records to someone real, someone close. Someone who had to be tracked down and held to account, punished in absentia, a long-dead whipping boy for a more recent crime.

Hannah, Annie and Captain William H F P Bains

It was some kind of dodgy scam but Jane almost fell for it.

Her mind was elsewhere, full of thoughts of Thomas Ramsbottom and the repercussions of a father's betrayal. She was checking her inbox quickly and the message asking her to verify her email account had seemed plausible and convincing. It was professionally laid out and well-written, without the jarring grammatical errors normally committed by small-time cybercriminals on the other side of the world. It warned of a recent security alert and recommended she login again to check her settings. It was tedious computer admin and she just wanted to get on with her research. She was just about to click as requested when she woke up and remembered she was supposed to be more careful. Tommy had once shown her how to hover the mouse over a link to see its real destination. Sure enough, the latter part of the Internet address looked reasonable but it began with a website name that was decidedly suspect. She thought about forwarding the email to her provider, but decided she couldn't be bothered. These things went out in their thousands. Let someone else report it if they wanted to. Nothing much ever seemed to happen anyway. The would-be phisher would simply create a new address and Jane's inbox would still be riddled with spam tomorrow.

She was back in Nottingham, sitting at her dining table and now found herself frantically hunting for her laptop's power cable. Its battery life certainly wasn't what it used to be. Tommy was right: it was getting old. She made a mental note to buy a new one when this case was complete.

Plugged into the mains, she could finally focus on searching for evidence of Thomas Ramsbottom journeying overseas. Betty said the family rumour suggested America, but Jane had remote cousins who emigrated to Australia and Canada at around the same time, so she kept her options open. She began with a narrow time frame, the 1871 to 1881 period from his last English census appearance to the date his wife began calling herself a widow, and then gradually threw her net wider. There were no Thomas Ramsbottoms who seemed to fit. There was one candidate living in Ohio on the 1880 US federal census who briefly seemed promising. He was roughly the right age, but his American children were in their early 20s and they and he turned up living in the same state ten years earlier.

Jane gave up on looking abroad and returned to the UK. As Betty had proposed, maybe he hadn't moved far after all. Jane searched for shortened forms of his first name, including Tom, Tommy, Thos and Thom. Ramsbottom was not a surname that was often misspelled, but she used wildcards to pick up other possible variations such as Ramsbotham and Ramsbotom. No matter what she did, the man seemed to have disappeared. Jane knew there could be gaps in the records. Historically, files had often been damaged and lost, paperwork being perpetually susceptible to flood and fire. Sometimes people were hidden by faded ink or incorrect transcription. Instinctively, however, Jane felt she was missing something. Her quarry must have left some trace somewhere.

Jane began to wonder if he could have changed his name. Her grandmother's Aunt Annie had been born Hannah, but she preferred to be called Annie and this was the name she reported to officialdom throughout her adult life. On electoral registers she was Annie and she was Annie on her death certificate. She was born some 60 years later than Thomas. If she had gotten away with living under an effective alias in the burgeoning bureaucracy of the 20th century, then presumably Thomas would have found it even easier. And besides, Jane knew that English law had always allowed people to call themselves what they wanted so long as it wasn't for the purposes of fraud. Why Thomas would have adopted a different name was open for speculation. Perhaps he didn't want to be found by his wife's angry family. Clearly, if he changed his surname, the options were myriad. A change of Christian name was more manageable.

Jane simply omitted a first name from her searches and found him almost immediately. She'd become stuck in a way of working and it was an obvious step she should have tried much earlier. A Jos or Joseph Ramsbottom had reportedly arrived in New York in March 1873 aboard Royal Mail Ship Algeria. The steamer's manifest listed the 500 passengers on board and was submitted to the state's immigration authorities when she berthed. It was to be hoped that her master, William H F P Bains, employed better seamen than he did scribes. The writing was as unnecessarily elaborate as the number of the captain's initials, and it took Jane some time to decipher the exuberant loops and swirls. Jos Ramsbottom was described as a 37 year-old male labourer from England travelling in steerage. Jane zoomed in on his first name as it was partially obscured by a letter swooping down from the line above. On closer inspection, it wasn't Jos as the transcriber had supposed, but Thos.

Jane leaned back in her chair and grinned. Thomas Ramsbottom hadn't changed his name to escape the wrath of his wife. He didn't need to: he'd put 3,000 miles of ocean between them. Here he was, exactly the right age, leaving England for America soon after the birth of their last child. Jane felt sure this had to be her man.

'Got you, you selfish, good-for-nothing bastard,' she said out loud.

Castle Garden

The pilot, a weather-beaten rock of a man with a salt-stiffened white beard, had taken command and was guiding the huge iron liner slowly and carefully through the maze of channels formed by shifting bars and rocky shoals. Sails tightly furled, the single funnel puffed faint wisps of smoke that drifted off on the light breeze. The sun was rising in a clear sky and the sea was placid for the first time in days. The ship no longer throbbed with exertion, but ploughed effortlessly through tidal currents that might have troubled a lesser vessel.

People began to gather on deck and watch expectantly as the narrows began to open out into a vast bay flanked by gently sloping countryside, pale winter brown in the morning light. They steamed past smaller, isolated communities and then a murmur of anticipation broke into a huge cheer as their destination came into sight. In the distance, a mighty city rose from the water, flanked on either side by sisters of almost equal scale. Their shorelines were a forest of masts and behind them churches and factory chimneys rose above the rooftops. The foundation piers of some future great bridge could just be made out, promising competition to the flotilla of small boats that were already busy plying their trade across the waterways. It was a spectacle that shouted prosperity and opportunity, a New World.

In better spirits, he might have taken out the pencil and pad given him by the minister's wife and tried to capture the scene, but he had been feeling sick for the entire passage. The crossing from Liverpool to the Irish port of Queenstown had been relatively calm, but even then the nausea had begun. Once on the open Atlantic, the captain and the weather confined them below deck and the crashing, rolling seas had him reaching for that foul-smelling bucket, day and night. The ship was only half full, but the section of steerage reserved for single men was still cramped, dark and airless. The narrow bunks were hard and seemed to be infested with something foul and lousy that made him itch beneath the clothing he hadn't removed in a fortnight. Now, he wanted to share the elation of his fellow passengers, but he was too weak. He seemed to ache everywhere and there was an odd rash breaking out on his stomach. And he didn't understand why he had woken up hot and sweating on a cold March morning.

There was a sharp slap on his back and he turned to see a younger man with bright blue eyes and dark-brown curls grinning with excitement.

'Now isn't she a fine sight! Even grander than Dublin Bay herself, don't you think?' beamed the Irishman.

The other man simply nodded without enthusiasm. He had never seen Dublin Bay but didn't have the energy to make the observation. He just wanted to be left alone. Instead he received another slap, this time to the shoulder.

'What's the matter, sheep's arse? We're not feeling sick again, are we? You Englishmen aren't cut from the same cloth as us good, strong Irish boys, now are you now? Sheep's arse?'

The glint in his blue eyes faded slightly when the Irishman became aware of a third figure standing behind him. He turned and was confronted by a heavy-set man with a bulbous face and hands like shovels, shovels that had been battered from years of hacking black rock from narrow seams.

The Irishman made an exaggerated pointing gesture towards the newcomer. 'And top of the morning to you too, sir! I was just saying what a fine sight—'

His cheerful lilt was interrupted by a less melodious voice. 'I heard what you were saying, lad. That joke's getting wearisome.'

'Ah, it's just a bit of craic.'

'I'll give you a bit of a crack,' said the third man humourlessly. 'Now leave me and my pal be. Or you'll be getting off this here boat with a fat lip.'

The accent was thick and unfamiliar. The young Irishman struggled to distinguish the exact words, but their meaning was clear. He smiled, bowed his head and pretended to doff a cap that he wasn't wearing. He then sauntered off towards another group of men talking animatedly further down the ship.

The sickly looking man put his hand on his forehead, lifting the fringe of his straight blonde hair. His fingers had once been delicately formed, but they too bore the calluses and scars of manual labour. 'Thank you, Henry,' he said.

'I know you're not feeling right, Tom,' said his companion, 'but I've told you. You need to stand up to these folk. Don't let them mither you. Once they start they don't let up.'

'I know, I know. I've been there before. It's just...' replied Tom, searching for an excuse. 'I'm feeling worse if owt. I just want to get off this damned beggar of ship. Stand on something that isn't forever pitching and swaying.'

Henry turned to face the urban sprawl that was starting to fill the skyline. 'It won't be long now, lad. We'll soon be on that train and on our way to Ohio. We'll be digging American coal before you know it.'

The Cunarder dropped anchor in midstream off the southern tip of the main city. She was met by steam tugs and lighters, and her passengers and their trunks were transferred to a landing stage alongside an old circular fortification with casemated walls imposingly built of red sandstone. Built to repel attack from the British, it now greeted them, along with immigrants from all over the world. Prior to its establishment by the State of New York, new arrivals had often fallen victim to exploitative scams, being sold tickets for fictitious trains, money at exorbitant rates of exchange or rooms in non-existent tenements. Castle Garden housed state officials, agents of the railroad companies, exchange brokers, multilingual letter writers, licensed boarding-house keepers and a labor exchange. Beneath the glass-domed rotunda people could also store their baggage and would sleep on its floors and benches if they had no bed for the night. Those arriving sick were ferried to state hospitals on islands in the East River. It was a well-intentioned service, but as ever, bureaucracy demanded compliance and control, so that it became a confusing ordeal amongst a crowded mass of people and a Babel-like cacophony of languages. For Yiddish-speaking Eastern European Jews, *kesselgarten* became a generic term for disorder and chaos. Nonetheless, this was a time before passports, visas and immigration law. Ellis Island would not open its doors for nearly 20 years. If you made it to New York you got to stay. You just had to pass through Castle Garden first.

Tom and Henry joined a long queue and shuffled towards their first interview. A finely dressed gentleman was asking questions. He was flanked by other, clearly lesser, men whose role was presumably to police the line and ensure no-one slipped by unchecked. As the two miners approached, it became obvious this was a brief medical screening. Henry told his pale companion to stand up straight and look strong. Tom promptly collapsed to the floor.

Windows on a life

Jane had found Thomas Ramsbottom, hopefully her Thomas Ramsbottom, crossing to New York, but she immediately lost him again. She shouldn't have been surprised: her earlier searches had found no trace of him living in America. She focused in, revitalised by the ship's manifest and its 1873 date of arrival, but he still eluded her. Most specifically, she could find no-one amongst the 50 million individuals in the 1880 federal census who looked like any kind of match.

Assuming he hadn't simply slipped the enumerator's net, what had happened to him in those seven short years? Had he died? Had he changed his name, perhaps in a deliberate effort to hide away and build a new life? Had he stayed in New York or moved on, maybe travelling to the territories then expanding in the west? Jane had some experience tracing a branch of her mother's family who'd emigrated across the Atlantic. She knew that different states, sometimes different counties, maintained their own records of birth, marriage and death. Some were digitised, some not. Not knowing where Thomas had been headed made the task much more difficult. Where exactly did one start?

Jane decided to take stock of everything she knew about him and the world he lived in. If she could build a profile, some clue might emerge.

Thomas Ramsbottom was born in Lancashire in February 1836. His parents were of a denomination that does not practise infant baptism, so the church record was simply a registration of his coming into the world. His father was a hand weaver and his address was given as Quebec. Jane was initially thrown by the Canadian connection, but research showed it to be the name of a farmstead high on the Pennine hills, presumably named after General Wolfe's famous victory the previous century. The Internet provided a view of the building as it now looked. It had been refurbished and gentrified but its antiquity was clear. Even today, its location was remote, the surrounding countryside windswept and bleak. It would have been a cold and lonely place to live and give birth in one of the last winters of Georgian Britain.

On the 1841 census, the Ramsbottoms and their five children were still living at Quebec, but Thomas's father was described as a labourer and the house was also shared by an elderly farmer and his wife, presumably the owners or main tenants.

By 1851, Thomas was a 15-year-old coal 'drawer' along with his 13-year-old brother, Benjamin. The family had moved to a small hamlet, little more than a ramshackle cluster of buildings, a few hundred yards away. There were three more children and Thomas's father was now elevated to the rank of 'labourer and farmer'.

In 1856, 20-year-old Thomas married Sarah Hargreaves, a woman three years his senior. The ceremony took place in the Anglican parish church despite them both being Baptists. The original marriage register had been scanned and it gave a Jane a tantalisingly personal link to the past. The bride and witnesses had touched that page and signed it with awkward and scruffy crosses, their marks indicating their presence and agreement. Thomas alone had been able to write his own name. But this was not the faltering script seen on some of the adjacent entries. It was confident, fluid and elegant. The man who had been working down a mine since he was 13 or younger had the most beautiful handwriting. Where, thought Jane, had he learnt that? She looked again at the photo of him and his family taken some 15 years later. His fair hair and delicate, attractive features seemed to say sensitive and artistic. This was surely not the face of a man who laboured beneath the ground, filthy and sweating and bruised. Studying the expression more closely, however, she thought she could see another side to his character, an 'I'm clever and handsomer than you', an arrogance that might explain a subsequent act of selfishness.

Jane found herself on a tangent, researching the schooling available to ordinary people in early Victorian England. It was a time of population explosion, when workers had large families, partly in response to the insatiable demands of the new mills and factories, and there was a move away from the countryside and into industrial villages and towns. Prior to a parliamentary act of 1870, elementary education was mainly provided by voluntary bodies with greater or lesser religious affiliation: the Church of England had its National Schools, British Schools being the main non-conformist, non-denominational rival. Both those institutions were eventually established in the area where Thomas grew up – one still stood and was now a care home for the elderly – but on the earliest map available, dated 1849, neither was marked. At that time, only the Sunday school of the Baptist church was indicated as a place of learning. Thomas's wife, Sarah, and most of their children now lay in the graveyard of the same church. Jane could only assume that was where Thomas had been taught, not only biblical scriptures, but also to read and write. If Sarah had attended alongside him, she had not benefited equally. Perhaps boys were treated differently, or perhaps Thomas was a clever and gifted child singled out for special tuition. The economics of his background soon condemned him to a life of manual toil, but those bright genes might have found their way to his youngest son and be the reason he could hold his own amongst more privileged classmates at medical school.

Returning to the marriage register, Jane noted that Sarah's father was a farmer and mason, whereas Thomas's was once more reduced to being a simple labourer. Maybe he was prepared to exaggerate his status to a census enumerator but not to a man of God. Two decades earlier, he had been a hand weaver. He would have worked in his own wide-windowed cottage producing cloth from the fleeces of local sheep, on the face of it a more rewarding, independent and creative occupation. Jane assumed he was forced to seek unskilled menial work when industrialisation and mechanisation had supplanted the old handlooms. She found an article describing a nearby uprising just before Thomas's birth. Mills and power looms were destroyed and the army summoned to quell the disturbance with cavalry sabres and artillery. Six people were killed and the 41 lead rioters were initially sentenced to death before being transported to Australia for their futile attempts to thwart the inevitable destruction of their livelihood and lifestyle. Perhaps Thomas's father had taken part or at least sympathised with their cause and could not bring himself to be subjugated by the new machines and chose to work on other men's land.

Thomas and Sarah had their first child, George, towards the end of 1856, less than nine months after their wedding. Jane stared once more at the family photograph. George was a mirror of Thomas, blond and handsome. Sarah was altogether more swarthy and plain, looking much older than her husband, far more than the three years that actually separated them. The dates said they had to get married. Jane wondered if it was something Thomas had always resented, such that it precipitated his subsequent flight to America while he was still young enough start a fresh life.

Jane continued to work her chronological way through the records. In 1861, Thomas and Sarah had three children, and he was still a coal miner. Ten years later, there were six children and he had switched to working in a cotton mill. 14-year-old George was also a mill hand by this stage. Jane found herself consulting the old maps again. When Thomas and Sarah had married, he had moved down from the hilltops and they established their family near her father's farm on the outskirts of a small but growing village. Blackwell Holme was set in a steep valley which cut into the moors, and above it lay a colliery with a straight, mile-long tramway leading down to the road. The coal presumably powered the four mills which were in reasonable walking distance. One in particular was right on the Ramsbottoms' doorstep, at the head of a long gulley. Its location suggested it might once have been water powered but even the earliest map showed a separate building labelled 'Nabb Engine', Nabb being a geographical feature close by. It was a name that led Jane to a potentially pivotal revelation in the history of the Ramsbottom family.

She found an online document headed 'More Boiler Explosions'. Amongst a gallery of disasters was a somewhat blurred photograph showing an early three-storey mill with a tall, square chimney. One end of the building lay in ruins and several figures, including what looked like two top-hatted constables, were standing amongst the rubble. One had climbed onto a dark cylindrical object lying at a 45 degree angle to the ground. At first Jane thought it was a section of a second chimney, but then realised it was a steam boiler that had been blown off its base. The photograph was annotated 'Nabb Engine Mill, June 1872, 4 killed'. Armed with the date, Jane searched a collection of 19th-century newspapers and the full story emerged.

The Blackburn Standard reported on the inquest into the deaths, held a week later in a nearby pub, the Graver's Arms, and with a jury formed 'of the most part of men conversant with boilers'. Evidence was presented that the blast had occurred at 10:00 am when about 100 hands were at work. The 30-foot long boiler was 'forced' a distance of 60 yards, knocking down the boiler house and embedding itself in the ground. A second boiler was tipped on end. A five-foot length of steam pipe was blown through the weaving shed and the 'buildings presented a most ruinous appearance'. There were a number of injuries and four fatalities. The boiler engineer, a warehouse boy and a throstle spinner, a girl of 16, were killed instantly. A 15-year-old weaver named as George Ramsbottom 'expired the same night from grievous scalding about the body and face'.

Jane had known that Thomas and Sarah's eldest son had died in 1872, but seeing his name in the fuzzy black and white of old newsprint still came as a shock.

The article continued at some length, discussing the technicalities of boiler construction and steam pressure. The conveniently dead engineer seemed to be getting the blame for 'incidents of intemperance' and 'neglecting his duties' rather than his employers and their somewhat aged equipment and lax management. Jane merely scanned the text, her head full of images of a handsome boy, looking so full of life in the photograph that might have been taken only days or weeks before his death. In her mind, Jane saw that beautiful face horribly burnt as he died in his distraught mother's arms. Sarah was already pregnant at this stage. It was perhaps little wonder that she would name her last child in memory of the one she had lost so painfully.

George Ramsbottom, the second George Ramsbottom, was born later that year. Despite his humble origins he would somehow rise to be a man of medicine. His great-grandson, Guy, would continue in the same profession and enjoy a very different status and lifestyle to that of his early forebears. Jane was no nearer understanding how that initial switch from labourer or mill worker to doctor had been funded, though she felt she had a better understanding of the characters involved. And her antipathy towards Thomas Ramsbottom, who ran off to America leaving behind a grieving wife with a young baby, was intensifying. She needed to track him down more than ever. But she was struggling to do it on her own.

Help

Hi Jane

Sounds like you've made some solid progress. Forgive me, but do you mind if I don't look at this properly until next week? That new contract I took on has turned out to be a bit of a nightmare. There's a new version of client's chosen software development tool (technically it's messaging middleware) and it's riddled with bugs. I'm having to find workarounds, but we've got a major project milestone coming up close of business this Friday (effectively that means first thing Monday morning) and I've got to burn the candle at both ends to meet it. And I can do without being dragged away to attend their stupid meetings. It's getting me a bit stressed again to be honest, but if I can finish this component, I'm hoping it's going to be relatively downhill thereafter.

Sorry to moan. Here are a couple of quick thoughts re finding Thomas Ramsbottom:

1873 wasn't a great year to emigrate to the US. It was the start of what they used to call the Great Depression until it was overshadowed by the 1930s.

In my experience, people didn't often make such life-changing journeys completely on their own. They went with a brother or a cousin, or they already had family over there. If you dig around the tree you might find some links to help you better understand where Thomas would be heading to in the States.

I'm sorry can't give this more time at the moment. I feel really guilty for letting you down.

Apologies

Tommy x

Hi Tommy

I tried to call you, but I think you might have your phone off.

Don't worry about the family history thing. I'm not working to a strict deadline and it's my responsibility not yours. You've given me some good pointers and I'll work on those. Ultimately, if I can't find what happened to Thomas Ramsbottom in the States, the world won't come to an end. It's only a job; it's certainly not life and death.

Tommy, sweetheart, I'm worried about you. You'll make yourself ill again if you stress too much. If the client chose duff software (messaging middleware?? WTF?!!), surely that's their problem? They can't expect you to slave all hours to keep their project on schedule. I know you're a computer genius and you've got your pride, but they'll have to let their dates slip. Isn't there a project manager running this thing? Tell him/her to do their job. Give me their phone number and I'll do it. Okay, I know you'd never let me, but maybe you should be brave and have that conversation with them.

You've been here before, you know you have. It sounds just like what you described in those group therapy sessions. I understand what you do is all about logic, intricacy and minutiae, but you let yourself get consumed by it. Sometimes you need to take a step back. You push yourself too hard in the expectation that once you've solved the current problem then it'll be okay 'next week'. But a new set of issues will come up and you'll be so damned tired your ability to cope will start to evaporate. You know you get obsessive about things, Tommy. You don't want to get weird again. The answer can't always be to work round the clock. Please try to take a break, even if it's just going for a walk and getting away from that bloody computer.

Lecture over. Please call me back.

Love Jane xx

Time out

Jane had been living on instant coffee and tinned soup. She was out of both. She realised she also needed a break and having some healthier food in the fridge would probably be a good idea too.

There were a few clouds in the sky, but they didn't threaten rain. Jane threw her shopping bags onto the passenger seat then climbed in and lowered the roof. Her head was getting clogged with names, relationships and dates and a good blast of fresh air might clear out the fog of detail and hopefully let her focus on the bigger picture.

She scanned left and right, and seeing only an absence of traffic, pulled the bright-green Mazda out into the road. She couldn't resist blipping the throttle and hearing the engine growl as she accelerated sharply away.

If she were drawing attention to herself, it was unintentional. Nonetheless, she was being watched.

The face had quickly pulled back from the window for fear of being seen. It now leant forward again and the eyes flicked from the disappearing car back to the house on the other side of the street. The evidence had been taken in and a calculation made. She would be gone some time.

And the eyes saw something else. The favourite expression of a lecherously crude school friend came to mind. The face mouthed the words, 'sex on a stick,' and then quietly sighed.

Unpleasantries

Jane had reached the far end of the supermarket. It was designed around a wide central aisle with shelving and refrigeration units radiating off to left and right. She habitually meandered back and forth down the side further from the entrance, before returning on the other, which was nearer the tills and the way out. Apart from a few rebellious individuals fighting against the tide, most people seemed to follow the same route. There were no signs or arrows offering directions; it just seemed natural. Was it a case of following the crowd or were there subliminal cues in the layout to which most human brains automatically responded? She suspected the latter. And for some reason, the retail thought controllers put the alcohol halfway round. Was that so there was still space in your trolley, but there would already be sufficient food and other products onboard to avoid you looking like a sad wino who was just loading up with booze?

Jane glanced down at her own collection of items: a few toiletries, dairy products, pre-packed fish, one portion of chicken and a big tin of instant coffee. She used to buy a lot more, but then Dave had eaten like a Shire horse with a gut full of worms. He also liked a beer, or four, and was ridiculously fussy about the brand and type. As far as Jane was concerned, it all tasted roughly the same, bad, and once in a glass an IPA or golden ale was indistinguishable from a lager. Dave had taken great pains to explain what he would or wouldn't drink, but whenever Jane did the shopping on her own, they'd inevitably have moved everything around and she always seemed to pick the wrong one.

'I told you that stuff was horrible! It's virtually undrinkable,' was his most common assessment, 'Maybe you should buy own beers in future,' her standard response.

Looking at the collection of bottles and tins now, she almost missed the excitement of taking something home and awaiting his verdict, like a child presenting a school report to ambitious but supportive parents. And now, right in front of her, she recognised Dave's favourite brand, the one she had so often failed to find. She thought of buying it for old time's sake, but resisted. When exactly would it get drunk?

Directly behind the beers were two long shelves of wine bottles. Jane had a slight preference for sauvignon blanc, but in truth would drink pretty much anything as long as it was white, chilled and not too sweet. She wasn't a serious drinker, in either sense of the word, and had long ago resisted the temptation to develop a more sophisticated palette. It seemed like an unnecessarily expensive affectation. And who could tell the difference after a glass or two anyway?

She was studying the sauvignons, following her default formula of finding the second-least expensive, when her eyes drifted onto a woman a few feet away, transferring several fizzy proseccos into her trolley. She was wearing heavy makeup and had short hair two-toned in blonde and coppery brown. Her clothes looked expensive, but in a tacky, blatantly labelled, designed for someone a damn-sight thinner than you kind of way. Jane's subconscious immediately pigeonholed her as common. She felt a brief pulse of guilt and then realised the woman looked familiar. It was two or three seconds before the face registered; Jane immediately turned away, but it was too late.

'How do you think you're staring at?' snarled the woman.

'Sorry, I thought I recognised you,' replied Jane, somewhat disingenuously.

'Oh, you recognised me, alright. What were you expecting – a few more scars? From when you kicked my head in?'

Jane turned squarely towards the other woman. She was not going to be intimidated, not by present hostility or by its echo in the past.

'Christine, I didn't kick you, I punched you. Rather too hard and a few too many times, but you'd been picking on me for months.'

'That's because you were a right stuck-up bitch. You and your, what was it, tennis or summat? Right Miss La-di-dah. "Oh, I don't want to wear makeup, I want to look after my complexion." Stuck-up cow!'

Jane noticed that, despite the vitriol, her old, bullying classmate was keeping her distance.

'Christine, it was a long time ago. We were 15. You pushed me, over and over again, and I finally reacted. I got expelled for it. I'm sure you didn't suffer any permanent damage.'

'Didn't suffer damage? The right side of my face was swollen for weeks.' Christine's accent was as hard as it had ever been, but she managed to stop herself shouting, opting instead for the threatening, spitting whisper favoured by hard men in East End soap opera. 'You could have blinded me,' she continued. 'I'd have got compensation these days. And you'd have been locked up. You were barmy, that's what you were.'

'Christine, look—'

'Don't you Christine me! You always thought you were better than us. Well, I've done alright for myself. Look at that.' She thrust her left hand forward, revealing talon-like manicured nails and a large diamond solitaire alongside a wedding ring. 'My other half's got his own roofing business. Doing very nicely, thank you very much. You're not married, I see.'

'No, I'm not married.' Jane almost added 'anymore' but decided this woman didn't need to know her life story.

'I'm not surprised.' Christine smiled smugly. 'Too full of yourself. But you see, I know who... what you really are.'

Jane closed her eyes briefly and sighed. 'What am I?' she asked, impatiently shaking her head.

'Criminal trash. I told my mum to get the police on you. She said your dad had been some kind of local gangster. He'd buggered off to London with some tart, but we didn't want to risk him coming—'

'You knew my dad was in London?' cut in Jane, her tone now more aggressive.

Christine's smile broadened as she realised she'd hit a nerve. 'My mum's boyfriend had some dealings with him. He was an unpleasant so-and-so, by all accounts. Bit like his daughter.'

Jane felt an old rage building up inside her. This stupid, common, ugly woman who had been a stupid, common, ugly girl, who had tormented her at school and made her life hell... This stupid, mocking, grinning woman had known for years what Jane didn't, what she had just found out in the last few weeks, that her father was only in London, by choice and with a cheap bit of skirt, not remorsefully exiled thousands of miles away on another continent.

Jane felt herself beginning to shake as she struggled to retain her composure, desperate to bottle up the inner demon screaming at her to hit, to hurt, to punish. She walked round her trolley and stood directly in front of her tauntress. A head taller, Jane lowered her face so it was inches away from Christine's now unconvincing smile.

Jane spoke quietly and slowly, but her hair trigger was betrayed by the tremor in her voice. 'Christine, please understand something. And this really isn't a threat. That... what was it? That barmy teenager you bullied and teased and goaded hasn't gone away. I keep her locked in her own little room, but every once in a while she kicks down the door and there she is, lashing out uncontrollably. She's almost been my downfall more than once. I don't want her to come out again. And nor do you, trust me. One of your piss-common nails might get broken. Or maybe I'll give you that scar you wanted.'

Jane raised her left hand and ran two fingers down Christine's now deadpan face, smearing the mascara on both sides of her right eye.

The tension was broken by a cough.

'Ahem. Excuse me, ladies. 'A nervous-looking supermarket manager in an ill-fitting black suit had joined them next to the wine shelves. 'Is everything alright here?'

Jane stared into Christine's eyes, challenging her to cry foul and ask for help. But the rules of the playground, and the street – never grass, never snitch – still held.

Christine nodded rapidly. 'Yes, we're fine. Just old school friends catching up, reliving old times.'

The manager looked relieved. Jane wordlessly turned away and resumed her search for the second-cheapest sauvignon.

Half an hour later, she was unloading her shopping bags from her car, angry at herself for nearly losing control, but trying to take comfort from the fact that she hadn't, even under the shock of a deep wound being cruelly re-opened.

From the window across the road, the same gaze that had watched her leave made careful note of her return. The conflict in her head was not apparent in her expression. She still looked like sex on a stick.

Victorians

Jane sought distraction through work and re-read Tommy's email and its comment on the economic climate when Thomas Ramsbottom had arrived in America. She had never heard of this earlier Great Depression, but Wikipedia soon provided illumination. Now sometimes called the Long Depression, it began with an event known as the Panic of 1873. It was the first worldwide financial crisis and its causes were rooted in an economist's glossary of banking house failures, unsalable bond issues, contracting money supply, deflation, destabilised business investment, gold standards and stock market bubbles. Much of the terminology seemed familiar from more recent crashes, but Jane didn't try too hard to understand it. She was more interested in its impact on jobs, particularly for new immigrants.

Thomas Ramsbottom had docked in New York in March. After a period of growth following the end of the American Civil War eight years before, financial panic arrived in the USA on a Black Thursday that September. Thousands of businesses failed and there were a million unemployed across the country, with one in four New York labourers out of work that first winter. Immigration rates were reduced to a trickle. Thomas seemed to have timed his life-changing flight at almost the worst possible moment.

So was destitution Thomas's fate? Did he die broke, frozen and unknown down some New York back alley on an icy December or January night? It was a possible explanation, but overall the downturn's impact on ordinary people seemed less catastrophic than the 1930s and Jane's intuition told her Thomas was a survivor. She began to wonder what a 36-year-old coal miner cum cotton weaver might turn his hand to, should he be sufficiently desperate. The idea of him joining the army occurred to her. It was a time of conflict with Native Americans and she was briefly sidetracked by the fantasy of him being hacked to pieces by Sioux at Custer's Last Stand in 1876. She quickly dragged herself back to plausibility but not before checking the names of those who fell at the Little Bighorn.

Having established little more than Thomas could have faced unexpected challenges soon after his arrival, Jane focused her attention on Tommy's suggestion that most emigrants didn't travel alone or might already have relatives in America. The latter rang true to her. Her great-great-aunt had won a 1920s local newspaper competition paying for young single women to sail to Australia, on the expectation they would work in service. The girl's heartbroken father had only let 21-year-old Myrtle go because one of his brothers had moved to Sydney in the aftermath of the First World War.

Jane worked her way through all of Thomas Ramsbottom's siblings, aunts, uncles and cousins. There were one or two inevitable gaps, but the evidence was that the family stayed put in Lancashire. Uncle George broke the mould, joining the 17th Regiment of Foot and fighting in the First Anglo-Afghan War, but he was discharged at the age of 46, just before his comrades were despatched to the Crimea, and appeared on the later censuses as a Chelsea Pensioner living back home with his relatively exotic wife from Kent.

At one stage, Jane held out high hopes for Thomas's brother Benjamin, who seemed to disappear from the records a few years before Thomas boarded his ship in Liverpool. Having buried his first wife after six years of childless marriage, miner Benjamin moved to the next village and married a widow with three children. They had two girls together but by the next census she appeared to be on her own again. Eventually, Jane found Benjamin hidden by a poor transcription of particularly bad handwriting. He was a boarder in a house a few streets away. Evidently the marriage had not worked out. Digging deeper, Jane exposed what had to pass for the complete story. In the days before divorce, the wife ended up living with a wealthy grocer. Benjamin stayed on his own and worked as a collier until he was 74 when his leg was broken, crushed between coal tubs. Presumably estranged from his daughters and their families, he died in the workhouse. As ever with genealogy, it was a complex life encapsulated in a mere handful of dates and events. It seemed sad for Benjamin, but there were no doubt nuances that would colour one's sympathies. Perhaps Benjamin was a drunken abuser, or perhaps he simply didn't live up to his predecessor in his second wife's affections and expectations. Such details were probably lost forever, but it seemed Benjamin could be ruled out as a candidate for co-conspirator in his brother's escape across the Atlantic.

Having found no clues in the Ramsbottom family tree, Jane tried a different tack. Looking at the manifest of RMS Algeria, the passenger names seemed in no obvious order, other than steerage being separated from the more well-heeled 'cabin' occupants. There was no attempt to sort names alphabetically, or by nationality, through individual families were grouped together. On that basis, it seemed likely that travelling companions would be side by side on the list. Ahead of Thomas was Henry Pickup, a 42-year-old labourer from England. Following were Wilhelm and Peter Schmitt, two men in their twenties from newly unified Germany, presumably brothers. They too had the catch-all occupation of labourer. For the first time Jane noticed the column headed 'Died on the Voyage'. Paging through all 500 passengers, she found it completed only once. A one-year-old male infant, the only child of a young Polish couple, had survived the long journey across Europe, the North Sea and northern England, to die only three days out of Liverpool. His future prospects could have been the spur that pushed his parents to leave their divided and annexed homeland, but he had been sacrificed in the attempt.

Assuming Thomas did not have an unlikely friendship with a pair of German brothers, Henry Pickup seemed the most probable candidate for further research. There was no indication where in England he was from, but a website showing the distribution of surnames in Victorian England suggested the Pickups were concentrated in the same area of Lancashire as Thomas's family.

General searches for Henry Pickups living in Lancashire threw up several inconclusive matches, so Jane decided to focus on the 1871 census, taken just two years before a man of that name boarded RMS Algeria. Unfortunately, she could find no-one who had any obvious associations with Thomas Ramsbottom. Having seen people missed by transcription errors, she decided to work through the scanned census records page by page. The district where Thomas lived was recorded across 49 sheets. The forms were completed by hand by the census enumerator, in this case a certain John Piccope. Jane noted that his title, Mr, had been pre-printed. Mrs or Miss Piccope need not apply for the role. Mr John Piccope wrote clearly and legibly, and Jane was able to work through the 200 or so households relatively quickly. As she did, she followed her progress on a contemporaneous map, imagining the enumerator walking from door to door on a damp April day nearly 150 years earlier. Henry Pickup still evaded her, but Jane noticed that one cluster of buildings, not far from where Thomas lived, seemed to have been omitted from the survey. On closer inspection, some kind of historic parish boundary swept down to cut off that section of the hillside. Jane identified the adjacent census district and found she had been there before. She was back with the barely legible handwriting that had caused her problems locating Benjamin Ramsbottom when he had been the focus of her research.

The writing was bad, but some of the transcriber's errors were unforgivable. Many people were supposedly born in a place called Lane which turned out to be Lancs, the common shortened form of Lancashire. One woman was apparently called Ake, but zooming in her name was clearly Alice. Jane could only assume the transcription had been offshored to someone who was being paid by the page and had the barest knowledge of British geography and people.

Again guided by the map, Jane soon found the properties she was looking for. And there, widowed and living with his mother, was a 40-year-old coal miner Henry Rickup. Jane upped the magnification and studied the first letter of his surname. It certainly looked like an R, but it could also be a P. She quickly searched the birth indexes to see how many Rickups had been born in Victorian England. There was one solitary girl, registered in Manchester in the 1840s. Rickup was an even more obscure surname than Jane had suspected. So obscure that she felt certain this man could only be called Pickup. Everything now depended on what the records said he did next. Unfortunately, he continued to maintain his low profile.

His mother, Drusilla, was still alive in 1881 but was now living on her own at the same address. Drusillas were helpfully rare and from her there was a link to another researcher's tree. Unfortunately it was marked as private, meaning Jane wouldn't be able to access it without the owner's permission. Judging by the numbers of sources and citations attached it was well researched and documented, so Jane sent off a brief message expressing her interest. She didn't expect a reply for a day or two, at best, but to her surprise the response was almost immediate, if decidedly brusque.

Hi

Online right now. Prefer not to grant access. Please justify.

Tjharvey3

Hi

Thanks for coming back so quickly.

I'm trying to find out what happened to an ancestor named Thomas Ramsbottom who emigrated from the UK to New York aboard RMS Algeria in 1873. I have reason to believe his travelling companion was Henry Pickup, born 1831. Henry was a coal miner from Blackwell Holme in Lancashire. Thomas was his near neighbour and had also been a miner. I assume they were therefore ex-workmates and friends. The trail goes cold after they arrived in the States. I can see your tree is very detailed and it looks like you've done some work on the Pickups, certainly on Henry's mother, Drusilla. I would be very grateful for any help you can give me.

Obviously, if there is anything I can offer in return, please ask. I am based in the UK, not that far from Lancashire, and will probably be visiting Blackwell Holme in the near future. I'm not sure where you are yourself, but am happy to provide local input if I can.

Many thanks in advance

Jane Madden

Hi Jane Madden

This is a summary of what I have on Henry Pickup. What you can't find from basic research comes from a letter kept in a family bible now held by one of my cousins in Canada. Your reference to a travelling companion makes sense and his identity adds value to my own tree.

- Henry Pickup 1831-1873.
- Coal miner, Blackwell Colliery.

- Widowed in 1870. No children.
- Aunt and uncle already living in mining community in Nelsonville, Ohio.
- Henry emigrates to join them in 1873. Arrives Ohio but dies of "ship's fever" shortly after.

Google will tell you ship's fever is typhus, not to be confused with typhoid. It's transferred by lice, though they didn't know that then. It was more prevalent in days of sail because of longer journey times in cramped holds. I assume it took Henry longer to show symptoms – maybe he caught it later than or, indeed, from Thomas Ramsbottom. It was obviously a fatal strain, hence your finding no further record of either man.

I am in Omaha City. I do not have a photograph of the Pickup family grave in the old Baptist cemetery in Blackwell Holme. When you do make your journey there, please supply.

I have attached a transcription of the letter.

Regards

Taylor J Harvey

The letter

My dearest sister,

It is with the heaviest of hearts that I communicate to you this day. I should have written sooner but was awaiting a happier outcome than the one I am obliged to report. Indeed, I was hoping another would have words for you rather than I.

Your Henry arrived with us near two weeks since, having been delayed in New York owing to the sickness of his confederate and who was moved to one of the State Hospitals on the City's islands. There, the doctors diagnosed Ship's Fever, though that is now much less known since the speedy passage of the steamers replaced the arduous crossings under power of sail. Henry stayed with his friend until hope and his moneys ran out and he had only enough for his journey to us here in Ohio. He had full intention of returning to see to the necessary arrangements, but he, too, began to ail. He had grown into a full strong man since last we saw him, but Reuben and I could both see all was not well. Your Henry would not have it at first, but very soon took to his bed. We got him what medical care we could, but this is not a great City like New York, and even in their fine hospitals Miracles cannot always be trusted upon.

I have not yet spoken the words, but you will have read them already. Your Henry passed into the care of the Lord yesterday evening. On Tuesday last, he had seemed to rally from the Fever and spoke so fondly of you, and commented he could see your face in mine such that it gave him great solace.

This letter's scribe is our minister and good friend, Reverend Atkins. We have knelt and prayed together for Henry and for you, dear sister. I have no more words in me other than to hope you are in good health and can bear this sorry news with fortitude.

Ever your loving sister,   Peggy

The angel

He awoke more tired than he had ever felt, as if all life had been purged from his mortal body. But he also felt a serenity, the weightless freedom of one reborn without care, without sin.

And then there was the light, a blinding radiance that flooded and drowned everything. At its heart, its very source, was a silhouetted figure. Vast, powerful, wild haired and bearded, ancient yet ageless, it raised a hand in greeting. Or was it a blessing? Or a farewell? To one side, a screen of ephemeral tapestries, with the glowing colours of stained glass, floated and fluttered on the softest of cooling breezes. To the other, a wall of purest white stretched unendingly down an eternal gallery. He could vaguely discern the outlines of others like himself, reclined, immobile, somewhere between life and death, awaiting judgement.

And God sent an angel to his bedside. The light quietened and her face emerged from the dazzling mist. It was a face more beautiful than he had ever seen, could ever see. Its smile radiated compassion and unquestioning love, and a porcelain hand reached out to stroke his face. Its touch filled him with renewed strength and he tried to lift himself. The angel shook her head gently and opened her lips. Her voice was like music. It rose and fell, and soothed.

He lay back, closed his eyes, and the cruellest of sleeps stole him away.

He dreamt of falling. He was tumbling and spinning down the blackness of a seemingly bottomless abyss. The dark was total, yet he could clearly see rocky walls racing past his face, the stone carved into grotesque shapes: obscenities and writhing, gargoyle-like monsters. And as he dropped, his temperature climbed. He began to burn.

As good as it gets

Hi Tommy

This is just a quick email to:

One, moan at you for not phoning me back.

Two, thank you for pointing me in the right direction. I won't bore you with all the detail as I know you've got a lot on your plate, but I think I've found the man who Thomas sailed to America with. He was called Henry Pickup and he died of typhus shortly after arriving in Ohio. His aunt wrote a letter back home explaining what happened. It was rather sad and I can understand why the family kept it all these years. If only we could find more documents like that. Anyway, it says his 'confederate' had fallen victim to the same illness and was left dying in a New York hospital. I've been digging around and I think he would have been taken to the Verplanck State Emigrant Hospital on Ward's Island. I haven't been able to find any definitive confirmation that a Thomas Ramsbottom died there in 1873, but I've read that its records were destroyed in a fire around the turn of last century. Ultimately, we're left with slightly circumstantial evidence but I think it's as good as we're going to get. (I still have a nagging feeling he could have survived and began a new life, perhaps had another six kids with some poor dupe of a woman, but I'm sure I'm just being silly.)

The point is, I've pretty much got to the bottom of things and I don't want you to even think about it anymore.

Hope you're making progress with your project and PLEASE DON'T WORK TOO HARD!

Love

Jane xx

Emma

At short notice, Sarah had asked Jane to make up a ladies' four. Cynthia had been called in to work on her day off, as one of the other GPs had childcare issues. That left the tennis players one short for their regular Thursday afternoon doubles match and Jane was drafted in as replacement.

She threw her tennis bag in the boot of the Mazda and briefly thought about lowering the roof again. The sun was shining brightly, but she looked at her watch and saw she was in danger of running late. It would only take seconds, but she decided against. It was probably too hot and she might be more comfortable in the shade.

Sarah's club was exclusively expensive and offered a selection of surfaces from traditional grass through to synthetic carpeting and asphalt. The ladies chose to play on artificial clay as it slowed the ball down and the higher bounce gave them more time to get across the court. None of them were teenagers anymore.

Joanne had two children at prep school and ran a small Internet business from home. She was herself a ball-shaped woman, but deceptively agile and with an appropriately bouncy character. She was playing alongside Emma, who was somewhat less smiley. A daily gym session had banished all padding from her frame and she sought to distract from her lack of curves by drawing attention to her long slender legs. Jane was sure she had a belt wider than what passed for Emma's tennis skirt.

Renewing their schoolgirl partnership, Jane and Sarah made reasonably short work of the opposition. Jane's rustiness had largely worn off by the second set, which was fortunate as Sarah's stamina was not what it once was and she was beginning to fade in the heat. Joanne took the defeat well, but Emma was a woman who saw competition in everything she did. Just walking down the street, she would speed up if someone was making faster progress than her. She was decidedly peeved that the tall, athletic interloper with the off-white whites was so much better than she was. Her line calls had become increasingly suspect and she even shouted out a foot fault in one of the later games.

Jane had encountered enough gamesmanship in her youth to not rise to the bait. She left it to Sarah to register the mildest of rebukes.

'Are you really sure, Emma darling? I don't normally overstep the line, but it's hard for us to see of course. Still, it's your call. Now, what's the score again? Oh yes, forty love, second serve.'

After the match, Joanne rushed off as her au pair was having a crisis with the dishwasher, leaving the other three women to repair to the club's lounge. At the bar, Sarah insisted on buying the drinks. She and Emma decided they'd earned a small G & T; Jane opted for a sparkling mineral water. The steward said he'd bring them over and the women, still wearing their tennis clothes, made for a large wicker sofa on a veranda looking out over the courts.

As they sat down on the green and white striped cushions, Emma explained the gin was also merited because she had cause to celebrate. Her husband had just been promoted to the board and it promised a significant increase to their income.

'You're not married?' she said, pointing to Jane's left hand.

Jane stared at her ring finger, searching for a vestigial mark. 'Not anymore. Divorced,' she mumbled. It was the second time her marital status had been queried recently and it prompted her to turn towards Sarah. 'I ran into Christine Jackson in the supermarket a day or so ago.'

Sarah raised her eyebrows. 'Still a total and utter chav, I presume?' Sarah's expression slipped into one of concern. 'It didn't... I mean, it went okay. She behaved herself?'

Jane nodded. 'Yeh, yeh. I'll tell you later.'

'Who's Christine Jackson?' asked Emma, feeling left out of the conversation.

Sarah chose to answer a different question. 'Jane's husband was a police inspector. Very tall, very handsome.'

'Very unfaithful,' added Jane. 'Well, not that unfaithful, I suppose. Only with one person, as far as I'm aware anyway.'

'Once is enough,' cut in Emma firmly. 'So, have you replaced him? I would, and quick. I wouldn't want him thinking I was moping around without him.'

'Not yet. I'm guess I'm busy setting up my new business. Too busy to have time for men and all that painful dating stuff.'

'Not that she hasn't had offers,' said Sarah, looking up as their drinks arrived.

Jane accepted her glass and mouthed her thanks. She waited until the steward had gone and then responded. 'What offers have I had exactly?'

Sarah swallowed a sip of gin as she quickly assembled an argument. 'Well, the client on your last contract, the rich Anglo-American businessman. You had dinner and everything. He definitely had the hots for you.'

Jane sighed. 'It was lunch, and I think I had the hots for him and misread the signs. And then I met his beautiful, successful wife and realised I wasn't in the same league.'

'Jane Madden, don't put yourself down,' scolded Sarah. 'You're very much first division, or is it premier... championship these days? Whatever it is, you're in it. And now that tart has left him, Dave would have you back tomorrow.'

Emma looked horrified. 'Is that your ex? You can't go back to him! That would be total capitulation.'

Jane shook her head slowly. 'It's not going to happen with Dave—'

'Well, Tommy's hopelessly in love with you,' interjected Sarah, simultaneously wincing as she realised she was betraying a confidence.

'Tommy's not in love with me. We're just friends. Good friends, but friends.'

'Who's this Tommy?' asked Emma, clearly enjoying the gossip.

'He's someone…' Jane paused while she weighed up how much to reveal. 'I wasn't very well a while back and he was having treatment at the same place. We got on. He's so nice. He helped with some family history stuff I was doing. It took my mind off things. But, we're totally different. He's got a brain the size of a planet.'

'You're not exactly stupid, Jane,' said Sarah, putting a reproving hand on her friend's shoulder.

'I'm not saying I'm stupid, but he's one of those cerebral people who's awkward socially. He's not my type and I'm certainly not his. He's got a girlfriend, well, an online girlfriend. But they talk about programming and computer games, things like that. I'd bore him to death. Very quickly.'

'He's a good-looking man.' Sarah's words come out hesitantly, as if her mouth and brain were out of step. 'But he's just a bit shy. He confided his feelings to me at that auction we attended.' She winced again. 'I'm sorry, I'm sure I wasn't supposed to tell you. It just slipped out. He knows it wouldn't work – you are too different – but he's totally besotted with you. I mean, gaga.'

'No, he's not. I'm sure you're putting two and two together and making five. We were all a bit drunk—'

Jane's denial was interrupted by an earnest sounding Emma. 'Am I the only one to think it's a bit creepy? I mean, a grown man having kind of a schoolboy crush. That's the sort of thing that leads to stalking. I mean, forgive me, but you said yourself he's had mental health issues.'

'I'm not sure I said that.' Jane's expression had become pained. 'Look, he's a really nice guy. I wasn't feeling great a while back and he got the train all the way from London. I hadn't even told him my address. He worked it out from my grandparents and online copies of old electoral registers—'

'And that's not stalking?' said Emma, somewhat triumphantly. 'He sounds like he's one of those who lives on his bedroom computer, looking at God knows what. I'm not being funny – you might find the wall is covered with pictures of you, taken with a telephoto lens when you're not looking.'

Jane raised her hands to take charge of the conversation. 'Look. First of all, Tommy isn't in love with me. I know him best and he just isn't. Secondly, he's not some kind of nutter I need to be frightened of because he's spying on me. So, please, can we change the subject?'

'Just keep him at arm's length. That's all I'm saying.' Emma downed her gin decisively. 'Now, can I get you girls another drink?'

Shredding

Jane slammed her front door and went into the kitchen to make a cup of coffee. Eventually its soothing warmth began to calm the fury that had started to build as she drove home. Reliving the post-match conversation in her head had made her far angrier than it had at the time. Jane had now wound herself up to thinking Emma was a bitch of the first order. She was a bad loser who tried to get revenge for her on-court thrashing by bragging about her wonderful, bloody husband and suggesting Jane's only real male friend was some kind of creep. It hurt all the more because of a secret Jane knew and kept. There had been some difficulties at one of Tommy's previous employers. But he'd not been well and it sounded like the female complainant simply misunderstood what was really a cry for help.

Jane was cross with Emma, but also angry with herself for letting the woman get under her skin. Nonetheless, if they ever played again, Emma had better keep her head down. Bodyline tactics didn't just apply to cricket. A smashed tennis ball can leave a nasty bruise. Maybe a black eye.

Jane sat down in front of her computer and tried a relaxation technique she had been taught by an otherwise useless therapist. It was ineffectual when the red mist was well and truly down, but seemed to help when she was starting to regain control. She held the inside of her wrist and felt the smooth skin under her fingers. It was the trigger to take her mind back to an event from her childhood when she felt safe, secure and happy. Her mother was on one of her honeymoons, but Jane had gone away with her grandparents and had got up early to cycle along a deserted seaside promenade which ran at the bottom of gently sloping, grassy cliffs. It was a beautiful, cloudless morning; the air was still and warm.

A low sea wall curved into the distance, and over it the faintest of waves hissed softly as they tentatively encroached on the remaining sliver of golden beach. The water was almost perfectly flat and reflected the sky in a shimmering, hazy blue. Jane breathed steadily and easily. Her pulse slowed.

After a few minutes, Jane opened her eyes and reached for her coffee. It had gone cold, as had her anger towards Emma.

'But your backhand's still crap,' she said out loud, before lifting the lid on her laptop and logging on.

It was yet another dodgy email. They seemed to be arriving with tedious regularity and she deleted it quickly, not wanting to let it fire her anger again. But then she had second thoughts. Was this one unusually targeted and personalised?

She'd recently switched her electricity and gas supplier. She'd never bothered in the past, but she knew that was what you were supposed to do and had, indeed, saved money on her monthly bill. She didn't understand why the utility companies couldn't just give you their fairest price. It might something to do with injecting competition into an otherwise artificial market. Or maybe big business was just happy ripping lazy people off. Either way, she was now with one of the smaller players. A week or so ago they had sent her a letter confirming the transfer and they'd apparently followed up with an email asking her to download an 'account management' program.

Somehow, something hadn't seemed quite right. Sure enough, when she'd checked, the link was actually to a suspiciously named website, presumably somewhere in Russia or the Far East. Or maybe it was in some spotty teenager's bedroom in Basingstoke.

But how did they know Jane had moved to this particular company? Was it just a coincidence? Was the spammer taking a chance and hoping that relative obscurity would work in their favour? And they'd included the first four digits of an account number. The rest was asterisked out, purportedly as a security measure, but presumably every customer's number began the same?

Jane wondered if she should recover the deleted email and look at it more carefully. But her patience felt at a low ebb and she found this aspect of modern technology painfully dull at the best of times. If there had been some sort of hack it wouldn't only have affected her and hopefully she'd just avoided the worst of the consequences. And then a different thought occurred to her. Could this be the first step in an attempt at identity theft? Could someone have been through her recycling and found the discarded welcome letter? She was guiltily aware her shredder had been broken for some time now. Perhaps she wasn't always as thorough as she could be tearing out personal details from any official correspondence she received.

She looked at her watch, sighed frustratedly and decided she was being overdramatic. She would simply stay vigilant, and the lesson was that she needed to buy a new shredder with some urgency. And then there was her aging laptop with its unsupported software. Should she get a new computer at the same time? That sounded more expensive and harder work. The shredder would have to do for the time being.

The unusual item of spam had tested her nerves, and at least it had taken her mind off the exchange after the tennis match. She was briefly reminded when she saw she had a bona fide email from the man Emma had warned her to be wary of.

'Stuff you, Emma. And buy a proper skirt while you're at it,' said Jane.

LostCousins

Hi Jane

Sorry about not ringing. You know I'm not good with phones and my other excuse is that I've been away for a couple of days. They called an urgent project meeting, up quite close to you. I could have done without it, but they managed to make some important decisions which have taken some of the immediate pressure off. There are a few short-term problems to sort out, but I think I can see the light at the end of the tunnel. You're right, of course, about my tendency to get obsessive about things, but I've been taking a bit of time out. It's helping. I think.

But going back to your family history research, I'm seriously impressed with what you've found. You're good at this stuff.

One quick thought on your man, Thomas Ramsbottom, and his possible survival in America. Given the evidence, I think it's almost certain he did die soon after his arrival in New York, but have you considered getting your client to do a DNA test? You might want to ask his cousin to do one as well. The down side is that it'll take a while for the results to come through. But what you'd be looking for is a match with someone living in the States who is descended from a mysterious Englishman with no past before the 1870s. The relationship would be something like a half 3rd cousin which is pretty close in genetic terms. I know I've talked to you before about DNA, but I don't know how much you've done with it yet. This masterclass is a very good place to start – though hopefully you're up to speed with most of this already?

Tommy x

Tommy's link took Jane to LostCousins.com, a website designed to facilitate contact between lost or distant cousins researching the same ancestors. The specific page was a detailed guide on how to use DNA for family history research. It was from a regular newsletter containing news and tips that went out to a distribution list with tens of thousands of email addresses worldwide. As Jane read it she felt stupid, stupid for not subscribing to the newsletter herself and stupid for not thinking of DNA before. Tommy had been right when he said she needed more training. He was wrong, however, about having to wait for samples to be processed. Both Guy Ramsbottom and his cousin had already taken the test. Their results had been staring Jane in the face and she'd been ignoring them.

Her excuse was that she hadn't got round to having her own DNA analyzed yet. Initially she'd dismissed it as only useful for giving an ancestral ethnicity profile. It might be fun to be told she was 60% English, 25% Scottish/Irish, 10% Scandinavian and 5% Sherpa, but she'd heard the results were of questionable accuracy, with different companies giving different breakdowns when presented with the same genetic material. Nonetheless, this aspect of the test was what the advertising campaigns focused on and presumably was what had attracted Guy and his cousin.

Jane had heard an increasing buzz about DNA, but had always assumed she could call on Tommy's help if she needed it. It made her realise how much her business model relied on her friend. The more she now read, the more she began to appreciate DNA's power for finding broken links or breaking through dead ends in a family tree.

As Jane trawled other websites to delve deeper into the science it quickly became more opaque, a thick soup of chromosomes, autosomes, genes, alleles, chips, snips and centiMorgans. One forum article attempted to summarise the concepts.

'I've been researching my family history since the s-l-o-w old days of whirring microfilm readers and having to travel to London to wade through names printed in real-life, physical index books. And yet, after all these years, I still haven't found the link back to the blue blood that I know courses through my veins. Now I'm being told that DNA is the biggest thing in genealogy since the Internet. Sounds promising, but how does it work?

'I'm no biologist – and huge apologies to any propeller heads reading this - but we've all heard of the "double helix" and the "blueprint of life", right? We may also have heard that the human genome is made up of three billion "base pairs" of coded information that tells our cells how to develop and do the jobs our bodies need of them. We may know that 99.9% of that code is the same in every human being – or else we'd be chimpanzees, or bananas – but it's the tiny differences or "mutations" that make us individuals with differing appearance, abilities, susceptibility to disease and so on. We certainly know that we inherit our DNA from our parents – who's the father? Take a DNA test.

'But when we're researching our family tree, the question is more likely to be – who's the great-great-great-grandfather? Then it gets a little more complicated.

'First of all, let's explain that there are different types of DNA you can have analyzed. Only men have a Y chromosome and its DNA is passed down on a strictly father-to-son basis, generation after generation after generation. There's another type of DNA, I won't bother you with its name (but it's "mitochondrial"), which goes down the maternal line, pretty much back to Eve herself. So test both of those and you've covered everyone? Think again. They only cut narrow swathes through your ancestral past – every mother's father and father's mother doesn't get a look in.

'So the most popular type of test is the one which looks at the vast majority of our DNA, where we get 50% from dad and 50% from mum. (I just can't stop myself giving you names – my mum and dad were Maggie and Jim and this DNA is called "autosomal".) Okay, 50% from each, that makes sense. But which 50%? Nature deliberately splits it into chunks and jumbles it up in a process called "recombination". For reasons of genetic diversity (think Darwin), siblings, other than identical twins, don't get the same mix of DNA from their mother and father. If they did, all brothers and all sisters would look the same. Again, you knew that already.

'Going back a generation, our parents also got 50% of their DNA from their dads and mums. So a quarter of our DNA comes from our grandparents? On average, yes, but because of that mixing up, we don't necessarily get a full 25% from each of them; we might get more from some than others. The idea that little Kathryn favours Grandma may have a good scientific foundation. This is really important because it means it can be difficult to determine exactly how closely two people are related by the amount of DNA they share. The closer the relationship, the more confident the prediction can be. Also, some lines may fade away and become undetectable much sooner than others. Our DNA is the combination of a few hundred ancestors, but ultimately we have thousands upon thousands of forebears and only a small fraction can leave their genetic mark upon us. (But I sense my royal genes have fought their way through the pack.)

'So how does one of these DNA genealogy tests work? You send in a sample, say of saliva, which contains cells from the inside of your mouth. It gets analyzed by some high-tech wizardry (a machine) that looks at sections of the genome known to contain individual variations. Obviously your great-great-great-grandfather is dead (I'm guessing) and won't be submitting a sample any day soon. But one of his other descendants (your 4th cousin or 3rd cousin twice removed, etc., etc.) might have done. A computer compares your unique code sequences to all the others in its database. Significant areas of correspondence (measured in the delightfully named "centiMorgans") suggest there is likely to be shared ancestry somewhere in the reasonably recent past, say up to eight generations back.

'Okay, so the computer gives you a list of people to whom you're probably related. All that mixing up means it doesn't know what your relationship is; it just has a rough idea of how many degrees of generational separation are involved. It might take an educated guess you're 3rd cousins for example. Then what? Well, if you're lucky, your 3rd cousin will have a meticulously researched tree posted online and which takes you back to 1066 and William the Conqueror. Job done. Maybe. More likely, you'll just have a set of names, often anonymised, and with variable amounts of family information attached, often none at all. And there'll be a lot of these new cousins, like thousands. The computer will try to estimate how close you are to each one, but as we discussed above, it won't always be right. Even if it does correctly predict you and 'CHRIS355' are descended from the same great-great-great-grandparents, the DNA data alone doesn't reveal which.

'That's when the work, and the fun, begins. You need to employ strategies, like looking for common surnames, geographic locations, etc. to try to establish how you might be related to at least some of these people. If you can get other members of your family tested it will help. If your dad shares a match with you, it should be stronger as he's a generation closer to the past, plus you can eliminate your mother's half of your genetic background. And then you'll find yourself getting in touch with new family, perhaps all over the world. Some of them will be keen genealogists who will have fresh insights and stories to share. Perhaps you've hit a brick wall in your tree that traditional methods can't get through because people moved or the paper records are inconclusive or lost. But then you find you're genetically related to someone and the only possible link means the wall comes tumbling down.

'I'm a BIG convert. DNA testing is in no way a substitute for good old-fashioned family history research, but used in combination, the two together open up a new world of opportunities. I'll prove I've got that royal blood yet.'

Jane sat back and tried to digest everything she'd read. Guy and his cousin's results would identify a long list of people with whom they shared DNA. Jane had to sift through the matches, researching their own lineage where necessary, to try to find a back-door connection to Thomas Ramsbottom.

But what were the odds of finding someone?

Perhaps the most important thing she'd discovered was that well over ten million people had now taken the same test as Guy, a large proportion of whom were in the USA. There was at least a chance she could unearth an American line of descent from Thomas and prove he didn't die of typhus in that New York hospital.

It sounded like it had the potential to be a lot of work, but Jane justified it on the basis of self-education: this was an embarrassing gap in the skill set of a professional genealogist. In truth, she knew there was another impulse at work. Thomas Ramsbottom was a slippery, slimy bottom-feeder of a man. She wasn't ready to let him off the hook without trying everything she could to drag him from the depths of history and into the daylight.

Shared code

As predicted, there were thousands of people who had come up as matching some of Guy's DNA, though the vast majority were classified as distant cousins whose shared ancestors should, with any luck, long predate Thomas Ramsbottom. That left over 300 3rd or 4th cousins who were in the right sort of range. Unfortunately, not all of them gave their real name or where they were from. And only a minority had a family tree attached that was extensive enough to go back to the 1870s. Establishing how most of these people were related to Guy would be a challenge.

Top of the list of matches was Guy's cousin, Betty, whom Jane had visited in Lancashire. Betty and Guy had the same grandfather but different grandmothers, so they were technically only half cousins. Unfortunately, they shared less than the average amount of DNA for that relationship and the computer suggested they were somewhat further apart. It was Jane's first confirmation of the randomness of genetic inheritance.

There were various ways of analyzing the results and Jane began finding her feet by searching for recognisable family names, starting with Ramsbottom and then broadening out. There were a few hits, mostly amongst the remoter cousins. Some of the individuals were or had been living in the United States in the last 150 years, but each one Jane looked at turned out to be a blind alley and she soon abandoned this approach. After all, one of her working assumptions was that Thomas disappeared from the records because he changed his name.

There was an option to see which of Guy's cousins shared DNA with each other and Jane quickly realised it could be the key to unravelling this particular puzzle. The fact that Betty and Guy did not have the same grandmother was actually a boon. If Jane focused on people to whom they were both genetically related, she would know she was on the Ramsbottom blood line, for two generations back at least.

There were only a handful of profiles which came up as shared by both Guy and Betty without being too distantly related. Of those, several included at least some ancestral information and Jane busied herself working through them.

She had started late and by midnight she felt like she was going all round the world getting nowhere. She had discovered one family cluster living in Australia and New Zealand and then found a woman who had moved to Hawaii but had actually been born in New York State. Jane's hopes were raised and she eagerly traced the woman's parents and grandparents only to discover she was descended from one of Thomas Ramsbottom's nieces who had emigrated soon after the First World War.

It was tantalising close, but not the answer Jane needed to find. Tiredness amplified disappointment into despondency. Jane suddenly felt drained and lost. This was a useless waste of time. She was useless for even trying. All the evidence said Thomas died when he got to New York. She could spend days or weeks working through all this data. But it would be just because of a stupid hunch that Thomas survived. It was a wild-goose chase to hold a deserting father to account, a stand-in for her own, a man who didn't want her, didn't love her, because she was an ugly, big-boned, unstable, useless lump. It was time to give up, give up for the day, maybe give up the pretence of being a genealogist altogether. She was a fraud and it was only a matter of time before she was found out.

Jane eyes filled with tears and she clamped them shut. When they reluctantly reopened they caught a name towards the bottom of the screen. It was a match shared with Betty, but Jane had been ignoring it as it appeared to have nothing usable attached. It was just a name attached to a profile that had not logged in for over two years. But it was an intriguing name, nonetheless: Roxanne Wiser, it certainly sounded American. Jane wiped her face and breathed deeply. Maybe it was worth one last try.

The name was also helpfully unusual. Jane soon found a Roxanne J Wiser living with her husband Frank in Minnesota in a 1990s' phone directory. A US public records entry said she had previously been Roxanne J Arnold. That proved, however, not to be her birth name. The Minnesota divorce index said she and her first husband, David L Arnold, had parted company in the 1970s. She had entered the world as Roxanne Josette Armand in 1952 of an America father and a Swedish mother.

Roxanne's parents married in Montana and the record included the name of the groom's father, Lewis (actually Louis) Joseph Armand and, significantly, the fact he was a Frenchman. Montana did not consider the groom's mother's full name worthy of note, but fortunately it was on her son's social security record. Roxanne's paternal grandmother was called Hilda Catherine Gish, hailing from Illinois. Hilda had not stayed married to Louis Armand for long, having different husbands on both the 1930 and 1940 federal censuses. But that information was mere colouring. What was important about Hilda was that she appeared on someone else's online family tree. It proved to be the breakthrough Jane had been looking for.

The woman who researched the tree, 'L.Y.' was a descendant of Hilda's sister, Esther Mary Gish. Jane felt confident Guy and Betty did not share Roxanne Wiser's French and Swedish blood. That suggested that, whilst L.Y. had not taken a DNA test herself, there was a strong likelihood she was also genetically related to the Ramsbottoms.

Hilda and Esther's father was Georg Giersch from Siebenbürgen, then in the Austro-Hungarian Empire, but now Transylvania in Romania. Their British ancestry came from their mother, born Sarah Kathleen Ramsden in New York in 1874. Sarah was the daughter of Thomas Ramsden, an Englishman who appeared to have no traceable past before his marriage the year before.

That was the year Thomas Ramsbottom sailed from Liverpool to America. The similarity in names was not lost on Jane. She felt sure L.Y. and Roxanne Wiser had to be descended from his second life in America. Jane had worked through most of the night but she had got her man.

The hospital ward

Thomas opened his eyes and was briefly disoriented. For two weeks he'd been in the fever ward, drifting in and out of consciousness, but his surroundings had changed. The wooden rafters that he stared at as they twisted and blurred had been replaced by a smooth plaster ceiling. And he could hear voices, people communicating not just coughing and groaning. Then he remembered being moved. His temperature no longer raged and they needed his bed. He also recalled being given something to help him sleep and, he was told, to ward off diarrhoea, whatever that was. He lifted himself onto his pillow. His muscles ached like he'd been hauling coal trucks all day, but the debilitating, draining weakness was gone. He looked about and felt a strange melancholy despite his recovering strength. It was a bright April day and the windows running the length of the left-hand wall had been raised, allowing fresh spring air to flood in and guard against the miasmas the chief physician still held responsible for much disease and illness. Curtains billowed in the cool breeze blowing off the Harlem River.

Thomas pulled his sheets higher over his chest and surveyed the regimented lines of cots running down both sides of the long, white walled room. One or two were unoccupied, but most contained a man, either lying or sitting, occasionally in conversation with a neighbour or visitor, but mostly asleep or alone with their thoughts. At the far end, a cluster of uniformed orderlies and two doctors in fine suits were gathered around a patient. Their hushed words had the solemn tone of finality and impotence.

Also watching the scene were a man and a woman standing by the bed next to Thomas. From behind, the man cut an intimidating figure. He was a little over normal height but as wide as he was tall, with unkempt reddish-brown locks streaked with white and grey. The woman was contrastingly delicate, sharing only the colouring, albeit without the trappings of age. She was wearing a rich-blue dress that reached to the floor, a checked shawl and her hair was tied back in a simple ponytail.

The man turned first. He had a heavily lined brow, weary eyes and a battered nose, but beneath was a darkly extravagant beard that argued the vigour and strength of his youth had not deserted him. Seeing Thomas awake, he raised a hand in acknowledgement, but no smile was apparent beneath the whiskers. He spoke a name, 'Mary', and the girl followed his voice and looked round.

Thomas felt a tremor in his hands that could only partly be blamed on the after-effects of illness and medication. Mary was in her mid twenties and simply the most beautiful thing he had ever seen. His world had been that of a small, isolated community where the faces were hardened by toil and largely interchangeable. He had heard of society belles and the alluring wives of rich men, but their orbit was far from his own. His experience of photography was restricted to formal studies of scowling families. He had visited an art gallery once in his life, but the women in the paintings were from a different age, remote and lifeless. This girl was real and breathing, a dream made flesh. But there was also a fragility about her, the quality of a porcelain doll.

'You're awake, darlin'. How are you feeling now?' Her Irish lilt was all music and warmth.

Thomas found himself involuntarily smoothing his matted blond hair. 'Tired, but I think I must be much better.'

'We've been wondering when you'd be back with us,' she said conspiratorially, looking over her shoulder. 'They seem to like the laudanum in here. It's strong stuff, takes you away with the fairies. They had Patty on it for a while.'

'Patty?'

'Sorry, let me introduce ourselves. I'm Mary Sheehan and this here's my father, Patrick O'Brien. We're over from Ireland in case you haven't guessed. Mary and Patrick are such unusual Irish names after all.' She grinned and then stepped to one side and pointed to the bed behind her. 'And this fine lad's my brother, Patty.'

A boy in his late teens waved a salute. 'They brought you in late last night,' he said. 'You've been asleep all day – I was worried you might not wake up. We lost a Frenchie in that bed yesterday,' he added cheerfully.

Mary gave her brother a silencing look and then turned back towards Thomas. 'Don't mind Patty. I'm sure you won't be following after that Frenchman. You'll be out of here in no time.'

Thomas's mind was working slowly. 'Mary Sheehan, not O'Brien?' he said, not noticing the frown that moved across Mary's father's face.

'I was married. Not for long. He... he died. He was a good looking fella, bit like yourself.'

Mary was not intending to flirt and she flushed with embarrassment. She glanced out of the window and then continued. 'Da thought we should try our luck in New York. My uncle's already here. And what do they call you now?'

'Thomas...' He hesitated, his mind going back to his experience on the ship. '...Thomas Ramsbottom.'

Mary's father let out a sound that started as a snort and then tried to disguise itself as a cough.

'It's the name of a town in Lancashire,' added Thomas, defensively.

'We're from County Wexford – we wouldn't know our way round England. And there's lots of names over here you wouldn't recognise. Those foreign fellas often change them. To sound more American, you know?'

Mary's blue eyes twinkled an apology. 'And what's brought you so far from home, Thomas Ramsbottom?'

Thomas had to think for a moment. The ship, leaving Liverpool, his past life seemed very long ago. 'We're heading to Ohio, the coal fields. My friend and I are miners. He's got kin there.'

Mary looked surprised. 'I wouldn't have you down as a miner. That's a dirty, dangerous way to earn a crust.'

'I was in a cotton mill for a while.' Thomas paused again. 'There was an accident. I don't like to think on it.'

'There's plenty of other work for a fit, young man, right here in New York. They've got all the streets laid out, mile after mile, neat and square, but there's a city to build in amongst them.'

Thomas didn't reply. He'd once hoped for something better than manual labour, but it seemed a futile and alienating thing to say. Laudanum's shadow and dark memories caused his heart to drop. He was suddenly close to tears.

Sensing his discomfort, Mary changed the subject. 'So, where's your friend now?'

Thomas shrugged. 'I'm not sure. I think he may have continued on his way. I guess he's thinking I'll follow after him.'

'And you've got no family to worry about you?'

Thomas shook his head. 'No, there's no-one', he replied truthfully, hearing 'in America' implied in the question.

It started as honest confusion and became a lie.

The party

Jane hadn't wanted to go in the first place. Now she positively resented the invitation. All the same, she knew she couldn't burn a bridge that had only been built so recently. She packed her smallest suitcase and threw it in the boot. It contained two dresses. One was the supposedly tasteful number she had worn to the auction where Duff had bought the fire engine. The other was a shade of blue that was verging on electric and had interestingly asymmetrical orange arms. In Jane's eyes it was a proper party dress; it suited her better and was much more fun. Her mother would hate it.

She remembered the route well enough to eschew the services of irritating robot woman in her phone's satnav, but the traffic was even worse than on her previous journey and crawled all through the New Forest and down to the Dorset coast. When she pulled up outside her mother's house, she was late and she was tired. It had taken five hours and her mood had not improved. She had driven all that way to meet a group of people she wouldn't like. Tomorrow she would have to drive all the way back again.

A voice Jane didn't recognise answered the intercom and the heavy iron gates rolled back. Jane found that space for a single vehicle had been left on the gravel area in front of her mother's bungalow. Jane parked the Mazda and climbed out, carefully opening the door so as not to scratch the car alongside. It loomed over her and seemed ridiculously large and ostentatious. Even Jane recognised the badge as that of a Rolls Royce. And next to it was a smaller, sleeker, prettier two-door coupé in a shade of bright lemon-yellow that she did very much approve of. Again, she found she knew the emblem on its grille. It was the trident of a Maserati, never again to be confused with the W of a Wartburg.

'Darling! Thank you for coming.'

Jane looked up to see her mother standing at the door, a glass of something sparkling in her hand. Jane immediately assumed it was a rather good champagne. Guests in Maseratis and Rolls Royces presumably didn't drink prosecco.

Jane waved a greeting. 'Mother, sorry I'm a bit late. There was a nasty accident on the A338. Tailbacks for miles.'

'Well you're here now, darling. And everyone's dying to meet you.' Her mother scanned Jane's clothing and frowned slightly. 'I'm assuming you've brought something nice to put on? I'll show you up to your room, so you can get changed.'

Jane read her mother's expression and immediately knew she which dress she would be wearing. She also found herself wondering if 'your room' meant precisely that, somehow her possession in her mother's dominion. She quickly decided not. It was not a large house. It was a guest room and hers for one night only.

Jane was awoken by the screeching of a seagull. She sat up in bed and checked her mobile phone. It was well past 9:00 am. She felt like she'd had the best night's sleep ever. The party had finished by 10:30 pm and she'd only sipped the champagne, partly because of her reluctance to develop expensive tastes. And the bed was unbelievably comfortable. She normally struggled to sleep when away from home, certainly for the first night or so, but the mattress and the quilt and the pillow were unusually cosy and comforting and warm. She could only assume she was used to the bedding equivalent of cheap fizz.

She looked around the room and saw her frock hanging over the back of a chair. She had played it safe and it had been the right decision. All the other guests had been elegantly glamorous and Jane would have stood out like the sorest of thumbs. The watchword had been sophistication not fun. Just as she was congratulating herself on her restraint, another thought came into her mind. She winced at its memory and decided she needed to get up. Perhaps a hot shower would wash it away unnoticed like a temporary and unobtrusive blemish.

Cleansed and dressed, Jane descended the stairs from the small first floor to find her mother in the kitchen staring out of the window onto the wide expanse of Poole Harbour. The house was immaculate and there was no evidence of the previous evening's revelry. Jane had offered to tidy up, but had been told that was what the hired staff were for. It was certainly a change from the bomb sites she had awoken to after parties she and Dave had held in the past.

'Morning, Mother,' said Jane. 'Sorry I slept in a bit. You been up long?'

The older woman was already aware of another presence in the room and turned her head slowly. 'Darling, glad you got a good night's rest – you young people have such hectic lives. I have been down a while.' She stood and began walking towards a wall of cupboard doors. 'I'll make you a coffee and what would you like for breakfast?'

When Jane had visited Dave's parents bacon and eggs were always on offer, but she knew that was beyond her mother's scope.

'Toast would be fine?' suggested Jane.

Her mother looked disapproving. 'I'm sure we've got some bread somewhere. I don't normally... How about fresh fruit and yoghurt?'

'That would be lovely. Thank you.'

One of the cupboard doors revealed a huge fridge whose shelves were only lightly stocked. Slices of fresh pineapple and melon were produced and laid alongside a small serving of Greek yoghurt. Jane's mother then turned her attention to the coffee. She did not check her daughter's preferences. She knew they still matched her own: a tiny bit of milk and no sugar. It was part of a regime that had thankfully stopped the teenage Jane developing her father's bulk.

The conversation faltered as her mother worked, and Jane focused on the view. It remained as wonderful as the first time she saw it. The perfect lawn flowed into the shining ripples of the bay. Yachts bobbed at anchor off the wooded islands. A waterside hotel still wore the crenellations of its fortress core. There was serenity, yet there was life. Boats already motored back and forth. Sails were being raised in preparation for escape out into the English Channel and beyond.

'There, darling,' said her mother, laying a pure-white, slightly dished plate in front of Jane. It was accompanied by a cream linen napkin and a spoon, knife and fork. The coffee was served in something that was bigger than a cup but far too stylish to be called a mug.

'Thank you, this looks wonderful,' replied Jane, looking up and smiling.

Her mother sat alongside cradling her own coffee in her hands. It was unclear whether she had already eaten or whether breakfast had been sacrificed entirely in her ongoing mission to avoid the spread of late middle age. If one had to choose between figure and face, she had opted for figure, though she wouldn't even enter her own kitchen without her immaculate and understated make-up helping fight the other front.

'So, did you enjoy the party last night?' she asked.

'Yes,' lied Jane politely, before adding a degree of qualification. 'Though everyone was rather more rich and glamorous than my normal circle of acquaintances. I've never seen so many jewels on display.'

'Rich, glamorous and old,' said her mother. 'That does seem to be demographic on Sandbanks. Certainly the ones I mix with. That was why I so wanted you to meet Hugo.'

Jane smiled unconvincingly. The blemish she'd hoped had gone unseen was threatening to be exposed.

'He's much nearer your age,' continued her mother, 'and utterly, utterly charming. And, between you and me, he could probably buy out everyone else at the party last night. He owns a hedge fund.'

'Yes, so he said. I did ask him to explain what they were exactly. I got very lost very quickly, but it did sound like a licence to print money.'

Jane's mother put her coffee down on the table. 'Indeed, and, amazingly, he's single at the moment.'

'And has the second fastest boat on the South Coast,' said Jane.

'It is a beautiful, beautiful boat.' confirmed her mother enthusiastically.

'The man with the fastest boat is a Japanese banker who doesn't know how to handle her.' Jane's sarcasm was now only thinly disguised. 'So Hugo's boat is effectively the fastest and he was very keen to take me out on her today. He said we could cruise over for lunch on the Isle of Wight. He knows this fantastic fish restaurant in Cowes.'

'It is a nice restaurant, darling. It would have been a lovely day out. Why on earth did you say no?'

'He wasn't my type. Too full of himself. I like confident men, but there's a limit. So I said no. And I had to keep saying no, because he kept on and on at me.'

Her mother shrugged. 'Men like that are used to getting their way. Talking people round. It's what makes them successful. I don't suppose he's used to being turned down.'

Jane stared out of the window. 'I got that impression.'

'So why did you have to say that silly thing, darling?'

Jane's gaze was still directed unseeingly towards the view. 'I meant it as a joke. A put down, but a joke. It just came out more strongly that I intended. It did the trick though.'

'But threatening to gouge his eye out? He made a joke of it too, though I could tell he wasn't 100% sure. He said you were, and I quote, "charmingly feisty", though I was far from convinced he was charmed.'

'Oh, Mother! I'm sorry if I upset your friends and they now all think I'm a mad, crazy bitch. I guess I don't fit into your world. I did try, but... I am a mad, crazy bitch sometimes. That's not a surprise to either of us.'

There was a long silence. It was finally broken by Jane.

'How did my father lose his eye?'

'In a fight of course. He was hit in the face with a broken bottle. God knows what he did to the other man. All he'd say was, "Don't worry your pretty face, sweetheart. I sorted it. That's all you need to know." Or maybe it was, "I sorted him." Either way, your father's face was sorted too. They could probably tidy it up much better these days, but I think he was proud of it. That hideous patch he wore. He really did fancy himself as some kind of pirate.'

'I went to see his sister.'

Jane's mother's brow dropped in disbelief. 'You went to see that awful woman? What was her name? Stella?'

'Stacy.'

'That was it, Stacy. God, she was rough. Why on earth did you want to see her?'

Jane finally looked back from the window. 'To see if she knew where my father was. To see if they were in contact.'

'And?'

'She said not. I'm not sure if I believe her. She said I was better off not getting involved with him.'

'Well, I agree with her there.' Jane's mother took her daughter's hand and her tone became conciliatory. 'What exactly do want from him, darling? An explanation, a reason for why he abandoned you? Reconciliation?' A cuddle from your long-lost daddy? I warn you he may not be as cuddly as you might remember.'

Jane felt the other woman's touch. Its warmth seemed alien and out of place. 'Maybe I want revenge. Maybe I need to punish him. I am a mad, crazy bitch after all,' she replied.

'Is that one of your jokes again, darling?'

Kids

The constable was rather short and decidedly fresh faced. Jane knew a classic sign of age was that policemen looked younger, but she hadn't realised she'd reached that stage yet. Perhaps this officer had only just qualified. Or maybe he was genetically blessed, or cursed: it wasn't an advantage looking like an innocent schoolboy when confronting an angry drunk outside a Nottingham bar on a Saturday night. This PC might need his CS spray more than most.

He wouldn't be needing it right now, of course. He was on a mundane burglary call-out, more admin and paperwork than policing. Nonetheless, he was wearing his stab vest. It was a sad indictment of modern society that this had arguably replaced the helmet as the trademark symbol of the British bobby, now they mostly patrolled by car and wore peaked caps or went bareheaded.

He smiled amiably and introduced himself as PC Zahid Kahn. He flashed a warrant card, though it disappeared so quickly it could have been his gym membership for all Jane knew. It didn't matter, she had reported a non-urgent crime and here was a uniform on her doorstep. PC Kahn obviously thought he could handle this on his own: Jane could see his colleague outside in the patrol car, busy on the radio.

'Hi, come in.' Jane said cheerfully. 'I wasn't sure they'd send anyone out. You hear stories of break-ins just being logged on the phone these days. Only even-numbered addresses being investigated, that kind of thing.'

PC Kahn looked hurt, a sensitive disposition seemingly joining his baby face in his list of non-ideal job qualifications.

Jane quickly backtracked. 'Sorry, not having a dig. It's the cuts, I know. I was on the force myself. Down in the Smoke.'

The smoke?

Jane grimaced. 'Sorry, London. I momentarily slipped back into my old mind set. That's how they talk in the Met. It's still a very macho culture. A bit Sweeney, you know?' Seeing a blank face she elaborated. 'Part cockney rhyming slang, part sexist stereotypes.' She affected a growl in her best EastEnders' accent: '"She was a right tea leaf, not to mention a total slag." That kind of thing. At least it was before I left.'

PC Kahn finally seemed interested. 'Was that why you did leave?'

'No, it was the usual reasons – shift work, antisocial hours. Tired of dealing with lowlife.' Jane reeled out her usual excuses. The truth of a mental breakdown and the assault and near blinding of a prisoner in custody was not something she needed to broadcast.

'I'm on a fast track programme. I'm hoping to make detective soon,' said the PC enthusiastically.

'I'm sorry to tell you that's when you get to meet the real scumbags. And I don't just mean the DIs!' Jane waited for a response and then decided she needed to apologise again. 'Just joking. My ex is a DI. "Guvnor" in Met parlance. And he's only a part-time scumbag.'

PC Kahn allowed himself a smile but then remembered his workload. 'Where did the break-in occur, Ms Madden?'

'It's Jane. Are you okay if I call you Zahid?'

The young constable didn't seem totally sure, but Jane just carried on and gestured that he follow her down the hall. 'It's in the extension at the back. My grandfather built it years ago. I really should have had the French doors replaced with something more robust. Never got round to it.'

They entered the room and Jane pointed to the doors. 'They've been forced with one of those big screwdrivers, I think. It's probably just kids. They've raided my drinks cabinet and nicked a small flat-screen TV I had in the corner. It doesn't look like they went through the rest of the house. They were probably nervous and scarpered quickly with the first things they found.'

'They didn't take your laptop,' said the PC in a puzzled tone.

'I can tell it's been moved,' replied Jane. 'But they probably saw how old and knackered it was and decided not to bother. Actually, they might have done me a favour if they had taken it. I've been told it's unsupported or something. It still works though.'

The PC shook his head. 'Cybercrime is where I'm hoping to end up. I've got an IT degree. Someone who knew what they were doing would probably be able to get into that thing quite easily. They'd have access to all your personal data.'

Jane frowned. Everyone seemed to have it in for her aged computer. 'Well good job they were more interested in a couple of bottles of gin and vodka,' she countered.

PC Kahn had moved over to the doors. The wooden frames were splintered around the central lock. There was a depression about half an inch wide that could easily have been made by the flat blade of a screwdriver.

He looked out into the garden beyond. 'Those walls and all the foliage make it quite secluded at the back. But I saw when I arrived that you'd got access down the side. I presume you were out at work when it happened?'

'I mostly work from home,' said Jane, 'but I was away for the night. I stayed at my mother's near Bournemouth.'

'And you live here on your own?'

Jane nodded.

'It might have been a good job you weren't in when they decided to try their luck,' conjectured the PC.

'Because I'd have killed them you mean, Zahid?'

The constable looked at Jane sternly. 'They might have been kids, but kids carry knives these days. Particularly the ones up to no good. We would always advise the public to exercise caution.'

Jane was about to argue she wasn't afraid of juvenile yobbos, but stopped herself. 'I guess you're right,' she conceded.

The PC was trying the door lock. 'You'll need to get a carpenter in to make this temporarily secure.'

Jane waved her hand dismissively. 'There's some two-by-one in the shed. When you've gone I'll screw it across at the top and bottom. That'll do the job.' She tilted her head slightly to one side. 'I guess you're not going to call in forensics?' she said tentatively.

The PC still had his back to Jane and was scanning the window panes. 'I can't see any sign of fingerprints. I think you're right, it is just kids and even they know to wear gloves these days. Shame you don't have CCTV.'

'But no house-to-house enquiries?' As soon as the words left her mouth Jane felt guilty. 'Sorry, just kidding again, Zahid. I am grateful you've come round. I know it's not the crime of the century.'

'We take all crime seriously, Ms Madden, but we do have to prioritise our resources, especially in the current climate.'

'Of course. I understand.'

'Look...' a doubtful expression crossed PC Kahn's face. '...well, there is a counselling service for crime victims. Sometimes the psychological effects can catch you unawares. Having strangers violate your home can be very unsettling.'

Jane grinned, sympathetic to the process the young officer was obliged to follow. 'Don't worry, Zahid. I have my moments, but this isn't going to stop me sleeping tonight.'

L.Y.

Jane sat down at her dining room table and admired her handiwork. The lengths of untreated pine were fixed into the wooden doors with the chunkiest screws she could find. She'd tried to get the battens square, but the lower one had a slight but noticeable droop down to the left. It didn't matter. It was just a stopgap and no-one would be forcing them again in a hurry. She would have to get someone in to give her a quote for new doors with proper multipoint locks. They'd probably need to do the windows too. It wouldn't be cheap. The insurance might cover some of it, but there went any hope of buying a new laptop.

Which was a shame, as it seemed even slower than usual logging in to her email. For once there was no spam in her inbox, just one new message with an intriguing subject line: 'Thomas Ramsden 1842?-1900'.

Dear Jane Madden

It was a great pleasure to receive a message from across the Atlantic. My career was in finance, and I was based in London for several years and met my English husband there. He turned out to be something of a disappointment, but I won't hold that against you. ;-) It is always interesting to make contact with a fellow genealogist, particularly one who may have new insights into an old mystery. I have been researching my family tree for many years now, although I have recently been concentrating on my East European roots. It is some time since I looked at the man I know as Thomas Ramsden.

First of all, let me say that I was aware of my second cousin Roxanne Armand. I have pencilled in that branch on another copy of my tree that is more complete than the one I choose to publish online. Personally, I have always been wary of DNA tests, though I confess I do not really understand the science or the potential consequences of having your data held somewhere on the great cloud that is the Internet. That said, I follow your reasoning that if Roxanne shares genetic ancestry with your client, then it is very likely I do too.

Assuming we can rule out the Transylvanian side to my family, that points to my and Roxanne's great-great-grandparents, Thomas Ramsden (sic) and Mary O'Brien, being the link. I appreciate the tact in your message, but I concur that Thomas is somewhat, let us say, 'suspect'. Poor Mary was from Ireland and I know quite a lot about her. What I know about Thomas leads me to believe that abandoning his family and subsequent bigamy were wholly in character. I believe him to have been a deeply wicked man. I can only hope his tainted blood is sufficiently diluted in my own.

My Thomas Ramsden claims to be six years younger than your Thomas Ramsbottom, of course, but that is a relatively small deception and brings his age closer to Mary's. I have had a brief look for evidence of an official change of name, Ramsbottom to Ramsden, but can find none. But then, I have no record of exactly how or when Giersch became Gish in my family. The stories of emigration officers at Ellis Island casually anglicising surnames are mythical, but many people just made an informal change to fit in with their new neighbors. They registered their children with their Americanized name and it stuck. I'm sure someone like Thomas Ramsbottom would have had no compunction about lying to a city clerk when obtaining his marriage license. No offence to your client, but if I were saddled with a name like that I might change it too. It's not one I've come across before. I think it Trumps my ancestral Bumgartens and Assbergs!

So what can I tell you about Thomas Ramsden/Ramsbottom? You will have seen what is on my public tree, but I have omitted the more damning details. I am happy to share them with you, but ask that you do not make them generally available on the Web. It is sufficiently long ago that I feel no inherited shame or guilt, but some other descendants might not agree. I subscribe to the philosophy that we do not 'own' our family trees.

I have some precious notes made by mother, probably in the late 1950s. I recognise her handwriting and can date them by the fact she was interviewing her own grandmother, Sarah Kathleen Ramsden, who died in 1959. My mother acknowledges Sarah was apt to be slightly confused, but she was still able to remember her early life and her extended family: cousins, aunts, uncles and so on. It was finding these notes after my mother prematurely passed that got me started with genealogy.

As you've seen from what I have put online, Sarah was the daughter of Thomas Ramsden and Mary O'Brien and her lifespan takes us right back to the 1870s. Sadly her own mother died when she was four and the primary influence on her young character was Thomas's second wife (or should that be third?), Ester Giersch. Ester had actually been Sarah's nursemaid. It seems poor Mary suffered from what we would now call postnatal depression and couldn't cope on her own. Thomas had somehow inveigled himself into the employ of an early New York photographer, and when the old man died (conveniently?) took over the burgeoning business. It flourished, but mainly because of Ester's acumen and drive. She seems to have been a powerhouse of a woman. Thomas was a waster who liked taking artistic pictures, perhaps even had talent, but Ester pulled the strings and made it all profitable. They ended up with a string of studios across the city. Sarah was a beautiful, beautiful girl. When she was 17, she married Ester's nephew Georg Giersch, who became known as George Gish.

George was somewhat older than his new bride and Ester moved him in to take over the business and effectively paid off Thomas, who then disappeared from the scene. Sarah said she remembered her father crying when he left, but Ester told her that was from weakness and shame.

And this is where the story takes its darkest turn. Ester said Thomas had killed Sarah's mother, Mary. The poor woman's body was found floating in the East River.

In my mother's notes made a lifetime later, she's put an exclamation point and question mark after the word killed. Sarah seemed vague on the exact circumstances. I don't know whether Thomas's mistreatment drove Mary to drown herself or he physically held her head under. Sarah certainly couldn't remember exactly what Ester said, but the message was clear. Her father later tried to get in touch, apparently, but Sarah understandably cut him out of her life.

I found a grave for a Thomas Ramsden of the right age in White Plains, just north of New York City. He died in 1900, a few days into the new century. He was supposedly only 58, but it now seems he was really 64. He had escaped the fiery pit of hell long enough.

So there you have it. If we combine what I know of Thomas Ramsden's later life and your information on Thomas Ramsbottom's beginnings, we have the picture of a complete monster. And I thought my no-good ex-husband was a scoundrel! But seriously, I am really grateful you got in touch and that we have been able to complete the puzzle together. It reminds me why I find genealogical research such a fascinating hobby. All those skeletons just waiting to be unearthed!

With fond regards

Linda Esther Yarborough

PS They were a family of photographers, so I have quite a few pictures taken around that time. I have attached one that captures all the players in our drama.

The more I look at it, the more I can sense the underlying tensions and secrets.

There were actually two files attached to the email. The first was a scan of Sarah Ramsden's death certificate giving the cause of death as 'Asphyxia due to Drowning'. The deceased was described as a white housewife of Irish birth who had been resident in the United States for five years. Her lifeless body was found on Blackwell's Island, which Jane established to now be Roosevelt Island, a narrow strip of land in the middle of the East River, just south of where it is joined by its Harlem sister.

If the certificate was poignantly haunting, the accompanying monochrome photograph induced a range of emotions from triumph to sadness, to a vague, questioning uncertainty. Jane sat and stared at it for a full 15 minutes, zooming in on the faces, looking for indications of character or emotion. Or guilt.

It featured four people in what appeared to be a grandly furnished drawing room, but on closer inspection was a painted backdrop. Seated at the front were a smartly dressed couple. The man had his hand resting on the woman's and both were smiling, though her expression looked forced, seemingly betrayed by eyes closer to tears than laughter. But she was stunning, with shining dark hair contrasting with the palest of skins, her slim figure cloaked in an elegantly simple dress.

The woman standing behind was altogether sterner in appearance. There was no attempt at warmth and her plain features had a hardness that could be read as ambition. She was more matronly in build and in her strong arms she carried an infant child. The little girl was looking slightly away from the camera, but facially appeared to be a mixture of her two seated parents, and all the prettier for it.

Jane looked again at the man. Proud, confident, happy? Perhaps. He had aged slightly since last she saw him, but still looked younger than his years. He was still blonde and attractive. His clothing now suggested modest success, but he was still Thomas Ramsbottom.

Blackwell Holme

'I love the colour of your car. What do they call it – I mean this particular shade?

Jane thought for a second or two. 'From memory, I think it was "Spirit Green". Doesn't really tell you much.'

'Ooh, I think it does. It tells you a lot. Do you believe in spirits, Jane?'

'No. I guess I'm not very imaginative in that department.'

'I don't think they're imagination. I think they're all around us. To an extent that's why we're making this trip, isn't it?'

Jane looked across at her passenger. Guy's cousin Betty had an expectant gleam in her eyes.

Jane's attention returned to the road ahead before she replied. 'Thanks again for coming with me at such short notice. I guess I am hoping to find ghosts of the past. Sometimes places talk to you.'

Betty nodded her agreement vigorously. 'Well, you were practically passing by my front door and it's a long time since I've been up to Blackwell myself. Not driving doesn't help. It'll be fun showing you around. My Sundays are normally quite dull and this is all very exciting!'

Jane smiled at her passenger's enthusiasm. 'I've walked around it on Internet but you can't get everywhere and it's just not the same. And it's often good to talk things through with someone else. It can help clarify things in your own mind.'

Betty had said she only knew the convoluted route taken by the buses, so Jane had her phone's satnav providing directions. She had muted the voice and was glancing at the screen cradled on her dashboard. It told her to pull into the right lane at a set of red traffic lights, prior to turning up a relatively minor road that climbed higher into the moors. The day was overcast and there was a vague drizzle landing on the windscreen that confused the car's automatic wipers into unnecessary activity. With the low roof closed, Jane was having to bend sharply forward to see the signals.

'I promised to update you on what I'd found out,' she croaked huskily through restricted breaths. The lights changed and Jane straightened and turned the wheel. 'Here we go,' she said, mainly to herself.

Having failed several driving tests, Betty was sensitive to the difficulties of junctions, right turns in particular, and had temporarily ceased her normally relentless chatter. She resumed with gusto.

'Yes, on the phone it sounded like you'd got some real hard proof. I guess that's the difference between you professionals and us amateurs. Or should that be, we amateurs? Anyway, doesn't matter. I'm afraid I get so excited when I think I've found something or someone new, you know, a record of a marriage, another child, the name of a parent, that I don't necessarily check that it's, well, 100% right. I add it to my tree and then look for the next one. I might even celebrate with a cheeky chocolate biscuit!' She smirked and looked across for approval. 'If I've been naughty and bought some,' she added contritely.

Jane eyes flicked sideways again and caught the tail end of the grin. 'We all make mistakes from time to time,' she conceded. 'Genealogy is relatively easy when people stay put. When they move, certainly when they leave the country, it gets a bit more challenging.'

'And you said my great-great…' Betty shrugged away the calculation. '…whatever it was, great, something, grandfather adopted an alias as well?'

'That's right. "Bottom" was changed to "den" – he became Thomas Ramsden.'

Betty's eyes narrowed. For some reason that name resonated, but Jane was still talking and the thought passed.

'It's as if he really didn't want to be found. Which, of course, having been a total bastard, he didn't.' Jane felt a twinge of guilt and quickly added, 'Sorry, I shouldn't be so rude about your antecedent. It's just... well, everything says he wasn't a very nice man. But we've all got some crap in our ancestral closet. It's not our fault and it doesn't change...' She momentarily hesitated as she pondered the truth of what she was saying. 'It doesn't change who we are.'

'I couldn't agree more. That's so, so right,' gushed Betty. 'We are who we choose to be. I'm a big believer in karma. "According as you act, and according as you behave, so will you be. A person of good acts will become good." And good things will happen to them. That's my mantra.'

'Shame about our bad acts,' mumbled Jane, her words lost under the noise of the engine as it laboured with the incline.

The road had become lonely as it crossed a barren hilltop, the treeless landscape dominated by tufts of reed and yellow-green marsh grass growing in peaty bog. Jane felt her mood starting to mirror the desolation and pulled herself together.

'So, let me tell you the full story,' she said.

'I'm all ears.' Betty folded her arms over her seatbelt and sat up as straight as she could in the low bucket seat.

'Okay,' began Jane. 'So, last time we met I told you that your death record for Thomas Ramsbottom was wrong. It wasn't our man. And you said you'd heard a suggestion he might have deserted his family and gone to America?'

'Yes, yes. I remember. I thought he looked too nice in that photograph, but I've never been a good judge of men.'

'Well,' continued Jane, 'I found a Thomas Ramsbottom on a ship's manifest arriving in New York in 1873.'

'How exciting!'

'Yes. His age was right and it turned out he was travelling with someone who lived in the same village. They were heading for the coal fields of Ohio. His companion had family out there already.'

'Thomas had been a coal miner hadn't he?'

'That's right,' confirmed Jane. 'He'd also worked in a cotton mill. But there'd been a boiler explosion that killed his oldest son.'

'How awful!'

'His wife was pregnant at the time and they named the new baby after the boy who died. And then Thomas swans off to a find a new life, leaving her and six kids in his wake.'

'Dreadful, simply dreadful. Can't some men be so, well, dreadful?' Betty sounded almost close to tears.

'It was a long time ago,' consoled Jane. 'They're all long dead and I think they were probably better off without him. I'm afraid he had more lives to wreck in America.'

'Really? What exactly did he do?'

'He never made it to Ohio. He contracted typhus fever on the boat, or it's possible he picked it up before he left. Typhus, as opposed to typhoid, is spread by body lice, though they didn't know it at the time. All they knew was it was something to do with poor sanitation and overcrowding.'

Betty simply nodded her head. It was unseen by Jane, who was having to concentrate on the road as it twisted and undulated with the contours, but she took the other woman's silence as a cue to continue.

'That's by the by, I guess. But Thomas was sent to a New York state hospital on his arrival and survived. His friend didn't exhibit symptoms until later and reached

Ohio. Unfortunately he died there soon after. Thomas, meanwhile, has met a beautiful Irish girl, lies about his name and age, and marries her. Judging by the dates, she was pregnant on their wedding day. So he started off with adultery and then thought he'd try bigamy too.'

'Gosh!'

'Mmm,' agreed Jane. 'You and your cousin Guy took DNA tests, and a match over in America led me to a woman who is descended from that pregnancy. She told me the story. Thomas and his new wife had the one child, a little girl, but she grew to despise her father and was raised by her stepmother. Who was from Transylvania, would you believe?'

'That's exotic.' Betty's mind was distracted by partially misplaced images of aristocratic vampires, gothic castles and torch-wielding mobs before a more relevant thought occurred to her. 'If the girl had a stepmother, does that mean Thomas married a third time?'

'Uhuh. This one wasn't, well, any great shakes in the looks department, but she was quite the entrepreneur. Thomas somehow got his greedy hands on a nascent photography business, and this last wife made a big success of it.'

Betty's face took on a puzzled expression. 'So did Thomas simply make another bigamous marriage? I mean, did he just walk out on the Irish girl?'

'If only. According to my American contact, should I say, your American cousin, he is supposed to have killed her. I can show you her photograph. She was so, so beautiful and yet you can sense she's so, so fragile. She was found drowned in the East River in New York. To say it was a crime is...'

Jane left the sentence hanging as her mobile phone indicated they had arrived at their destination. She turned the Mazda through some iron gates into a small car park and killed the engine. The two women climbed out and walked up a short path until they were standing at the door of plain, square building that looked like a large house with an odd arrangement of windows.

'They outgrew it, of course,' said Betty looking up at the freshly cleaned stone walls. 'They built a new chapel down the road and this one fell into disrepair. You know they were all Baptists, obviously?'

'Particular Baptists,' said Jane. 'Not that I really know the difference.'

'It's to do with particular atonement… salvation limited to the elect few,' replied Betty with the abrupt authority of someone who knows the words but would prefer not to be challenged on their precise meaning. 'And I think they were less antagonistic towards the Church of England than the General Baptists. I'm afraid I'm not really one for organised religion. I like to pick the best bits from different faiths. Eastern spirituality is my main guide in life.'

Jane didn't feel minded towards a theological discussion and tried the door. As she expected, it was locked.

'In the photographs it looks like the renovation will be impressive when it's finished,' said Jane as she turned back to face Betty. 'All those wooden box pews and a gallery running round the floor above. But it was the graveyard I came here to see.'

'Follow me,' said Betty decisively.

Behind the chapel was a screen of stunted, windblown trees and then a cobbled path climbed up to a rounded hummock covered in gravestones and bordered by a high drystone wall. The path was noticeably cambered and had drainage channels running down both sides, suggesting that heavy skies were very much the norm. Brooding, bleak hills rose all around adding to the feeling that inclement weather was never far away.

There was one imposing memorial set apart from the others, close to the chapel. It commemorated a Victorian minister who had 'guided' the people of Blackwell Holme for many years and had died saving the life of a young child. Jane realised Reverend Richards would have been there at the time of Thomas Ramsbottom and, presumably, have known him well. She was contemplating what assessment he would have made of Thomas's character when she was distracted by a shout from Betty.

'It was over here somewhere. Shouldn't be able to miss it.' She had gone on ahead and was walking across the lush grass between the ordered lines of monuments. She stopped, retraced her steps and then followed a different row. 'There it is!' she called and marched over the crest and down the other side. Jane quickly followed and found Betty bending in front of a particularly large stone with an ornate classical pediment.

It stood out from those around it in size and decoration and also from being a glossy black, rather than the weathered grey of the local gritstone. Looking about, Jane could see only one other memorial in a similar marble. That was tucked by the wall in the furthest corner of the cemetery and by contrast seemed particularly plain and modest. Jane's eyes were strangely drawn towards it but were refocused by Betty reading out loud.

'Here lies George Ramsbottom, 1856 to 1872, the finest of sons, tragically taken too young. Also his mother, Sarah Ramsbottom, died 1898 aged 65.' There was a pause and a sigh. 'And then there's one of Sarah's little baby grandsons, aged just two months, poor lamb.' Betty turned and looked up. 'Is it what you expected to see?'

'It's very grand isn't it?' answered Jane indirectly. 'I wonder who paid for it?'

'My great... erm, I mean, Sarah's son? The one who became a doctor? He could afford it.'

Jane frowned in concentration and began reasoning out loud. 'Trouble is... Sarah's name looks like it was inscribed after George's. Remember George here was her eldest boy who died in the mill explosion. So the gravestone was for him originally and then Sarah was added when she died in 1898. And then her grandson after that.'

'That makes sense,' agreed Betty.

'So,' continued Jane, 'the gravestone would predate 1898. Now by my reckoning your great-grandfather – also called George – would still be at medical school. His comfortable income would surely come later?' She shrugged. 'I don't know. I need to think about it some more.'

Jane took a photograph with her phone and then Betty showed her the graves of other relatives who had stayed in the area. Nearby was the burial plot of the family of Henry Pickup, Thomas's ill-fated travelling companion on his voyage to America. None of the memorials were as impressive as George and Sarah's, and after more snapshots the two women left the churchyard by the back gate and made their way into the village.

The first toll road over the moors had been built late in the reign of George III. It followed the course of a fast-flowing stream, crossing it several times and hugging its banks before abandoning it and climbing up and over the head of the valley. The roadway linked two ancient hamlets and they had eventually merged into a single community a mile long and often only as wide as a single terrace of houses, lateral development restricted by the steep slopes on either side. What now passed for the village centre had a scruffy pub and a single corner shop which advertised itself as 'Proper Convenient, Proper Cheap'. A Chinese takeaway provided the only other local source of nutrition and distraction. Apart from the

Anglican and Baptist churches, there were two other more substantial buildings. A primary school sat behind a high, modern steel fence. Its stone frontage had been scrubbed clean at some point, but the side walls were still blackened by the soot of a century or more. Any doubts as to vintage were dispelled by two doorways, with 'Boys' and 'Girls' respectively carved above them and a central gable with 'Board School 1878' in the same lettering. Almost directly opposite, and with the river culverted beneath it, stood the towering, four-storey bulk of an old mill. Its huge square chimney, banded in iron, was set slightly back but had evidently been docked and it now barely reached roof height. One large sign proclaimed, 'To let. Storage facility with modern lift.' A smaller notice read 'Graver's Hall Sofa Company', but it wasn't clear if that business was still in operation. There was an air of abandoned emptiness, though that could have been due to it being the day of rest rather than bankruptcy.

Just along from the school a side turning led into a narrow lane that rose up and out of the village, following the clough carved by a small tributary that could be seen joining the main stream close to the junction. A solitary road sign indicated no more than it was a dead end.

'It's just a hundred yards or so up here,' said Betty pointing the way.

Three quarters of a mile later, having passed a small modern housing estate, the lane forked. The tarmac section led down towards what looked like a salvage yard in the distance. An unpaved track continued upwards and Betty gestured towards it, her voice seemingly lost to the exertion of the climb.

'I'm glad I wore my sensible shoes,' laughed Jane.

'I only have sensible shoes,' replied Betty, with breathy seriousness.

They rounded a corner and Betty stopped, placed her hands on her hips and stretched her back. 'I'm sure it wasn't this far last time I came, but there it is – Father Richard Barn. I haven't a clue who Father Richard was, but it certainly doesn't look like a barn now.'

She was right. What had appeared to be a collection of farm buildings on the old maps had been transformed into a single luxury home, set back behind rather forbidding tall steel gates. Old outhouses were now a stable block, and a paddock was laid out with coloured rails for jumping. The large central section of the house had been extended outwards with a vast glass-roofed conservatory, but its origin was still discernible. There were three cars parked outside. As usual Jane struggled to identify them, but it was obvious they were big, expensive and, judging by the monstrous tyres, four-wheel drive, no doubt a prerequisite for accessing this place in the depths of winter. They also shared very similar metallic grey paintwork. Their owner or owners clearly had money, but in Jane's eyes, no sense of colour or fun.

'I can't help you with Father Richard,' said Jane, 'but the earliest record I can find of this place is a marriage register entry from 1794. The bride lived here. Even then it must have been converted into accommodation. By the time of the 1841 census it was split between four families, including Sarah Ramsbottom and her parents. She lived here more or less all her life. Her father was farmer...' Jane was looking at her phone and scrolling through pages of notes. 'Yes, that's right. A mason and farmer of 20 acres, though I don't think that's a lot. You'd call it a smallholding these days, and he wouldn't own the land. He died soon after Thomas ran off. Fortunately Sarah still had her mother, who appears to have taken over the running of the farm, assisted by a labourer who also moved into this place. A labourer with the quintessentially northern name of Ashworth Tattersall. Interestingly, when Sarah's mother passed away, Ashworth seems to have got the rights to the land.

On the 1891 census, he's listed as a farmer of 20 acres and Sarah is now reduced to his housekeeper.'

Betty looked suspicious. 'Remind me how old this Ashworth Tattersall was? Relative to Sarah, I mean.'

Jane checked her phone again. 'About a year younger. Why do you ask?'

'I think I assumed housekeeper was a euphemism for common-law wife, that's all.'

Jane lowered her phone and stared at the house as if it might be persuaded to tell tales on its previous occupiers. 'And who could blame her?' she said eventually. 'Interesting she never actually remarried, though. She said she was a widow on the censuses, but maybe she didn't really know whether Thomas was dead or alive.'

Jane's eyes remained fixed on the stonework of the old parts of the building. She thought about using the intercom on the gates, but decided against it. She doubted they'd get a warm welcome and didn't suppose she'd learn anything from the converted splendour, even if the builder had retained the odd original feature as a talking point. Instead she turned around and took in the setting. Two lines of ugly electricity pylons marched across in the mid-distance and that salvage yard was only partly hidden. The outlook wasn't perfect from an estate agent's perspective, but it was certainly a view and you could see almost the entire valley across to the hills beyond. Jane called up the Victorian Ordnance Survey map on her phone. Marked directly below where they now stood was the early cotton mill whose boiler explosion had claimed the life of young George Ramsbottom. It had barely left a trace on the modern landscape. There was an odd kink in the lane where it had been redirected around the corner of the building and the overall footprint was now a flat, scrubby patch of waste ground, fenced off but used as a dumping ground for rusty farm machinery. Steam power requires a ready supply of water, and there had once been a small reservoir but that too had gone, although the vegetation in its place looked suspiciously boggy. The map clearly showed a separate structure marked Nabb Engine. One of its huge boilers had been blasted 60 yards and embedded in the ground. Jane scanned the adjacent fields for tell-tale craters but was disappointed. She then remembered she had a copy of the grainy photograph from the contemporary newspaper report. Looking at it on her screen, she was reminded how substantial the mill had been. There was a wide, three-storey weaving shed with a chimney behind that must have climbed to 150 feet tall. Today, not a brick remained visible. Only the terrace of back-to-backs built to house some of the workers, now incongruously remote and isolated 50 yards down the lane suggested this was at one time an industrial scene.

And then Jane's thoughts turned to Sarah Hargreaves, pregnant and so close by on that June morning in 1872. Father Richard Barn would have rocked and shook. What windows it had would have blown out and she herself might have been thrown to the ground. It would have been like nothing she had ever experienced, yet she would have surely known what had happened. And feared the worst. And would they have carried her teenage first-born son back to her, his beautiful face hideously scolded and burnt? And would he have died in her arms somewhere in the original core of the luxury residence that Jane now stood outside?

She was again tempted to try the intercom, but resisted. She would simply be imagining scenes that might never have happened. Instead she passed her phone over to Betty.

'All this was just down there,' said Jane, waving her hand to indicate a rough outline.

'Isn't it amazing how nature reclaims its own,' replied Betty, her eyes flicking left and right.

Jane nodded. 'It was disused but still standing in the 1930s, but by the time you get to the 1960s' maps it's all gone.' She turned and pointed to the hill above them. 'And way up there used to be a mine. I suspect that's where Thomas Ramsbottom once worked. That long, straight ridge running diagonally across those fields of sheep is the path of a tramway. They used it to transport the coal down to a loading staithe on the road. At the far end there's a low, modern building. I think that's over the old pit entrance. Next to that wind turbine.'

'Isn't that symbolic of our progress? I mean, away from fossil fuels towards green renewables? Very appropriate, very exciting,' said Betty, grinning appreciatively.

Jane's mind was elsewhere and she declined to echo the enthusiasm. Betty saw the lack of response and asked a more pertinent question. 'Thomas left the mine, didn't he? And went to work in the mill. I can't remember what he did there. Surely he was too old to begin again as a weaver or a spinner?'

Jane pressed the screen of her phone and quickly brought up Thomas's profile and then the 1871 census. 'I've never really thought of that before. Oh, here it is. It says he was a, quotes, Eng Ast. I think I googled it but was none the wiser."

'English... no, Engineer. Engineer's assistant?' suggested Betty.

'Yes, that's obvious now you say it.' Jane stared into the distance as the cogs turned in her head. 'At the inquest, the boiler engineer got the blame for the explosion. He'd been killed too and couldn't defend himself. You don't think Thomas could have been culpable in some way? Maybe it's no wonder he ran away to America. And then when he gets there he ends up killing his second wife. God, what a man!'

The cross

On their journey home, Jane took them an alternate route, driving further up the valley and across the face of a strangely misshapen pike that dominated the skyline. It was pockmarked by ugly, alien-looking recesses, presumably ancient quarries now taken back by the grasses and the moss. But it was a different testament to human destruction she had come to see. She parked by the road and they climbed a short flight of steps to a stone cross standing alone on the hillside and visible for miles around. It was dedicated to the local men who had perished in the Great War of 1914 to 1918. Jane knew that two of Thomas Ramsbottom's grandsons were numbered amongst them, but the cross's commanding position had exposed it to the worst of the Pennine weather. Nearly a century of blasting by wind, rain, sleet and snow had eaten into its panels and only a ghostly suggestion of lettering remained. The brave young soldiers, surely better men by far than their grandfather, were remembered no more.

The Harlem River

Before he left her shores Thomas Ramsden had never visited his homeland's capital, but he had heard that the hub of Victoria's empire was even more crowded than downtown Manhattan. The engineers of London were bypassing the gridlocked thoroughfares by digging down and running railways beneath the streets. But that great metropolis was built on soft clay. Its challenger on the far side of the Atlantic was rooted in solid rock. Outcrops still towered above some of the undeveloped streets that had been driven through the terrain to fulfil the decades-old master plan of a vast, ordered grid. The cost of tunnelling warranted an alternative solution, and New York had gone up rather than down. The new elevated railroads rattled along tracks raised high on steel columns, like a seemingly endless bridge over a sea of horses and carriages and handcarts.

Thomas had his head leant against the carriage window, wafts of steam from the locomotive drifting past. His eyes were looking downwards at the long, straight line of Third Avenue below. They were looking, but not seeing. As the train chugged northwards the scene became a patchwork of newly completed tenement blocks in brownstone or brick, wooden shanties squatting on vacant lots, and open land, sometimes waiting to be raised or lowered to match the grade of the street. Out towards the East River, away from the transport system that was driving speculative development, building was sparser, with isolated factories, yards and gasworks dominating the landscape.

Once Thomas might have been eagerly dissecting the view, imagining it captured on his photographic plates. Today he was lost in the darkest of thoughts. They were interrupted when the train pulled into the East 106th

Street station and he had to force himself to disembark. He slowly descended the steep, covered staircase down to ground level, fellow passengers impatiently pushing past. The voices were Irish, Yiddish and Italian but he heard none of them. He walked the two blocks to First Avenue, before turning northwards. Somewhere beneath his feet he crossed the old Harlem Creek, but that one-time obstacle to northerly progress had been buried and would soon be forgotten.

Looking down 109th he saw his destination, stretching into the Harlem River, the short pier where he had set foot on the mainland for the second time. The first, at the old fort of Castle Garden some eight miles south, had been the briefest of landings before he was shipped off to a fever ward, isolated on Ward's Island across the water from him now. When he left that place and the ferry brought him the short distance to this point, he had been a different man. The typhus had been purged from his body and he had been glad to be alive. For the first time in his life, he had been in love. And passion's unfamiliarity had made a weak man weaker and a fool more foolish.

The wooden jetty beckoned him and he couldn't resist its call. He found himself at its tip, staring across the narrow strait. The water was a cold, impenetrable grey, its surface chopped and lively in the cutting wind. A man who flung himself into it would not last long, particularly one raised far from the sea, whose thrashing limbs would drag him under rather than keep him afloat.

And there, imposing and proud, stood the Emigrant Hospital, its wards stacked into five parallel wings each redolent of a cathedral nave fronted by twin towers that held water cisterns in place of bells.

That was where he had met her for the first time.

His eyes dropped towards the seawater fizzing and slapping at the planks beneath him. This was the scene of his worst crime, for which he knew he must be forever damned. He had pushed her and the tidal currents had taken her. They had dragged her fragile body out towards the ocean through the confluence of Harlem and East Rivers cruelly known as Hell Gate, to be washed ashore on another of New York's Islands of the Undesirables. He looked south but its narrow profile could not be made out in the murk and mist. When she had been taken ill after their baby's birth, one of the so-called doctors had suggested her transfer to Blackwell Island's lunatic asylum. It was a bitter irony that she was found close by its doors as if begging posthumously for its dubious ministrations to relieve her torments.

At that moment, he wanted to follow after her, his guilt too heavy to bear. But his body resisted, locking rigid, unable to throw itself forward. As always, it seemed he didn't have the courage, not even for the ultimate act of cowardice. He heard himself cravenly making excuses. What would become of his daughter? He had abandoned his other children. He must not repeat that sin.

But there was someone who knew his secret and her silence had a price. He would pay it. He deserved punishment in this world as well as the next.

Stolen goods

'Well thank you so much for the day out. I thoroughly enjoyed it,' enthused Betty as she opened the car door outside her house.

Jane smiled. 'No, thank you again for coming and showing me around. It really was a great help. There are lots of background things that seem much clearer now.'

'Anytime. I mean that. If you want a partner in crime for your future genealogy cases, I'm your woman. I've found it all very exciting.'

Jane hesitated before answering. 'I'll bear it in mind. But I do already have a partner. It's just he's otherwise engaged right now. I guess he's one of those silent partners.'

As she said the words, Jane felt the joke falling flat, to her ears at least. She wondered if she was the one being silent. Tommy was uncommunicative by nature, but she hadn't tried to contact him for some time. She really ought to find out how he was coping.

Jane's thoughts were interrupted by her phone ringing on the dashboard. She glanced at its screen, but the number was withheld.

'I'll be off and let you answer that'. Betty waved a quick goodbye, shuffled out and shut the door.

Jane lifted the phone from its cradle. 'Hello?'

'Is that Ms Madden?'

'Yes. Who is this please?'

'Oh, hi again, Ms Madden. It's PC Kahn. I came round to your house after your recent break-in?'

'Hello, Zahid. This is a pleasant surprise. Don't tell me you've caught the bastards?'

'Not as such, but I think we've managed to locate your property.'

'What, the TV? How do you know it's mine?'

'Well… We were attending a stolen motorbike that had been left down an alleyway round the corner from where you live. An elderly lady came out to speak to us and said someone had dumped a new-looking TV and a couple of half-full bottles of alcohol in her wheelie bin. She thought it was odd.'

'Presumably the TV's all smashed up?'

'No, Ms Madden. We've haven't tested it, obviously, but it doesn't look too bad, a bit of a scratch maybe. It's the same model as yours and, well, there was the bottle of gin and the bottle of vodka… It seemed too much of a coincidence.'

'Why would someone go to the trouble of breaking into my house and then just chucking everything away?'

PC Kahn seemed to take the question as being rhetorical. 'When would it be convenient for me to come round so you can identify your stuff, Ms Madden?'

Twitching curtains

Jane watched the police car drive away. The property was returned and the case closed. The TV was working and only slightly battle scarred, but the potentially tainted booze had already gone down the sink. It seemed a pointless crime and the insurance would not cover anyone's time or inconvenience. Fortunately, there was no anxiety or distress to be added to the unpaid bill. Jane's only emotions were irritation, confusion and anger at herself for not properly securing her home.

PC Kahn had opined that the young housebreakers had lost their nerve or had been compromised in some way and didn't want to be caught in possession of stolen goods. Maybe they intended to return for their loot and had not yet had a chance.

'The council won't be collecting the rubbish until next week. You could mount surveillance on the wheelie bin where they dumped the stuff,' suggested Jane, thinking aloud rather than being serious, or flippant.

'We don't have to resources to do that sort of thing, Ms Madden. It's hardly… Well, I know every crime has a victim and having one's home invaded and defiled is no laughing matter, but it's not exactly… There was no physical violence involved, no element of hate crime… I'm sure you understand.'

'Of course. I was just joking. No, not joking, just postulating that in an ideal world with limitless police officers, that might give you a collar. I completely understand you, and I, have to be a bit more realistic.'

'Indeed.' PC Kahn rubbed his nose as if stalling while he thought of how to make his exit. 'From a practical viewpoint, you have your crime reference number. Your insurance company will reimburse you for the damage to your property. I'm sure they'll advise the installation of better locks.'

'Don't worry,' agreed Jane defensively. 'I'll make sure I'm better protected in future. I do know it was a crime waiting to happen.'

PC Kahn's tone was hovering somewhere between admonishment and doubt. 'Well, I would have thought, as an ex-police officer…'

Jane was on her front doorstep reliving the conversation as the car reached the end of her road and turned the corner. It had suddenly occurred to her that the young Asian constable might have suspected her of an attempt at some kind of minor insurance fraud. But surely she would have added a non-existent diamond ring to the haul if that was the case? The potential slur made her want to track the culprits down herself and she briefly considered parking near the now infamous wheelie bin and keeping watch herself. The trouble was she wasn't exactly sure which one it was and the exercise would, in truth, be an awful lot of hassle with very little chance of reward. Even if she did find some youths going through the bins, they'd easily make up excuses. And it probably wasn't an altogether sensible exercise for a woman on her own.

She was about to go back inside when she saw a curtain twitch across the street. Mrs Metcalfe had no doubt been avidly watching the coming and going of police cars and imagining all kinds of juicy gossip. Jane's grandmother hadn't been particularly fond of her nosey neighbour. Jane herself wasn't overly concerned what Mrs Metcalfe thought or said, but decided to cross the road anyway. It she wasn't going to do her own stake-out, she could at least carry out a house-to-house enquiry.

Jane rang the bell and the door opened almost immediately. Mrs Metcalfe had lived opposite since Jane had been a little girl. She had seemed elderly even then; she appeared little altered by the passing years, though her quiet, portly and bald husband had died several years back. Jane had occasionally smiled at her in the street, but seldom said more than hello.

'Mrs Metcalfe, I hope you don't mind me coming over?'

'No, not at all. It's Jane, isn't it? How are you coping without your grandmother?'

'It's been a while now. I miss her still, but life has to go on. Look, I'm sure you've noticed that I've had the police round?'

Mrs Metcalfe avoided eye contact and blushed slightly. "Erm... I did see the car parked outside.'

'I'm afraid I've had a break-in. Through the dining room doors round the back.'

'Oh dear, how frightening!' Mrs Metcalfe looked genuinely anxious. 'And this used to be such a nice area.'

Jane realised she ought to say something reassuring. 'It was my own fault really. Flimsy security. Your double glazing is only a few years old, isn't it? Assuming it's the same at the back, they'll have put in proper multipoint locks. I'm sure you're nothing like as vulnerable as I was.'

'Oh, I hope not dear. I'm a woman on my own, of course. Since Jim died.'

'Yes, I know. I'm not sure if my gran ever told you, but I was a police officer myself for a while, down in London. If ever you're worried about anything, just give me a knock. I'll try to help if I can.'

'Thank you, Jane. That is kind of you. Did they take much of sentimental value? That's the worst, isn't it? My cousin lost her father's medals. They were practically worthless. Financially, I mean.'

'No, they didn't take anything that mattered. Just a TV and that's been found and the police brought it back to me.'

The old lady raised her eyebrows. 'So they've apprehended the culprits?'

'Not as such.' Jane felt disappointed she couldn't be more encouraging. 'The TV was dumped and a member of the public reported it. It still works though.'

Jane knew she had inevitably inherited many of her grandmother's prejudices but found herself softening towards this lonely old woman, nosey or not. She tried to phrase her next question tactfully.'

'I know you... live in the front. I just wondered if you'd seen anything suspicious. It would have been on Friday. I don't know… Dodgy kids hanging about near my house, a man or men maybe. God, it could easily be a gang of women these days.'

Mrs Metcalfe turned her eyes upward as she thought. 'The only man I've seen is your boyfriend. Yes, I think he was there on Friday.'

Jane frowned with confusion. 'My boyfriend? I don't have a boyfriend.'

'Well, he… what's the expression these days?' Mrs Metcalfe pulled a worried face before tentatively continuing. 'He was black. Well, a bit black. Afro American. No, not American, Afro Caribbean maybe. Or mixed, erm…'

'Mixed race?' offered Jane.

'Yes. A very nice-looking boy, anyway. I saw you getting in a cab together a while back, going somewhere fancy. He was in a dinner jacket and you had a lovely frock on. You made such a handsome couple. You need someone tall, don't you, and he looked just the right height for you. And he seemed kind somehow. I remember thinking he had the look of my Jim about him. Not that there was a physical resemblance, obviously, but Jim was, well, a really nice man.'

Jane briefly turned towards her house to visualise the scene. 'That was Tommy. He's a friend, not a boyfriend as such.' She paused as she processed what was being suggested. 'Sorry, you're saying you saw him as recently as Friday?'

'Yes. I remember thinking your car wasn't there and he must have missed you. I've seen him a couple of times in the last week or two. There was one time he seemed to have inadvertently thrown a letter or something into your recycling bin. I've done it myself more than once. He was having to sift through all the bits of paper.'

Jane's mind instantly went back to the suspiciously targeted spam she'd recently received purporting to be from her new energy supplier. She'd been half-convinced someone had found an item of correspondence, but had blamed herself for not having a working shredder. Buying a new one had seemed an easy, lazy way of putting the problem aside, filing it under 'done' rather than thinking it through properly.

With some discomfort Jane pressed further. 'Are you sure it was Tommy, not just someone who looked like him?'

Mrs Metcalfe thought for a while and then nodded. 'Despite my age, I've got good eyes. I had my cataracts done three years ago and it was wonderful. And yes, I'm pretty certain it was him. Same build, same colouring, same gentle face. He's had a haircut, of course…'

The red light

Jane couldn't sleep. She'd been working late again, typing up her notes from her visit to Blackwell Holme. She wanted to document her thoughts and observations while they were still fresh in her mind. Rather than sitting downstairs staring at her amateurish repairs to the French windows, she had taken her laptop up to her bedroom. Stripping off, for once she just threw her clothes in a heap on the floor. She put on her most comfortable M&S pyjamas, and propped up on pillows in bed, she tried to produce a structure and prose that she felt an educated man like her client, Dr Guy Ramsbottom, would be able to read non-judgmentally. Unfortunately, it had been a long day and her ability to write sentences in anything like decent English seemed to have deserted her. The more she tried, the more laboured her language seemed to become.

At just past one, she gave up. The information was pretty much there, and revitalised by a good night's rest, she hoped she would easily be able to tidy it up in the morning. There was also the chance her unconscious brain would process the facts – people, places, dates – and she would awake with new insights, or perhaps new questions, that eluded her in her increasingly tired state.

Exhausted as she felt, her mind refused to switch off. She had been trying to get into the head of Thomas Ramsbottom and now he refused to leave hers. Another man also kept elbowing his way into her thoughts, however much she tried to push him out. Mrs Metcalfe was obviously mistaken about seeing Tommy hanging around her house. He had said his work had brought him up north recently, but if he had tried to call on Jane at home, he would have said something. But if not Tommy, who was the tall, thin, short-haired lookalike who had supposedly been through her paper recycling?

Was it really possible he had specifically wanted to target her with a malicious email? Why would it be worth his trouble? Internet fraudsters surely relied on targeting the masses, counting on the small percentage who were ill-informed, gullible, forgetful or just plain stupid. Jane wasn't any of those but she was a nobody: she wasn't rich; she wasn't powerful; she wasn't a celebrity with potentially dark and dirty secrets that could be sold to the tabloid press. Why would she be singled out? It didn't make sense.

And it also didn't make sense that the same man could have then stalked her house, waited until she was out and broken in to steal a television and two half-full bottles of booze that he promptly chucked away? Jane wasn't used to feeling scared, but the more her tired thoughts looped around the idea, the more uncomfortable and threatening it all seemed.

She began to realise it was a mistake to work into the early hours without allowing herself time to unwind and relax. She thought about getting up and having a glass of wine, but decided that drinking yourself to oblivion was a lifestyle choice best avoided. It would also entail getting out of bed and going downstairs and her body at least didn't feel like it had the energy. She desperately tried to distract herself with mundane and happy thoughts, but it didn't work.

She rolled over and looked at her bedside clock. The glowing red numerals said 03:56. She couldn't believe she'd been awake for nearly three hours and suspected she had dozed for a while but woken up again. For some reason, her eyes were drawn to the colon dividing hours from minutes, and the twin LEDs seemed to swell and brighten with the focus. And then she saw there was another smaller pinprick of glowing red, offset to the right. Her curtains were heavy and blocked almost all of the street light outside. Her eyes took time to adjust to the gloom and she realised the mysterious third dot was coming from the top of the dark, oblong shadow that was her laptop. That made sense: she had brought it up with her and hadn't turned it off, relying on it slipping into sleep mode, its artificial intelligence untroubled by overwork and imagination. But then again, that didn't make sense: its status was signalled by the subdued white power symbol she could also see below the keyboard.

Jane squeezed her eyes shut. The last thing she needed was another mystery to pester and nag at her thoughts and keep her awake.

She rolled over again and then rolled back. She sat up in bed and reached for the light switch. This at least was a problem that was easily put to bed. She leant across to turn off the laptop, but then stared at the faint red LED above its screen trying to remember why it was there. And then it came to her.

The camera was on.

Collodion and albumen

Monsieur Rivard, always Monsieur never Mister, was a chemist by training. He had learnt the process for producing wet collodion negatives in Paris and right until his death argued for their superiority in terms of tone and subtlety over the new dry-plate technology. Clients would arrive at his studio, he would greet them and discuss their requirements, and then he would have his assistant arrange and pose the sitters under the north-facing glazed roof while he himself repaired to his darkroom. He would ensure the blank glass plates were thoroughly clean before carefully coating them in a syrupy solution called collodion. Judging when it had set, but not dried, he would then immerse them in a bath of silver nitrate. Suitably sensitised to light, they had to be used whilst still wet. The Monsieur would emerge, check the composition and expose the plates in the large wooden camera which he had imported from France. He would then bow and disappear behind the scenes to develop and fix the images, again before the plates had time to dry out.

In Thomas Ramsden, he had seen a man with artistic sensitivity, literate and numerate enough to help with the administration of a small business and also with the intelligence and patience to learn the complex techniques and alchemist wizardry of photography. As the aging Rivard weakened and failed through a painful tumour in his stomach, he increasingly relied on his assistant, until the younger man was running the studio whilst its owner was confined to his rooms above. On Rivard's death he left everything to Thomas. The Frenchman had devoted his life to science and art. There had been no time for family or lasting friendships.

That had been the highpoint of Thomas's fortune and happiness. For the first time in his life he was a man of means, a man worthy of respect, with a beautiful wife and an angelic child. But the cracks were always there, the edifice waiting to crumble. He was harbouring a shameful secret and his wife's postnatal malaise meant her moods could swing from grateful contentment to bitter, resentful despair.

And then, in a moment of selfish, lunatic weakness, Thomas had ruined everything. His daughter was motherless and the blood was on her father's hands. Zenith had become nadir. Now his only solace was in his work. He allowed it to consume him.

The gelatine dry plates were manufactured by George Eastman's patented machinery in the city of Rochester in upstate New York. As well as having faster exposure times, they allowed the landscape photographer to work in the field without lugging a portable tented darkroom as well as a bulky camera and tripod. He – it was almost always a he – could go back to his studio at leisure and there carry out the chemical transformation that made the plates into negatives from which multiple paper pictures could be printed. The processing steps remained complex, however, requiring equipment, skill and judgement, thus keeping them in the realm of the professional and only the most dedicated of amateurs. Eastman was still working on the technology that would become his Kodak camera and make photography accessible to a far-wider marketplace.

Thomas had returned after the studio had closed and gone straight to his darkroom, excited to confirm the success of his endeavours. Working methodically under a dim red light, he moved the thin sheets of glass between trays of different solutions, developing, stopping, fixing and then washing. He stacked the results to dry and nervously inspected them through a lens. He was well used to looking at negative images and his mind could visualise black where there was white and the shades of grey between. Apart from the smoky haze over the heart of the city, the pictures were pin sharp. He was delighted with their scope and detail. There was the north-south line of the widened Fourth Avenue, train tracks now hidden beneath the ventilation ducts in its central mall. To the west was the vast expanse of Central Park, isolated mansions and hotels starting to sprout along its borders. North west, the seemingly endless chequerboard of rectangular lots was still largely empty, waiting to be levelled, occasional farmhouses being the main signs of occupation. North east, the elevated railroad lines running down Third and Second Avenues were clearly visible along with speculative apartment buildings, factories, wooden shanties, rocky outcrops and yet more farmland. In the distance, the Harlem flowed into the East River like a spill of ink and beyond sat Ward's Island. Under magnification, the grand architecture of its institutions was clearly visible. Thomas found himself transfixed by the grey dots of the hospital windows. They drew him in until he could look no more, his energy and drive drained away. The process of transferring the images to his sheets of shiny, egg-white albumen paper would have to wait until the next day.

Thomas opened the darkroom door and was surprised to see his wife standing in the narrow hallway that led to the front of the studio. He could tell she was angry. For once, he knew he had given her cause.

'Ester, I'm sorry. I was engrossed in a study. I forgot. I should have come up to see you earlier.'

'Vorgot!' Her English was vastly improved and she had learnt to soften her German accent with clients and others she was trying to impress. She did not bother when in private conversation with her husband.

'Vorgot!' she repeated. 'Thank Gott young Georg can work your stupid camera. The Goldstamms were angry enough you weren't here. Filthy Jews! Frau Goldstamm had spent hours dressing up that ugly daughter of theirs. She looked like a… Hochzeitstorte… a wedding cake!'

'I found Georg's plate in the darkroom.' Thomas felt his throat dry as he prepared to deliver bad news. 'There are a few small flaws. And I'm still not convinced he has the eye. The pose does not flatter the girl.'

'With a face like that she is beyond flattery! You and your artist's eye…' Ester looked up at the ceiling in exasperation. 'How many times must I tell you? You may know your chemicals and your paper and your plates, but this is business. And Georg will make a fine businessman. So much better than you. He charmed the little Fräulein, and her gross mother. The picture will be fine. I'll make sure it's paid for.'

'But what about our reputation as a fine studio, a producer of quality prints that people will be proud to display on their walls and on their mantelpieces?' Thomas's pleas had the empty conviction of a guilty man already judged and sentenced.

'You should have thought of your reputation when you chose not to be here for your appointment. What was this so-called study you tell me you were engrossed in?'

Thomas relaxed slightly. 'I honestly think it is something of importance. It is what the new dry plates were invented for. Mr Bauer let me take my equipment onto the roof of his new home—'

'Mr Bauer who owns the brewery?' Ester sounded interested.

'The same. He let me photograph from his roof.'

'I don't understand this word "let". Mr Bauer is a wealthy man. He is paying you to photograph his roof? Isn't he?'

'Not immediately.' The enthusiasm was growing in Thomas's voice. 'But when he sees what I have produced, I'm sure he might want to. It will be a work of historic importance – the march of progress, the old city and the new.'

'The march of progress?'

'Yes, Ester. Please listen. Let me explain. I placed my tripod on Mr Bauer's roof. You've seen his house.' Thomas raised a bent hand above his head as if demonstrating the height of a towering child. 'It is on a hill and the tallest building on that part of the East Side. I rotated my camera through the arc of a circle until I had captured the whole panorama – eight images, north, south, east, west and the points in between. I have just developed the plates. They've come out really well. You can see Fourth Avenue sweeping up, the railroad emerging at 96th Street. Central Park and its reservoir are over to the west. To the north—'

Ester's patience had expired. 'To the north is ugliness! It is vacant blocks, a handful of proper buildings, those wooden shacks jammed with dirty Irish and Italian peasants. It's a construction site.'

'That's the point, Ester. In a few short years, the city will have swelled northwards. We'll have block upon block of high tenement buildings, all the same. Sure, there'll be grand houses by the park and along the boulevards, but we'll have lost what lies beneath, and how we got there. It's a moment in—'

'No!' Ester slapped her hand against her skirts to signal she had heard enough. 'Don't talk to me of years! We bought the new portable camera equipment because you told me if would free you to work outside the studio. You could take the scenic views of New York. Portraits only sell to the sitters. A picture of Castle Garden, or the new bridge, or the cathedral is of interest to many people. They send them home to say, "Look at my fine new city." This is good money for us. It is good business. No-one wants to see an ugly, muddy, unfinished mess!'

Thomas's head dropped. 'To Monsieur Rivard, photography was much more than business. Painting is dead, he would say, we are the new artists. Our work will last like that of the great masters. He saw I had talent – that's why he employed me. That's why we now have the studio. That huge piece of luck gives us the lifestyle we now enjoy.'

Ester wagged a finger to signal her disagreement. 'I give us this lifestyle! I run this business. I make sure the bills are paid. And I raise your daughter while you make your pretty pictures.'

'How is little Sarah today?' A sadness had entered Thomas's voice. 'She had a cold, I think?'

'That is my concern. I am her mother now. Since you killed—'

'Ester!' It was Thomas's turn to rise in anger. 'I forbid you! God knows who might hear. What if Sarah were to be listening.'

Ester moved closer as if challenging her husband to hit out at her. 'Never forget I know who you are Thomas Ramsden, or Ram's-arse or whatever it is you're really called. Who you are and what you are. And what you have done.'

Thomas just stared, silently reminding himself he was in a hell of his own making, perhaps even of his own choice.

Ester smiled, her dominance confirmed. 'I have decided we need to open a new studio, to expand. Georg will be the photographer. Another of my nephews is coming over, he too will learn. This new camera equipment is so easy, I could use it.'

'When? When do you want the new studio?'

Ester shrugged. 'Next year at the latest.'

Thomas looked away before responding. 'I've been thinking about visiting England next year'

'Home to England? Is that wise? There are those who might not welcome you.'

'I must go.' Thomas rubbed his brow as if he might push the idea back into the deeper recesses of his mind.

Ester hesitated, calculating. 'Go if you want,' she said eventually, 'but I will need papers. Legal papers. Our customers, our suppliers must know that I am the one in charge. Those men must understand I am the one they must deal with. I have absolute authority. While you are away.'

A small face suddenly appeared from behind Ester's wide skirts. 'Mama, I heard Papa shouting. I don't like it when he shouts.'

Thomas and Ester's eyes met in a wordless exchange.

Her step-mother ran her fingers through the little girl's hair. 'Your father can be an angry man. But don't worry, liebling, I won't let him be angry with you.'

Thomas looked at the child's beautiful face, half his own, half that of her poor, dead mother, and knew his daughter was lost to him.

He had brought it on himself. It was part of his punishment.

The digital camera

The parade of shops nearest to Jane's house had changed dramatically over the years. When she'd been a child, there had still been a traditional bakery, a butcher's, a greengrocer's, an ironmonger's and a newsagent's. The newsagent was still clinging on, but most of his custom seemed to come from selling cheap tins of booze to rather rough-looking men who hung around outside drinking and talking rather than paying pub prices. There were also two charity shops, an emporium selling odd bits of everything with cut-down prices reflecting their dubious quality, a nail bar, a tanning salon, an Indian restaurant and two cafés, one of which belonged to a vast chain imported from America. Recently, the old dry cleaner's had been replaced by 'Nottingham Tech and PC', advertising 'computer-laptop-mac-repairs, proprietor V Abar BSc (Eng)'. Jane had never been in but had walked past several times and seen the bespectacled Mr Abar working at a counter set right behind the shop window. He, clearly, was the business's main asset. From a distance, he could have been 20 or 40, and as well as his glasses he wore a tie and a bad haircut. It was a look that said 'computer geek' and, again, could have been a deliberate marketing ploy.

He'd seemed intrigued when Jane explained her concern and suggested she return that afternoon, when hopefully he would able to offer a diagnosis. As Jane re-entered the shop he greeted her with a gleam and a nod that said he'd got to the bottom of the problem and was very pleased with himself for doing so.

'Ah, Ms Madden. It was a good job you brought this in to me. You've been well and truly hacked. As I told you, this is an old laptop. You're vulnerable.'

'I know, I know,' replied Jane with only a hint of irritation. 'You're not the first… I've been meaning to replace it. Just haven't got round to it yet.'

Mr Abar tapped the keyboard a few times. 'We could upgrade the memory, but ultimately I don't think the processor is up to the current version of the O S. Replacement is probably your only option. I could help with setting it up and copying all your data across?'

Jane wasn't sure what O S stood for but got the drift. 'Okay, thanks for the offer. You said I had definitely been hacked?'

'Oh absolutely. Nasty, nasty, nasty. I ran a scan and found a keylogger—'

'A keylogger?'

'A program that records all your keystrokes, everything you type into the keyboard, and then sends it off to its master somewhere on the dark web.'

Jane's mind quickly tried to assess if she'd recently typed anything that might expose her financially. 'I use my phone for most things, like my banking app,' she said hesitantly. 'I use the laptop mainly for my work on family history. You know, research and stuff. I can't imagine anyone would be interested in that.'

Mr Abar shrugged. 'What about emails?'

'Again, I usually check those on the phone, certainly when I'm out and about. But, you're right, long emails I will type on the laptop. Though they're mostly boring work stuff. Again, who'd care?'

'Is your email account password protected, by which I mean – do you have to type your password every time you log in?'

Jane hesitated briefly, still distracted by her own thoughts. 'Not on the phone. It goes straight in. But on the laptop, yes. The app thing stopped working and now I go in via a browser. It did ask to save the password once, but I didn't do it for some reason.'

Mr Abar pointed a finger to indicate they'd identified an exposure. 'So they could well have your password and be signing in on their own computer. That could be the gateway to all your other accounts, banking, shopping, et cetera. They could have reset the logins via your email.' He raised his eyebrows as a shocking thought occurred to him. 'Obviously, I'm assuming you don't use the same password for everything?'

'I'm not that stupid,' said Jane scratchily. 'How can I tell if someone's been changing my other passwords?'

'Have you been locked out of anything? Have you noticed an unusual activity in your email account? Or anywhere else?'

'No and no. Oh God, what a mess!'

'Don't despair, Ms Madden. I've cleaned up your laptop and reactivated the anti-virus and firewall. They'd been turned off as well. Change your email password immediately and then check your bank transactions and anything else financial. I'd change all those passwords too. And there's a police website on which you can report potential fraud and cybercrime.'

'What a mess!' repeated Jane. 'How did this key… key log program get on there?'

'You probably downloaded it by accident from a malicious website or it came in on some dodgy spam.'

'I'm normally good about that kind of thing, though to be honest I have had a few suspicious things in my inbox lately.' Jane's eyes became thoughtful. 'Hang on. Is it possible someone who had physical access to the laptop could have bypassed the security and loaded it?'

'On this old thing, sure. You don't leave it lying around in public places do you?'

Jane shook her head. 'My house was broken into recently. They took some stuff and promptly dumped it. They didn't take this piece of junk.' Jane pointed accusingly at her computer. 'But I did notice that it had been moved.'

Mr Abar stroked his glasses. 'That would be a new one on me, but it's possible they loaded the keylogger. Maybe they were part-time hackers and were trying to expand their housebreaking business. Or vice versa. Oh, and we're forgetting something.'

Jane tilted her head as a silent question.

'The reason you brought it in the first place, Ms Madden – the video camera coming on.'

Jane exhaled slowly as if trying to delay more bad news. 'Oh yeh. I'm not sure how long it had been on. It's such a tiny light. It's only because it was night-time that I noticed it. Is it related to the keylogger?'

'Yes and no. They loaded a separate program to control the camera and, of course, the microphone. Maybe it was just some pervert who wanted to snoop on you. Watch you, well…' Mr Abar looked embarrassed. 'The Internet's full of weirdos. I spend a lot of time in chat rooms. There's something about the culture… You see people egging each other on, suggesting… stuff.' He swallowed audibly to combat a dry, sticky throat. 'Maybe someone, who's tech-savvy, has taken a fancy to you and gone to extreme lengths to snoop on your emails and see you… Well, you said the laptop was in your bedroom.'

The video call

Jane had reset her main passwords and Mr Abar had helped check her email account for any signs of damaging activity. Nothing was obvious, and he offered the opinion that they'd caught the problem in time. Jane was relieved but slightly concerned the shopkeeper was at the limit of his experience and expertise. Perhaps his BSc (Eng) signified a degree in civil rather than software engineering. Perhaps he'd bought it online from an unscrupulous institution masquerading as a university.

But there was someone she knew whose credentials were beyond doubt. Someone who was decidedly, definitely tech-savvy.

Back home, she found herself staring at her phone, strangely reluctant to touch it. Was it guilt for not chasing up to see how he was? Or was another emotion the cause of her unease? She berated herself for being influenced by other voices. She did not trust the psychological assessments of Emma at the tennis club or the eyesight of Mrs Metcalfe. She wasn't sure Mr Abar's idea of 'tech-savvy' would hold water in the wide ocean of IT outside a little shop in Nottingham. Yet their words ate away at Jane's certainties. She knew her doubts were misplaced; she had to trust her better instincts, her friendship and her loyalty. But still the voices nagged.

Jane typed a text and pressed send. She'd added an extra kiss, as if that would someone soften her motive, but immediately hated herself and wished she could draw the message back from over the airwaves.

'Tommy. I've haven't heard from you for ages. I want to see that you're ok. I know you don't like phone calls, so we might as well make you really squirm. Can we FaceTime please? Love Jane xxx.'

A minute or so later, a reply arrived.

'FaceTime? Wouldn't be seen dead with a poncy iPhone.

;-)

I'll do a video call on WhatsApp. Here it comes…'

Jane's phone began to buzz. She pressed the answer symbol and Tommy's grinning face appeared on the screen. Jane returned the smile, but it was a shallow, fragile facade. Her heart had suddenly crashed.

Tommy looked at her expectantly and so Jane was forced to speak.

'Hiya. Thanks for ringing me. I just… wanted to check how you were.'

Tommy's eyes creased as if he could tell something wasn't quite right. 'I'm doing okay. A few sleepless nights over this damn project, but that's business as usual. We're almost there. It'll soon be done.'

'Good. You're not letting it get you down too much?'

'No more than usual. I could do without them wasting my time in bloody meetings. But maybe it's good for me, forcing me to get out. You know how it is.'

'Yeh, I know, Tommy.' Jane's voice was lifelessly unconvincing. 'But no regrets about taking the job on?'

Tommy briefly looked away as if the question were painful. 'Wouldn't necessarily say that. The money's been really good, but I don't think I'd do it again. It's not worth the stress. I think it's back to the search engine thing I was doing before.' He touched his face nervously. 'Oh, and Jane…?'

'Uhuh.'

'I've been thinking. Maybe I could work more with you on the genealogy research. You know the idea of a partnership you suggested?'

Jane's expression hardened. 'Yeh, maybe. I'm still not 100% sure it's viable. I'm just about paying the bills. If there were two of us, it might not work out. Financially, I mean. And maybe I should give up anyway and get a proper job.'

'I understand,' lied Tommy, his shoulders sinking like man whose lifeline has been unexpectedly severed.

'Okay. I just wanted to see…' Jane closed her eyes. 'I just wanted to see you were okay.'

'Jane? Are you alright? You don't seem yourself.'

'No, don't worry about me. Everything's great.'

'Look, I'm up your way next week. One those damn meetings. I could come and see you?'

'Don't do that, Tommy. I'm fine and I'm travelling myself a lot. Probably wouldn't be around anyway.'

'Are you sure you're not getting down again. The two of us, eh?'

'Seriously, Tommy, I'm fine,' Jane said forcefully before turning her head as if distracted by noises off screen. 'Sorry, there's someone at the door. I'd better go. Thanks for the call. Bye!'

Jane hung up and threw the phone onto the sofa beside her. She had sought one answer and got another. And now her mind spun with a mix of disappointment, anger and betrayal, most of all betrayal. She just wasn't sure who was betraying whom.

She began to softly cry.

Liverpool

They entered the Mersey estuary on the dawn tide. The previous day they had been in Queenstown and Thomas had briefly lost himself to an alternative destiny, one where he had been able to bring his sweet, fragile Mary home to Ireland. It was a joy she, and he, would never know. After a sleepless night he had left the warmth of his bunk to don his fur-collared coat and stand on a lonely deck, watching the lights of England grow in distance. They dimmed as the March sun rose and the outlines of buildings became clearer. To the right were the fort and grand hotels of New Brighton. To the left was a seemingly endless line of docks with warehouses holding timber from Canada, cotton from the southern states, sugar from the Caribbean islands and sundry goods from all over the world. The confusion of cranes, masts and rigging led towards the church towers and chimneys of the great town far ahead. It had been elevated to the rank of city since last he saw it, but to his eyes its once impressive scale and grandeur were now dwarfed in comparison to the metropolis he had departed just over a week previously. If the entrance to Liverpool was not as spectacular as New York Harbour, the lack of excited passengers cramming the rails was more a testament to the near empty cabins and steerage deck of the mighty liner RMS Servia, which at her launch had been second only to Brunel's flawed Great Eastern in size. Her twin compound engines, double-bottomed hull and innovative electric lighting were financed by the prevailing traffic towards the New World. On her return journeys, her customers were few and her most valuable cargo was the sacks of mail beneath her decks. Thomas had hardly spoken whilst on board, other than to pass on his requests to the attentive and underworked stewards. In the Babel of New York, his class was defined by his relative affluence, obvious to all through the expense of his clothing. In this floating outpost of the British Empire, dress was secondary. His accent, muted as it was, labelled him unworthy of the interest of his fellow first-class passengers. Even the courtesy of the crew could at times appear facetious, the cost of his ticket not guaranteeing respect. He had been surprised his wife let him spend so much, but realised she considered it another investment, hoping he wouldn't return.

Thomas's isolation was of little consequence. He didn't seek anyone's approval and had always been happy enough in his own company. He passed his time reading, though his attention was all too often interrupted by conversations being rehearsed in his head. His novel was reaching a happy conclusion; the real-life scenarios that he imagined seldom did.

As Thomas took in the early morning view of the port city's skyline, he once again wished he had been able to bring his precious camera equipment. He was using his hands to crop the backlit horizon, seeing it captured in crisp monochrome, when he became aware of another person standing close by. He turned sharply to find a young girl, probably in her mid twenties and wearing a coat and bonnet that identified her as belonging to the lower ranks. Her access to this deck suggested she was a personal servant to someone who occupied one of the finer staterooms. Her beaming face indicated she at least was glad to be near journey's end.

Thomas touched his hat as an unnecessary gesture of politeness given the girl's status. 'Are you coming back or seeing England for the first time?' he asked.

The girl curtsied. 'Coming back, sir.'

'And judging by your voice, home isn't very far away.'

'No, sir, I'm from just outside Manchester. I'm so looking forward to seeing my mum and... I mean mother and father, sir.'

'Mum and dad are fine with me, lass.' Thomas's own accent was beginning to slip back, subconsciously mirroring the girl's. 'And how long have you been away?'

'We've been travelling America for a year – the master's been on business. We've seen some things, I can tell you.'

'I wager you have.' Thomas felt he should enquire what sights had turned her head, but his heart wasn't in it. He touched his hat again and began to turn away. The girl, however, was emboldened by his initial questions.

'We took the Union Pacific Railway. We saw a Wild West show in the state of Nebraska. Rough riders, indians, huge buffalo – it was right exciting,' she babbled.

'Indeed,' replied Thomas.

'And the sharpshooters…' she continued, 'They could hit dime pieces tossed in the air 30 paces away. It was a wonder to behold.'

Thomas simply smiled.

The girl suddenly remembered how she was supposed to interact with her betters. 'And you, sir? How long have you been away?'

'Me?' Thomas knew the answer, but still thought through it. 'Ten years. A little more, in fact.'

The girl raised her eyebrows in surprise. 'Your family must have missed you so. I mean, do you have family in England still?'

'Family?' Thomas looked down at his gloved hands. 'There's a word. Yes, I have family. But then again, I don't. I've been… I've been so far away.'

The girl misinterpreted the enigmatic reply. 'Letters can get lost, can't they? I'm sure your family are still there. It's not my place, sir, but I don't doubt they'll be ever so happy to see you again.'

'Happy?' Thomas paused as he studied the girl's features for the first time. At first he had thought her plain, but he now saw a disarming prettiness. Perhaps he just saw youth and innocence. Perhaps she just looked hauntingly familiar, an echo of his past. His mind wandered and he allowed himself to briefly fantasise about being young again, or at least young enough to woo a simple girl like this, to save her from a life of servitude, to build a different life for himself.

There was a blast on the ship's horn as the captain sought to warn the ketch cutting across his course. The Servia was steaming at slow ahead, but her steel bows would not turn easily and would obliterate any lesser vessel that came beneath them.

"Happy?" repeated Thomas when the air had cleared to near silence again. 'I wanted to make my fortune, to make my wife, her father, proud of me. For once. But things didn't turn out as I hoped.'

'I'm sure they'll be very proud, sir. You're a fine gentleman. The world can see you're a man of means.'

'Unfortunately I made an... error. Several errors. And now I'm between worlds and not...' He paused without finishing the sentence. 'Tell me, young lady, what do think is the most important attribute of personality a man – or indeed, in these modern times, a woman – can have?'

The girl looked uncomfortable. She was not used to having her opinions sought. 'I couldn't say, sir. A sense of duty? Faith in the Lord?'

Thomas smiled. 'Commendable, but I would say courage. Every day, every decision, every challenge. Courage.'

It was Thomas's turn to feel discomfort as he realised he was unburdening himself on someone whose social standing obliged her to listen respectfully to his musings. In truth, she probably thought him a silly old fool. And she had presumably now heard enough of his accent to know he was an imposter on an upper-class deck.

'Tell me, is there a boy waiting for you at home?' he asked, diverting the conversation onto what seemed safer waters.

'There was,' she answered sheepishly. 'A right grand-looking lad. I hope he's still there for me, but he's only written to me twice. I'm not sure he hasn't found another.'

'Take my advice,' said Thomas. 'If he has, let him go. And don't worry too much about handsome features – always look for someone kind, someone you can trust, someone… brave.'

They were interrupted by a shrill voice shouting across the deck.

'Betsy! Where are you girl? You are needed.'

Betsy curtsied again, offered a quick apology and scurried away. Thomas watched her and fleetingly wanted her to stay. And then his face sank.

'I'd surely let you down, too,' he muttered, his words drifting off on the sea air.

The seagull

It was another bad night. Jane finally got to sleep just before dawn and dreamt of her father. It began with a familiar scene, something that had played in her mind since childhood despite being rooted in false memory and deception. Once again, he was on that quayside saying goodbye, beneath the towering, arcing hull of the vast grey ship that was to carry him away to a distant continent, a journey he never made.

'Don't cry, little princess.' he said, his wild hair caught by the breeze. 'I'll come back when you're grown and I'll save you, save you from the demons in your head. I put them there and I can take them away again. I'll put my huge hands around their throats and squeeze out their venom and their bile until they are empty and lifeless, crumbling to ashes and scattered on the wind.'

And the screaming seagull came down and landed on his pirate shoulder. Somehow its hooked yellow beak shortened and twisted into a leering smile. Its monochrome feathers became flushed with red, green and blue. And then it laughed a cruel, mocking, derisive cackle.

'Don't trust him,' said the parrot seagull. 'Don't trust any of them. You're on your own, little girl.' The bird guffawed again. 'And I pity you for that – I've never met anyone more stupid, weak and hopeless.'

Jane's eyes shot open as the creature began ripping and tearing at the right side of her father's face. Her pulse was racing and she was sodden with sweat. The drama felt like it had lasted for hours, but only the last few fleeting moments seemed within reach. Jane was not someone who believed in the spiritual power of nocturnal imagery. She didn't try to chase the nonsense that had been taunting her dormant mind and instead looked at the clock. It was mid morning. She grabbed her phone from the bedside table, climbed from under the sheets and went downstairs. Hunched at the kitchen table over a cup of coffee, she replayed the conscious thoughts that had kept her awake for so long, hoping that a fresh day would provide the clarity that had eluded her in the darkness of night. But she was still dog-tired and soon found herself in the same morass of indecision and doubt.

The evidence had been slim, circumstantial, a coincidental nothing. But she had only asked the hateful question because she expected a resounding, incontrovertible 'no'. 'Perhaps' had caught her off guard and thrown her. And its arm had been strong and fast.

Jane knew her mood was sinking rapidly and her ability to think straight was being sucked down with it. She had been here too often before. Those ignorantly obvious words resented by every depressive began echoing in her head.

'Just pull yourself together,' they rang. 'This is silly. Just pull yourself together. Just think it through.' It wasn't working. It never had.

The more she tried to persuade herself that her suspicions were foolishly unfounded, the more she loathed herself for thinking them. Was she so weak minded that she let herself be influenced by tittle-tattle and ignorance? Was she being paranoid, irrationality overriding reason, when you start to think even your best friends are plotting, scheming against you?

But what if it was true? Just suppose… What was the old joke? Just because you're paranoid doesn't mean they're not out to get you. You have to confront him. A simple, honest, up-front conversation. That would clear things up. Quickly, painlessly. But he's oh-so clever, and oh-so sensitive. No matter how you tried to say it, no weaselling, 'I don't believe this for a minute' 'or 'I know this sounds silly' would disguise the doubts. That wicked word 'but' would reveal the truth. You'd hurt him forever and you'd be exposed as the untrusting, cruel, mad bitch you are. Barmy, just like Christine Jackson said. Barmy then, barmy now. Uncured and incurable.

Jane stared at her phone willing it to ring. She began rocking backwards and forwards as if the motion would calm her like a baby in her mother's arms. It was a full 20 minutes before the device buzzed with life.

'Hi Jane. Just got your text. Sorry hard to talk right now. At a bloody fire engine convention with that stupid old Duffer of mine. Can you believe it? What a bunch of nerds. Hope you're ok. Can I call you this evening? Sarah.'

Jane read the message wishing she'd sent a less composed request. Dared she say, 'No, I'm not okay; please tell the nerds to stuff their fire engines and please talk to me now, Sarah, talk me out of this spiral of stupidity?'

The phone began to ring. Jane's immediate reaction was an exhalation of relief. Her friend's intuition had overridden her social mores. Then she saw the caller's picture on her screen. It was someone whose shoulder she had cried on so often, someone who knew her better than anyone and had always helped her through her darkest times. Except one. The one where he had summoned the clouds and blocked out the light.

'Hi Dave.'

'Hi Janey. Look, I was at a loose end and I realised I hadn't spoken to you for a while. Just thought I'd call to see how you were.'

'I've been better, if I'm honest. I guess.'

Dave read the understatement accurately. 'What's wrong? Something getting you down, babe?'

'I'm being stupid again.' replied Jane hesitantly. 'It's just that he's had a haircut.'

'Haircut? Who's had a haircut? And what does it…' Dave sounded totally confused. 'I mean, haircut?'

'Tommy's cut his hair. It's really short. And it wasn't supposed to be. He was supposed to still have his Afro.'

There was a silence as Dave's mind tried to process the information. 'I don't understand. Is something going on between you two?' His tone changed to one of incredulity. 'You and Tommy?'

'No, there's nothing going on between me and Tommy.'

'So why do you care if the bloke's cut his hair? And why would it upset you so much if there was something going on. You're not the silly sort, Jane.'

'Mrs Metcalfe, across the road, saw someone who looked like Tommy, with short hair, breaking in. Well, she didn't see him breaking in as such, but she saw him acting suspiciously.'

'Sorry, Jane, are saying you've had a break-in or not?'

'Yes. And they didn't take anything. Well they did, but they just dumped it round the corner. But they hacked into my laptop. And well, as I said, Tommy has had a haircut. And I'm just scared he's working too hard, and it's making him unwell again and a bit, you know, obsessive. And Sarah says he fancies me, well, more than that actually, and—'

'Jane, Jane, Jane! Slow down a bit. You're losing me. Talk me through this. From beginning to end.'

Jane took a deep breath. 'Sarah reckons Tommy confessed he was in love with me—'

'No shit, Sherlock,' interrupted Dave. 'I was never convinced you were cut out to be a detective. Sorry, I don't mean that.'

'You knew Tommy had the hots for me?'

'For God's sake, Jane. He used to look at you like a little lost puppy dog. If he wasn't a wet dishcloth and totally out of your league I might have warned him off. Anyway, carry on with the story.'

'Well, I'd been getting more spam than usual. It looked like someone was specifically targeting me. Trying to get me to download something dodgy. When that failed they broke in, hacked directly into my laptop and tried to make it look like a burglary. They've been reading my emails and turning on the camera. Watching me.'

'Christ, Jane! Has this gone to the cybercrime boys?'

'No, of course not! I reported the break-in, before I knew, well I don't know… Before I thought it might be Tommy. But I don't want to get him into trouble. He's obviously ill again. Maybe. Or maybe I'm the ill one suspecting him.'

'Jane, come on. Think straight. Sure, Tommy could do the hacking bit. No problem. But housebreaking? Let's get real here. The guy's frightened of his own shadow. He's got no form, not the vaguest sniff of it.'

'That's not 100% true,' said Jane reluctantly. 'He came from a pretty rough estate. He had this older cousin who was bad news. Bullied Tommy along on a couple of break-ins when he was twelve or thirteen. The cousin ended up banged to rights, but kept quiet about Tommy's involvement. He still has nightmares about it coming to light. He told me about it once and made me promise not to tell you.'

Dave puffed doubtfully down the phone line. 'I still don't buy it. It's one thing being dragged along by someone else. It's something totally different having the guts to do it yourself. But we need to get to the bottom of it. If it's not him, it's some other stalker creep who needs a damn good slapping down—'

'I simply need to talk to him,' said Jane calmly. 'I just need to think how to put it. It's a horrible thing to accuse a friend of doing.'

'Do you want me to have a word?' offered Dave. 'If he's still at the same address, I could pop round this afternoon. I'd soon clear it up.'

'I don't doubt you would. I know you and your words. No, thanks for the offer, it's something I need to do myself.'

'Are you sure?'

'Yes, thanks, Dave. You've been a big help. Honest. Just talking it through has helped me get a bit of clarity. I'm feeling much better. You're right, it's serious and I need to pull my finger out and talk to him. I just need to work out the best way of doing it.'

'Sometimes you can overthink things. The direct approach is often—'

'Yes, thanks, Dave. But what you and I mean by directness is somewhat different.'

'Hmm.'

'Look, I'm going to go now. I owe you again. Thanks for ringing. Bye now.'

'You sure?'

'I'm sure. Thank you, but I need to go.'

'Bye, Janey. Look after yourself, hear?'

Jane hung up and then stared at her phone, wondering if she should make the call immediately rather than prevaricating any longer. After a short delay she went into her contacts and pressed dial.

The call was answered immediately, but not by Tommy.

'Dave, it's me again.'

'Hi Janey. Second thoughts?'

'Dave, I know what you're like. I know you just want to help. But I mean it. Please don't go and see Tommy. I'll never talk to you again if you do. You'll scare the life out of him and that'll hurt me more than he ever could, even if he has gone a bit weird. I can handle Tommy. Do you understand?'

'Yes, I understand. But—'

'No buts, Dave. I'll sort it out and let you know how it goes. Don't worry, just leave it to me. I'm not your responsibility anymore. Remember?'

'I remember.'

'Thank you. And, Dave… look, thank you for still caring.'

'Janey, how many times… I always cared. I think I should come and see you. I could drive up, at the weekend say. I'm worried. You're sounding a bit, well, not yourself. Not your good self anyway. And, if I'm honest, I miss you.'

'Let's not go there.' Jane's dismissal was automatic. 'I think I'd better ring off again,' she added quickly for fear of changing her mind. 'As I said, I'll let you know how it goes."

Jane hung up for the second time and slowly raised her eyes to the ceiling, where they fixed on a small cobweb in the corner above a cupboard. Everything, everybody, was flawed if you stared hard enough. Would it really be so bad if her ex-husband did come up? Perhaps she should have offered a more encouraging response. But she knew how impetuous he could be. She hadn't actually said no. And if she did find him standing on her doorstep, how would she react?

The meeting

It was only half an hour's drive away, on the right side of the city centre. Tommy's meeting was scheduled to finish at 3:00 pm and Jane arrived in the car park ten minutes early. He didn't actually come out until twenty past. At first he looked flustered, but on spotting her his face broke into something else, something she read as relief. Was he just happy to see her, or was it the expression of a man whose misdemeanours have caught up with him and no longer has to hide?

'Jane, I'm so sorry I'm late. It just dragged on. Some of the guys were upset and wouldn't shut up about it.' He quickly looked over his shoulder to check none of the aforementioned guys had followed him out.

'It's not a problem,' she answered with a shrug. 'I know meetings overrun. The sun's shining and it's… well, it's a rather soulless dump round here, to be honest.' She smiled unconvincingly at her own attempt at humour. 'I thought they had a flash head office in London?'

'They do, but it's cheaper to stick the computer staff out here in Derby. I guess it's the geographic equivalent of putting them in a windowless basement. Did you watch the IT Crowd on TV?'

'Not really my thing,' replied Jane, dismissively shaking her head. 'It all looks pretty new.'

'Used to be the site of the locomotive works for the old Midland Railway.' His eyes scanned the surroundings. 'I guess this is what all modern industrial estates look like. They know the buildings probably won't be standing that long. No need to make them interesting.'

Jane shrugged. 'So where can we get a cup of coffee?' she asked.

'The station's probably the best bet. It's just round the back.'

'Lead the way.'

As they walked, he began to expand on the reason the meeting had become heated. 'The company's been bought out. There've been rumours, but it happened really suddenly. They'll probably place a moratorium on all new software development. They'll want to save money by merging systems – easier said than done, obviously. In the meantime, we've been told to take a few days off until they know what's happening.'

'Gosh, after all that work you've put in.' She put a comforting hand on his shoulder. 'How do you feel about it?'

'It could be a relief, to be honest. Maybe the pressure's off. I'm just a bit scared they'll decide to resume again in six months and drag me back in.'

She still had her hand in place and pulled him to a stop. 'Tommy, sweetheart, you're an independent contractor. If you don't want to do it, just say you're no longer available. They can't expect you to be at their beck and call if they've pulled the plug on you.'

'You're right,' he grinned. 'With any luck I'm a free man. I'll be a poorer one, too, but I can go back to my old job and things will be okay again. I may have a bun with my latte to celebrate.'

There was a ubiquitous coffee-chain outlet in the station concourse and Tommy insisted on paying for the order. Jane declined the pastry and asked for her usual Americano with a splash of milk. She found a table in the window overlooking the passing traffic of passengers and waited for Tommy to bring over the drinks and sit down. He seemed to have had second thoughts about the bun.

'Erm, you said there was something you wanted to talk to me about face-to-face?' Tommy sounded nervously reluctant, as if he'd been building up the courage to ask the question.

'Yes, it was just good fortune you were in Derby. I'd have happily come down to London.'

'Is everything okay, Jane? You were a bit… well, off with me when we spoke on the phone. Is something wrong? Have I done something?'

'Why would you think you'd done something?' Jane's eyebrows knotted quizzically.

'I always think I've done something wrong. Part and parcel of being neurotic. I guess I shouldn't be so sensitive.'

'Someone's hacked into my laptop, Tommy. And I wanted to… get your advice.'

'Yuk! I did say it was vulnerable. What damage did they do? Have you got it with you? Do you want me to look at it?'

Jane took a sip from her coffee before answering. 'I took into my local PC shop. He's cleaned it up – probably destroyed all the evidence – but he found a, quotes, keystroke logger and a program that took control of the camera.'

'A keystroke logger?' Tommy's concern sounded genuine. 'So they'll have got your passwords. Which accounts have they taken over? Have you lost money?'

'As far as we can tell, they've just been reading my emails. God knows why. I'm not exactly passing state secrets.'

'Didn't your antivirus pick it up?'

'No they turned that off. I saw that the little camera light had come on. It was dark. In my bedroom.'

'They didn't deactivate the LED?'

Jane looked wrong-footed. 'Can you do that?'

'Of course. If you know what you're doing. They were obviously bloody amateurs. How did they get in?'

'I think they tried to get me to download dodgy emails at first. When I didn't fall for that, they broke into my house while I was out. They pretended to nick some stuff but the motive was to get at my computer.'

'Bloody hell! I said they were amateurs, but that's hardcore amazing!'

'Why? How would you do it?'

Tommy gazed at his hands as he thought. 'Several ways, I guess. Sit in that café across the street and hack into your wifi?'

'Is that easy to do? Would you find that easy to do?'

'It's not easy, but I'm pretty sure I could do it. Well, I could do it, obviously, because I know your wifi password. But even if I didn't—'

'You know my wifi password?' An expression of vague recollection crossed Jane's face.

'Yes. When I stayed with you for that charity auction. Duff's fire engine. You said I could read the password off the back of your router. You were pretty hungover at the time.'

'God, I'd forgotten that.'

'Obviously, whoever loaded the keystroke logger didn't have the password, but even so, resorting to a physical break-in is desperate stuff. Sounds like someone just googled "hacking for dummies" on the Web and, well, maybe housebreaking is their day job and that seemed like the easy bit. But... are you okay? Do you know why they did it?'

Jane stared into the dark coffee steaming in her cup. 'Dunno. A stalker maybe. Someone who wants to nose into my personal life, see me getting undressed, whether I'm alone or not.' She looked up. 'Maybe it's industrial espionage from a rival genealogist. But I suspect not.'

There were deep frown lines on Tommy's face. 'But it must have freaked you out a bit. It would me, but that's not too hard. You're much tougher than me.'

Jane's eyes dropped again. 'Sometimes. But then sometimes things get to me. I sometimes feel all the men in my life, the ones that matter to me, they've betrayed me. My father, Dave. Even my grandfather betrayed me by dying.'

Tommy rubbed his temple as a thought coalesced in his mind. 'You didn't think it was me, did you, Jane?'

She reached across the table and placed her hand on his. 'No. I don't think you're that kind of weirdo. You're one of the good guys. I trust you. It's just that it did freak me out and... why did you have to get your haircut, Tommy?'

'What?'

'The Afro suited you.'

'I don't... Short hair is much easier to live with.' He was talking quickly now, clearly wanting to dismiss what seemed a distracting irrelevance. 'When you took me to that hairdresser's in Nottingham it made me realise they're not that scary. Jane, I don't understand?'

She put her head in her hands and her words became slightly muffled. 'My neighbour has nothing better to do than stare out of her window all day. She said she saw someone who looked like you, but with short hair, hanging around my house. Well she said it was you. I didn't believe her and then you'd had a haircut. And I just... You know how sometimes, everything's going fine, you feel strong, and then the world sinks from under your feet. I'm sorry, Tommy. I'm the one who's guilty of betrayal.'

Tommy leant back in his chair. 'But you don't still think it was me, do you?'

'No. It was always stupid. Of course you wouldn't risk breaking into my house. You could send me anything and I'd load it. Because I fundamentally trust you. You're a nice guy. And my friend. Not some creep who wants to abuse me.'

'So what are you going to do next?'

Jane sat up straight. 'Not sure. Keep an eye out for blokes acting suspiciously who look like you? And when and if I see one...'

'Call the police?' offered Tommy.

'Uhuh.'

The conversation stopped and neither of them could meet the other's eyeline. Tommy broke the silence. 'So, tell me about your family history project. I've just remembered I'm about to be a free man with lots of time.'

'You don't hate me?' asked Jane forlornly.

'I'm the last person to condemn someone because they think crazy things from time to time. Tell me about your project. How far have you got?'

Jane breathed out slowly. 'Well, Thomas Ramsbottom, or Thomas Ramsden as he started calling himself. Now there was a man who betrayed just about everyone he came into contact with.'

Tommy looked pained again. 'I always think we can never really know these people. We have a few dates, snippets of information, but there's a tendency to fill in the gaps based on our own experience and prejudices. I'm wary of categorising people, living or dead.'

'Absolutely,' agreed Jane. 'But I'll make an exception for this bastard.'

Out and back again

Jane had slept, but only fitfully and was woken up still feeling tired. She switched off the alarm and tried to roll over again, but a mood of guilty remorse nagged for her attention and forced her to sit up in bed. She sought distraction from her thoughts and switched on the portable TV her grandparents had bought her when she was a teenager. It still worked well enough, but these days it required an additional remote control for the digital tuner that became necessary when the old analogue transmissions were abandoned.

Jane flicked between the main breakfast TV channels, but the news was equally depressing: young boys stabbing each other in London and politicians squabbling. The ITV presenter was presumably trying to liven things up by interrupting and shouting at a guest who seemed to have been invited because his intolerant views made him a ready target for the broadcast equivalent of a mediaeval pillory.

Jane shouted 'Prat!' at one or both of them and turned the screen off. She leant across and pressed the power button on her laptop. She still hadn't replaced it but now took the precaution of switching it off every night. Its tired disc and processor churned through the boot process and loaded layers of programming it had not been designed to accommodate, and eventually it signalled it was ready for use. Jane thought about checking the BBC News website, but realised the stories would be just the same. Dave would always head for the sports' pages, but Jane found them even less uplifting than articles about urban deprivation and limelight-seeking MPs parading ill-considered opinion as fact.

Instead she opened her emails. There was one she hesitated before reading. It was from Tommy and had arrived in the early hours.

Hi Jane

I've been doing some digging around into Thomas Ramsbottom aka Ramsden. It was a great bit of work tracing his DNA relatives, by the way – seriously impressed. And I have to concede he doesn't come out smelling of roses.

So, the first thing is that I don't think it's his grave in upstate New York like his American descendant believes. I'm pretty certain that belongs to a different Thomas Ramsden who also came over from England, albeit a few years earlier. He ended up living close to where he's now buried.

If our man didn't die in 1900, what happened to him? As yet, I don't know, but I do think he made a return visit to England. I say visit because there's a record of a Thomas Ramsden, New York photographer, coming over first class – it was before the three class system, so it was either that or steerage – to Liverpool in 1884 and then sailing back a few weeks later. He's confusing things by using his new name, ie Ramsden, but giving his real age.

So why did he come over? As this point we can only speculate. It could have been business related, though I'm not sure what form that might have taken. It was a long time before globalisation, and photographic technology and techniques in the States were on a par with those in the UK. Maybe he was sounding out a permanent return, but I can't find any record of another crossing.

Maybe, of course, he came to see his family. But would they have welcomed him back after what he appears to have done to them? It seems unlikely. Perhaps he tried to buy his way back into their lives. That photograph of his eldest son's gravestone in Blackwell Holme doesn't look like it was paid for by a widowed housekeeper scraping a living on a meagre farmstead.

And then, of course, there's Guy Ramsbottom's original question of how his ancestor paid for his medical education. One conclusion is that Thomas offered them blood money and then went back to his successful life in New York.

I'll keep digging and let you know what I find.

Tommy

PS Please find attached links to all my sources.

Jane read the email twice. Thomas's return to England seemed telling. They might never know for sure why he made the journey, but it was probably enough to go back to Guy and offer him a likely answer to the challenge he had set. There was no other money in his ancestral background. He and his immediate antecedents owed their status and careers to a man who had cheated, lied and reputedly killed to achieve his own elevation in society. But as doctors, the later Ramsbottoms had no doubt saved and enhanced countless lives. Good had come from evil. The circle of hell to which Thomas had been condemned might not be as unrelentingly grim as it could have been.

Jane scanned Tommy's words once more. This time she was looking for signs of her own forgiveness hidden between the lines. He was still talking to her, still wanting to help, but had she caused irreversible damage to their relationship? There was something missing in the text, something it took her a while to spot. But then, there it was. Or wasn't. The solitary 'x', the kiss he habitually put after his name when writing to her at least, had been omitted.

It was a trivial nothing, but it played on her mind. Did it signify affection replaced by distrust and resentment? She realised she needed his friendship more than ever.

The leaving of Liverpool

The station hotel was by no means the grandest in Liverpool, but it was a world away from the louse-infested doss-house where he and Henry Pickup had spent the night, sharing a room with a dozen other men of the lowest classes. Half of them had been blind drunk and they stank of alcohol, toil and unwashed filth as they snored, scratched, belched and farted through the hours of darkness. In many ways it was worse than the later confines of steerage, though it didn't roll nauseatingly on heavy seas. Was it possible that foul atmosphere had been the miasma that had infected them with the fever to which he and his travelling companion had later succumbed?

Early the following day, the two emigrants had lugged their limited baggage down to the waterfront and boarded the ship that was to take them to their new lives. Henry's had been pitifully brief, and whilst Thomas had recovered, his was newer and ultimately sadder than he could have imagined. He had changed his name, his age, his past. And now he was deserting that past once more. He would travel in comparative luxury but without the warmth of expectation that had sustained him on that previous journey. He was a man lost, and a part of him wished for a mighty storm that would lash the great steel steamship and drag it onto jagged rocks on some lonely, unreachable foreign shore.

Thomas sat at the desk in the window of his room and looked down on the busy street below. It was named for the mediaeval tithe barn that stored farmers' contributions to the Church, but that practice and structure had long since gone and the scene was unrelentingly modern. It was as busy as the Lower East Side and bustling with noise: men, women and children talking and shouting; clanking horse trams ringing bells to clear their path; and iron-shod cartwheels rattling over the cobbles.

The glass panes did little to block out the din, and he tried to focus his thoughts as he dipped his pen into the ornate brass inkwell. Sarah, his first and only true wife, had refused to listen to his pleas. Ashworth, the man who had taken his place, had bodily thrown him out. Now Thomas's only recourse was to commit his case to writing. He had thought of addressing her directly, but doubted she had learnt to read in the years since he had patiently, and fruitlessly, tried to help her overcome that hurdle. He needed an intermediary, someone who might act as advocate as well as simply verbalising the inadequate words he would commit to paper. There was only one person who had always championed his cause.

But how much of his true story should he reveal? Despite all his sins, he was tired of lying.

The Dennis

Duff's natural attire was a suit, shirt and tie; Jane had never seen him in overalls before. Even then, he carried off the look with some aplomb. The dark-blue boiler suit was crisply pressed and paired with a raffish cravat made him look like a character from a 1950s Ealing comedy, a gent maintaining his veteran car or a vicar about to take the controls of a museum-piece steam locomotive. A rag hung from his breast pocket like a handkerchief and a smear of oil across his forehead completed the picture of an enthusiast at work on things mechanical. He was talking to two other men who were more prosaically dressed in grubby old jeans and T-shirts. Their attention was focused on the rear of the large red fire engine parked at the side of the house.

'Hi, Duff!' shouted Jane.

He turned and immediately began walking towards her. 'Jane, darling, you're looking as gorgeous as ever. That's a very striking shade you've got on. Would you call that magenta?'

Jane looked down at her blouse. 'Reddy, purpley, mauvish maybe?' she suggested.

'Well it's delightful. Forgive me if I don't give you a hug.' Duff displayed his palms. 'I'm a regular grease monkey at the moment. Oh, how rude of me – let me introduce the chaps.' He twisted and pointed in the direction of his two associates. 'On the left you have Jimmy, heavy goods driver extraordinaire, and alongside him Kevin, wizard of the spanner and of the torque wrench.'

Jane waved. Jimmy responded in kind and Kevin gave a thumbs-up.

'It looks very technical, Duff,' she said, a slight question in her tone implying she was surprised to see him getting his hands dirty.

'Devilishly, so,' he agreed. 'I met the chaps at a rally. They know their onions and reckon we can get the old pump working. Imagine that. We can go to fetes and fairs, roll out the hoses, crank up the pressure, hang on for dear life and squirt a torrent of water across the village pond. The kids will love it!'

'So no regrets about buying the thing?'

'The Dennis?' Duff shook his head rapidly. 'Absolutely not. Made some smashing new chums, and it's the most fun I've had in images.'

Jane almost asked who Dennis was and then spotted the name spelled out in large chrome capitals across the bonnet. Here was a vehicle manufacturer who hadn't hidden behind an obscure logo.

'I didn't mean to interrupt you,' she said. 'I'd better let you get back to it.'

'Indeed. And I'll let you go and see my dearly beloved.' Duff paused and a naughty glint appeared in his eyes. 'Look, Jane. I don't suppose you could suggest to old Ginge that she adds a teeny-weeny bit of tint to her hair. It would be a wheeze if she really did match the engine. Personally, I think it would go down a blinder.'

Jane looked at him like a schoolmistress admonishing a wayward child. 'No, Duff, I don't think that would go down well.'

'Pity,' he said, his sincerity almost convincing.

He bowed, gestured to lift his non-existent hat, and returned to his fire engine. Jane continued to the front door and rang the bell.

Five minutes later, she and her friend were sat at the heavy oak table in Sarah's large farmhouse kitchen. Before Jane had been to her mother's bungalow in Sandbanks and then Guy's Ramsbottom's near mansion in the Derbyshire countryside, this room had been the most impressive she'd seen. Duff and Sarah's home was a converted barn and one end had been almost completely glazed, offering a stunning view over the farmland behind. On the floor above was the master bedroom; at this level was the kitchen cum living area. The architect had somehow blended wooden-beamed rustic with a futuristic wall of glass. It shouldn't have worked, but it demonstrably did.

They were drinking their coffee out of elegantly plain Wedgwood mugs. Jane had just related her brief conversation with Duff, omitting his proposal for his wife's hair colour.

'Did he introduce to his new friend Kevin?' asked Sarah.

'Only at a distance.'

''You were lucky. God, the man can bore for England. Drones on and on about gaskets, whatever they are. Still Dennis the fire engine keeps Duff out of mischief,' said Sarah, raising her eyebrows. 'Though I'm beginning to think he loves the thing more than he loves me.'

'Not possible. Duff adores you.'

'Mmm, perhaps. So, tell me about your life, loves and otherwise.' Sarah had lifted her mug but had second thoughts about taking a sip and continued speaking. 'Look, I'm sorry I couldn't talk when you messaged me. It was just a girly chat you wanted, wasn't it?'

'Kind of. Believe it or not, Dave phoned out of the blue and sort of pointed me in the right direction.' Jane's head dropped. 'But then I went and messed it all up.'

'Messed what up?'

'Well… I've a horrible feeling I've made Tommy hate me.'

'Tommy?' Sarah reached across and gently lifted her friend's chin. 'Not possible. We both know what he thinks of you. You're his Dennis the fire engine, though in somewhat more attractive female form.'

Jane winced. 'But what if I accused him, wrongly, of being a perverted stalker who broke into my house and spied on me? That feels like suitable grounds for hatred to me.'

'Jane? I know you had that break-in, but are you saying you thought it was Tommy?'

'No. Well, sort of. Not really.'

Sarah's brow furrowed. 'You're being a little opaque, darling. Start from the beginning.'

'I knew I would upset him. I lost sleep over how to say it and then blundered straight in and did exactly what I was afraid of.'

'Jane, sweetheart, that's not the beginning. It may be the middle. It may be the end, but it's not the beginning.'

'Okay, okay.' Jane tilted her hands upwards at the wrist in a gesture of surrender. 'So, the supposed burglar took my TV, but then dumped it. Because what he actually wanted to do was get at my crappy old laptop and hack into my emails. And spy on me using the stupid camera that's built into the thing.'

'Jane? Seriously?'

'Yes, seriously. And Mrs Metcalfe, nosey Mrs Metcalfe across the road, saw someone who looked like Tommy, albeit with a haircut, hanging about. Now, Tommy's been working too hard lately. Round the clock. It's not good for him – I've been worried he's making himself ill. So I thought, I'll phone Tommy, see that he hasn't been to the barbers, and that'll put my mind at rest. And I can nag him to take it easy. But he had cut his hair. It was short and I went all peculiar.'

'So you confronted him?'

Jane shuffled uncomfortably on her chair. 'Not immediately. In my heart I knew it wasn't Tommy, but I had to say something or it would have eaten away at me. So I tried to attack it in a roundabout way. But he's no fool. He's the cleverest person I know. And I'm the stupidest. He saw what I was getting at and now he must hate me.'

Sarah stroked her mug thoughtfully. 'I can't imagine Tommy doing anything like that either. But just to be sure, you're 100% convinced it wasn't him? I mean, all that computer wizardry is very much his area of expertise. Like gaskets are to Kevin the bore. Sorry, I don't mean to be flippant.'

'It's okay and yes, I'm 100% convinced,' replied Jane. 'Tommy breaking into my house to hack into my computer is like Kevin fixing an engine by hitting it with a sledgehammer.'

There was silence as Sarah considered the analogy. Eventually she responded. 'Did you apologise to Tommy?'

'About 50 times,' said Jane dejectedly. 'He said it was fine, understandable, that I had to say something. He still seems to be talking to me, but…'

The sentence was left hanging and Sarah completed it. 'But in the meantime, there's some deviant who's broken into your house so he can spy on you. That's serious, Jane. Have you told the police? What does Dave say?'

'I don't want to get Dave involved. I don't want my ex-husband rushing to my rescue. He's already threatened, well not threatened… I've a horrible feeling he's going to turn up at my house this weekend to check I'm alright.'

Sarah wasn't sure whether to encourage Dave's intervention or not. Instead she settled on an alternative strategy.

'We need to talk this through. And we need something stronger than coffee. I'll open a bottle.'

Jane looked reluctant. 'I can't. I'm driving.'

'Leave the car here,' Sarah said decisively. 'You can stay the night. Or get a cab. Or Duff will drive you home – assuming Kevin doesn't drag him down the pub like he usually does.'

Jane found herself acquiescing. 'Go on then. I could do with a glass of wine. Maybe two.'

Baptist ministry

Like the reigning queen empress, Elizabeth Richards knew she would be wearing widow's weeds to her deathbed. But whilst Victoria's Albert had barely lived to middle age, Reverend Harry Richards had been in his late seventies, still straight-backed and dignified, when he waded into the swollen moorland stream to rescue the young child who had lost her footing on its banks. He pulled her to safety, but succumbed to a chill that became pneumonia. Elizabeth's marriage and near half-century of exile came to an end, and she returned to her childhood home in Somerset, now being farmed by her late brother's son and heir.

Her own health was failing but Elizabeth had one task to complete before she was reunited with her husband. In his later years he had determined to record his memoirs and had enlisted his wife as scribe and editor, her command of the written word being at least equal to his own and her eyesight latterly far superior. He had assiduously kept a lifetime of documents, letters and sermon notes. Elizabeth was now seated alongside a trunk of paperwork and was scanning the final draft of 'A Baptist Ministry in the Barren Hills of Lancashire'. She would use their remaining savings to finance the publication of a few hundred copies. Neither of them ever expected it to reach more than a small select audience.

One of the later sections was still causing her concern. In it, her husband had mused on the nature and limitations of human versus divine forgiveness. He related a story of a weak and pitiful man who had sailed to America, abandoning his wife and family, returning prosperous and successful many years later. He had visited his wife, but she had understandably sent him away without listening to his litany of excuses. As a result, he composed a letter putting forward his case. Because his wife was illiterate, he wrote to the minster and asked him to act as go-between. That Revered Richards did, but his judgement and advice were suitably damning. He was not taken in by the lies and self-justification and saw through them to the full wickedness of the crimes that lay beneath.

As Elizabeth Richards read her husband's account, she again questioned whether anger and intolerance had started to colour his temperament in his final years. Had a once ambitious and driven man looked back on a career and seen only stagnation and waste in a desolate corner of nowhere? She also knew that she played a larger part in this chapter than was suggested by the words on the page. Thomas had written to her, not the minister himself. She had interpreted her one-time protégé's story with compassion. She had seen weakness and error certainly, but not premeditated malice.

She reached into the chest and retrieved the letter. Looking at it once more, her thoughts initially dwelt on the beautiful handwriting. Thomas had always had an artistic temperament and flair. He had surely been corrupted by manual labour; the boy had been meant for better things. And the words flowed and his explanation appeared coherent, to her at least. Victim or villain, whose conclusion was valid, hers or her husband's?

Elizabeth pondered her own recollection of events prior to Thomas Ramsbottom's journey to America. She remembered him as a gifted and sensitive child, bullied by his envious peers for being different. She remembered how he had been chased by oh-so plain Sarah and how she had been with child at their wedding. Elizabeth could see Sarah's father, an angry and drunken thug of a man and could only think how he would have reacted at the knowledge of his daughter's pregnancy. And then there was the hideous mill explosion that had killed that beautiful child 15 years later. The inquest had blamed the engineer, but outside the courtroom the whisper was that Sarah saw her husband as being culpable. Was it then those tongues first began to wag at her closeness to the burly farm labourer who would eventually become her second husband in all but the eyes of God and the state?

Elizabeth paused as she questioned her own motives. Thomas had been such a handsome boy. He had been so receptive to her teaching. They had shared a love of drawing and of poetry. 'Ah, love,' she thought. And she knew it clouded her judgement. She had loved Thomas as if he were her own son. And like any mother, she could not believe him truly false and black-hearted.

Elizabeth's thoughts drifted back to that humble cottage overlooking the fast-flowing stream and she could hear her husband uncharacteristically raising his voice in anger.

'Look what he did to that poor, innocent Irish girl when she found out their marriage was a bigamous sham! She had barely washed ashore on the banks of New York harbour and then he lied to and married some other poor woman. And now he wants to inveigle his way back home, leave his misdeeds on the other side of the ocean before they catch up with him! Well, let him face them!'

Elizabeth found herself mouthing a response that was less memory, more the amalgam of a thousand repetitions in her head. 'But he explains what happened, his motivations. The Irish girl was beautiful and kind. He fell in love. Probably for the first time in his life. And then… His guilt is one of, shall we say, human frailty.'

'Frailty! It's all deception and excuses! Wife, you are blind where that man is concerned! You always were. He is the child you never had. There! I've said the words.'

That sentiment had ended the discussion. Elizabeth had left the parlour in tears. And she wept now, but her mind was set. These were her husband's memoirs and they should be told in his way, not sanitised by an emotionally irrational woman who could not hope to understand the intellectual reasoning of a man who had devoted his life to ecclesiastical study. She would prevaricate no more.

Taxi home

Jane was woken by an awful racket that seemed to be making her bedroom windows rattle on their hinges. She checked her bedside clock; it was nearly 9:30 am. Slowly, through the deafening noise, the previous evening began to come back to her. She had stayed up late talking, and drinking, with Sarah. The conversation had lightened when Duff had returned from the pub and regaled them with droll anecdotes from his and their past. That Jane had heard the stories before made them all the funnier. She and Sarah could be players in the comedy, not just its audience. When Duff's repertoire and energy were exhausted, Jane had said goodnight and caught a cab. Now she wished she had taken up their offer of a bed. Whatever was going on outside could surely never disturb the remote tranquillity of Duff and Sarah's rural home.

Jane opened her curtains and looked down into the street below. 30 yards up the road, a section of pavement was surrounded by barriers and a Dayglo-vested man with a hardhat and ear defenders was shaking and bouncing over a pneumatic drill. Two similarly attired colleagues were leaning against shovels and watching. Something about their stance suggested they should have cigarettes in their mouths but neither did. Jane surveyed the scene looking for clues and quickly settled on a white van with a gas company logo on the side. Her curiosity satisfied, her attention refocused on her aching head and neck. She desperately wanted to slip back into the warmth of her sheets and sleep the pain away. There was a brief encouragement when the hammering stopped but the cacophony all too quickly resumed. Jane pulled out the drawer on her bedside cabinet and rummaged around until she found the pair of foam earplugs that had once been the counter to Dave's snoring. They proved of limited effect, so she gave up on sleep, threw on a T-shirt and her slouchiest jogging bottoms, and went downstairs. As she passed the bathroom she thought about brushing her hair but decided she couldn't be bothered. Should the postman come to her door this Saturday morning, he would have to take her as she was. He was always unrelentingly, perhaps unhealthily, cheerful. A grimace might do him good.

20 minutes later, Jane had forced down a single piece of dry toast, and was sitting at her dining room table with her laptop and her second cup of coffee. The gas men seemed to have finally got through whatever mass of concrete had been in their way and Jane dared to remove the earplugs. She was still struggling to concentrate and found herself distracted by the asymmetry of her temporary repairs to the French windows. She resolved to visit a nearby double glazing shop that afternoon and then turned her attention back to her screen. There was an email from Tommy. She had seen it come in on her mobile when she arrived at Sarah's, but had been more interested in its tone than its content. Now she was trying to study it properly.

Hi Jane

Just a quickie. They've called a final wrap-up meeting in Derby. I'm typing this on the train and will be arriving at the station any minute now. While I've been sitting here, I've been doing some digging around online and it's come up trumps.

I was looking at the census records for Blackwell Holme again and found the local Baptist minister was called Harry Richards. He was there for decades and must have known the Ramsbottoms well – most of them are buried in his churchyard after all.

Anyway, I did some research on the man and up popped his memoirs. They're out of copyright, obviously, and have been scanned in full on the Web.

Click on the link and zap down to page 89.

He's not given any names – 'to protect the innocent rather than those less so' – but if he's not talking about Thomas Ramsbottom, then I'm Steven Seagal. And/or a Dutchman. Steven Seagal's Dutch cousin? Would that be Rutger Hauer?

We're just pulling in. Let me know what you think.

Tommy x

Jane was often lost by Tommy's humour and cultural references, but resisted the temptation to google Rutger Hauer and opened the link as instructed. She found herself looking at the image of a relatively fresh cover sheet with a handwritten Dewey Decimal code and the crest of a college library at Oxford University. It was followed by a somewhat foxed title page that read 'A Baptist Ministry in the Barren Hills of Lancashire by The Late Reverend Harry Richards'. The heavy serif typeface and simple layout also spoke of age and Jane could almost smell the mustiness rising from the paper. She scrolled on and began reading the preface. The language was piously convoluted, containing phrases such as 'sublimely glorious exhibition of the divine Being's perfections' and 'the triumph of the gospel is inscribed as a monument in every transgressor converted from the error of his way'. It was going to take some effort to get through.

Jane reached for her coffee but managed to knock the cup and spill some of its contents on the table. Her fragile patience snapped and she swore angrily at herself and at the world. Then, begrudgingly, she stood up and went into the kitchen in search of a cloth. She was about to re-enter the dining room when she saw a shape at the window. She quickly hung back and watched through the gap between the half-open door and its frame.

A man was close up to the glass peering in. He was mixed race, tall and thin with short black hair. At a passing glance it could have been Tommy, but it wasn't. Jane had never seen him before in her life but knew him immediately. It was the man who Mrs Metcalfe had seen, the man who broke into her house and into her laptop and into her privacy.

Had she paused to think, Jane would have realised the sensible thing was to grab her phone from the hall table where she'd dumped it the night before and dial 999 while leaving through the front. She could enlist the protection of the workmen who were hopefully still out there, not off on a mid-morning tea break.

Not for the first time in her life, anger and indignation barged reason aside. This scumbag would not have a chance to get away.

Jane went to the side door and quietly turned the key. She stepped out and round the corner into her back garden. The man was now leaning his weight against the French windows, clearly wondering how well they'd been secured.

He didn't notice Jane until she spoke out.

'You won't get through those this time. Not easily anyway.'

He was visibly startled, but immediately tried to sound guiltlessly relaxed. 'Oh, hello, duck.' He smiled amiably but then coughed, betraying the anxiety in his throat. 'We're doing some building work in the area. I'm just knocking on doors seeing if folk have got any jobs that need doing. While we're here like.'

The excuse had rolled off his tongue with seemingly practised ease but Jane wasn't in a mood to be conned. 'Do you always sneak around the back of people's houses and nose through their windows?'

He adopted an expression of amused disbelief. 'It's not like that, duck. I rang your bell first, but the lady of the house is quite often round the back. In the kitchen or whatever.'

He was holding his nerve and Jane found herself hesitating as she considered the evidence. Judging by his accent he was a local lad. Duck was the all-purpose Nottinghamshire term of endearment, though he was laying it on condescendingly thick. His clothes were casually fashionable and most of all clean, and his trainers looked expensive. He was not dressed for any kind of building site. Jane remembered she'd come home the previous night by taxi. Her distinctive green car's absence from outside her house would suggest its owner was also away. This cocky, arrogant chancer might have tried the doorbell to double-check, but it wasn't the loudest and she'd been wearing earplugs to deaden the noise from the street. If he had been remotely monitoring her laptop he would want to know why it was no longer responding, why he could no longer read her private emails and watch her getting undressed.

Jane reached a conclusion and expressed it as concisely as she could. 'Bollocks,' she said, adding a scowl to communicate the perceived insult to her intelligence.

He read her face and his tone became more forceful. 'Now, come on, duck. You're overreacting. You're being a little bit silly here.'

Jane had picked up her phone on the way out and now raised it in front of her face. 'Maybe,' she said calmly. 'In which case you won't mind if I take your photo and then call the police.'

His composure cracked and he stepped forward and slapped the phone onto the grass. 'Don't muck me around!' he snarled, all pretence of friendly innocence abandoned.

Jane stood her ground. 'I'm not scared of a scrawny prat like you. Who the hell are you? What's going on? Why are you spying on me? Are you just a pervert or what?'

Angrily, he made a grab for her. As he lunged, she leant back, caught hold of his right arm with both hands and tried to use his forward momentum to pull him down and over her outstretched left leg. But he was too quick and the leverage in his long limbs too strong for her. After a brief struggle of yanks and pulls, she found herself facing away from him, being held around the neck, pressed into his body and with his mouth panting into the side of her face.

'I told you not to muck me about!' You should have listened. Bitch!' He spat the words into her ear and there was a tremor to his voice that suggested he was close to losing control.

Jane squirmed and writhed, but his grip tightened around her throat and chest. 'Let me go!' she insisted, gasping for breath.

'Stop fighting me or I'll hurt you,' he threatened, maintaining his hold. 'I mean it. I'll give you a proper slap in a minute. Just stop it.'

'Let me go,' croaked Jane. 'You won't get away with this. Let me go before things get too far out of hand.'

'Shut up! I need to think.' There was a palpable panic to his words now. He knew he had made a bad call.

'You'll be looking at prison unless—'

'I said shut up!'

This time Jane acquiesced, sensing his hesitancy to dig himself too much deeper. But his attempt at rational calculation was interrupted by another noise. It was faint, drifting through the open side door, but then it sounded again.

It was the doorbell.

Jane saw her chance. 'That's my husband. I'd run while you have the chance.' She stretched her neck free enough to scream out. 'Dave! Dave! Round the ba—'

Jane felt the side of the man's fist being jammed hard into her mouth, forcing it wide and choking the words. 'Shut it!' he said, lowering his voice. 'I know all about you. You're divorced. The bastard lives in London. It's just some poxy Jehovah's Witness. Now just let me think and maybe you'll get out of this in one piece.'

Jane tried to wriggle free again but he wrenched her roughly, causing her to wince and let out a muffled squeal. But as her eyes reopened, she saw another figure reflected in the dining room windows and coming towards them from behind. Suddenly there was a sharp yank and Jane found herself toppling backwards. She reacted quickly, coming down with the point of her elbow jabbing hard into her assailant's stomach. She span over to see him lying winded on his side. She grasped his wrist and pushed up with all her strength, bending his arm back and flipping him onto his face. She jammed her knee into him and increased the force on his twisted shoulder. He cried out in anger as well as pain.

Jane glanced up at her saviour and thanked him with her eyes. Had it been Dave he would have taken violent charge by now, but it was Tommy standing there and he looked confused and frightened. She turned her attention back to the groaning man pinned to the floor.

'Trust me, I'll happily snap your bastard arm,' she said, emphasising her threat with a blip of pressure. 'So talk to me. Who the hell are you?'

'Piss off!'

Jane had been pushing his head into the ground with her other hand. She now began to reach round the right side of his face, which was partly buried in the grass. Her nails formed into a claw beside his eye socket. She knew then that she was going to make him answer. Or maybe she was just going to make him pay.

Tommy saw her fingers move and began to reason urgently. 'Jane! Not his eye! Let's just call the police. Please, Jane.'

Jane looked up again and she saw the concern on her friend's face. Memories of previous lapses slowly filtered into her consciousness and her passions quelled. Her hand relaxed. 'Okay, Tommy,' she said. 'You're right. Call them.'

'No, stop! Don't do that!' begged the man on the floor. 'I'm here because of your father.'

'What?' Jane shook her head at Tommy to indicate he should wait and then brought her mouth closer to her captive's ear. 'Start talking. What do you know about my father?'

'He's thinking of coming home. His sister said you were sniffing around. He wanted to know whether, I don't know, whether you hate him. Whether you were likely to stitch him up with your police pals, maybe that ex-husband of yours.'

'My father told you to break into my house?' said Jane incredulously.

'No, of course not. Oh Christ! I'm going to get killed. Like, literally, killed. Even if I go back to jail, they'll have my throat slit while I'm in there.'

Jane's eyes flicked from side to side as she tried to grasp the threads of the story. It made little sense.

'Just explain properly. From the beginning.' She had begun speaking in her old 'good cop' voice, hoping it might covey leniency, a potential way out.

''Okay.' He was audibly trying to slow his breathing and steady his nerves. 'I've done time for thieving. It's a mug's game. I've always been good with computers and stuff so I thought I'd try to get into cyber. You get away with that, unless you piss off the Yanks by breaking into the Pentagon. So I told him I could do it.'

'My father?'

'No. I've never met your father. Billy…' He hesitated as he wondered if he was buying himself more trouble. 'Look, never mind about his surname. Though you probably know it already. He basically runs things round here. They go back a long way and your father was calling in a favour. Anyway, Billy said he'd put out some feelers, and I told him it would be easy to snoop on your emails. I just wanted to impress him.'

'Impress Billy?' Jane had never been stationed in Nottingham. She didn't know the local criminal hierarchy, though it didn't seem overly critical at that moment. 'Impress this Billy, and my father, by breaking into my house?'

No. I told you, Billy'd kill me if he knew. I sent you some, you know, like viruses. You were supposed to download them but you wouldn't take the bait. I didn't know what to do. I guess I panicked. I'd seen that knackered old laptop of yours and reckoned I could hack into it. It's all on the Web if you know where to look. I saw you going away and I had to take the chance.'

The means, motive and opportunity seemed on the cusp of plausibility, so Jane tightened her focus. 'So what do you know about my father?'

'Not much. Just what I've been told. Huge bloke, nasty with it. You wouldn't want to piss him off. Oh God! If Billy doesn't do me, he will. He lives abroad. There's something wrong with face. Had plastic surgery. I don't know. What do you want me to tell you? I've never met the guy.'

'Don't piss me about! You must know more than that!' insisted Jane, her inner cop switching from good to bad.

'That's all I have. Honest. I was just asked to find out about you.'

Jane felt rage surging within her again. 'So what about the camera? Why did you want to watch me like some kind of deviant? And what sort of father asks someone to do that to his daughter?'

'I was more interested in the microphone. I thought I might overhear you talking to people, saying stuff about your dad, you know. I think I mucked it up and turned the camera on too.'

Tommy, who had returned to listening in nervous silence, rolled his eyes in disbelief at the would-be cybercriminal's ineptitude.

The man's voice grew tremulous again. 'Look, I will get killed. Legs broken, minimum. If you call the police. If Billy finds out. I'm really scared.' He was whimpering now. 'You weren't supposed to know. I was just supposed to find out if you were still in touch with your husband. For your father. It's because of him. I was only meant to read a few emails. What you don't know doesn't hurt you. But I cocked things up.'

Jane relaxed her grip and gradually lifted herself off the prostrate figure lying beneath her. Tommy's look of anxiety briefly intensified as he saw the man was now free. It was unjustified. The face that turned up from the grass was one of defeat and despair.

'Just go,' said Jane.

'You won't tell anyone? It was for your father, honest. No harm meant. No harm.'

'Just go,' repeated Jane.

The tall, skinny man with the short hair and fashionable clothes, now muddied and dishevelled, climbed to his feet. He looked at Jane and Tommy questioningly. Then he ran.

Threads

Tommy and Jane were sitting at the kitchen table. Tommy was cradling a mug of tea and still looking in a partial state of shock.

'You're just going to let him go? Not call the police?' he said, disbelievingly.

Jane had her face in her hands. 'Yep. Well, probably. I need to think it through. It's a bit much at the moment. My father, I mean.'

'You were physically assaulted! God knows what he might have done to you. Maybe you should tell Dave at least.'

Jane lifted her head. 'He'd go apeshit. Not to mention bananas and ballistic. And…' She turned her gaze towards Tommy. '…why do I need Dave when I've got you?'

Tommy looked away. 'I was useless. I just froze.'

Jane reached out for his hand. 'Tommy! You pulled him off me. He'd have put up more of a fight if you hadn't been standing there. He didn't know what you were likely to do.'

'Nothing is what I was likely to do.'

Jane gently squeezed his fingers. 'Stop it. You're my hero. You were there when I needed you.' Her brow suddenly furrowed as she realised she hadn't asked the glaringly obvious question. 'Tommy, how come you were there, I mean, here?'

'I was in Derby yesterday. They insisted I went out with them to the pub, sort of to mark the end of the project. It would normally be my idea of hell, but they're my kind of people, geeks and nerds the lot of them. And I'm trying to make myself be more sociable.'

'How did it go?'

'It wasn't too bad in the end. Anyway, the project manager said he'd pay for me to stay overnight in a hotel.

And so this morning, because I was so close, I thought I'd come to see you. I did send you a text.'

Jane picked up her phone and saw there was an unread message on the status bar. 'Sorry, Tommy, I must have missed it. I was either asleep or there was all this roadwork noise earlier. I couldn't hear myself think.'

Tommy continued his explanation, albeit falteringly. 'I came because, well, there was a bit of a, I don't know, atmosphere between us last time. I just thought if I popped by, we could talk about what I found on Thomas Ramsbottom and, with any luck, we'd sort of be back to normal. Mates, I mean.'

'Oh, sweetheart!' The morning's drama finally hit Jane and tears began to well. 'You're the best mate a girl could have. I'd be lost without…'

Jane didn't finish her sentence; instead she reached across the table and hugged Tommy around the shoulders. Inevitably, his body locked with embarrassment.

Jane sank back in her chair and found herself uncertain what to say next. Tommy was quickly uncomfortable with the silence and decided to take his normal refuge in information and facts.

'So did you read Reverend Richards' memoir I sent you that link to?' he asked.

'I was about to when I got interrupted by our friend. I got bogged down in the introduction.'

'It gets better, well, a bit.' Tommy pulled out his own laptop from his bag and set it between them. His fingers began dancing across the keyboard as he spoke. 'The writing style is on the ornate side, but you just really just need to read that one chapter. Here you go…'

The morning's excitement had at least banished Jane's hangover and she quickly worked her way through the few short pages of text. There was reference to a letter that was not reproduced and none of the characters were named, but there were enough specifics to suggest this could only be the story of Thomas Ramsbottom. It seemed to confirm what had previously been supposition and rumour. And the picture it painted was dark.

'Wow,' she exclaimed, sitting back in her chair. 'We've got the bastard. Or else I'm Rutger whatshisname.'

Tommy smiled his agreement. 'And I've found some more.'

Jane stared quizzically at Tommy and he kept talking.

'That copy of the memoirs is held in a library at Oxford. It's part of an archive of Baptist history and heritage. According to their catalogue, they've actually got a collection of documents and letters left by the very same Reverend Harry Richards and his widow.'

Jane interrupted excitedly. 'So it's possible they've got the original letter sent by Thomas? We could read his own explanation of events?'

'Possible,' agreed Tommy. 'It's worth asking the question. And I did find something else while on the train this morning.'

'Tommy, you are amazing! What?'

Tommy had taken over the laptop again and was scrolling down the screen. 'Here it is. I've finally pinned down Thomas's death. He came home to England. For a second time, for good. Or bad. It turns out he met an unpleasant end.'

The archive

Jane had been to Cambridge, as a tourist not a student, but had never visited its academic and historic sibling. Her first impression of Oxford was that it was the less attractive of the two, mainly because a large, modern city had sprawled out from the ancient university at its core. From a distance, the various colleges still advertised their presence through the poet's dreaming spires that reached skywards like the raised arms of gifted children amongst a class of the ordinary and less privileged. Duff was an Oxford man, though it was something he seldom mentioned, mainly through modesty but also because he had not survived to his final year. He would offer 'the three Rs: rugby, rowing and roistering rather than reading, revision and restraint' as his standard excuse, though in bawdier circles 'roistering' was usually replaced by 'rogering'. One of Jane's senior officers in the Met had also studied PPE at Oxford. The superintendent had a one-way ticket to the top and was not a woman to have neglected her studies. Unfortunately, one of the Ps didn't stand for personality and she failed to qualify as a human being, no matter how bright she might have been.

Jane navigated the ring road and left the Mazda in the multistorey car park of a vast new shopping mall. She made her way past shiny shopfronts that could have been any town, anywhere and emerged into the sunlight following the directions on her phone. Soon the buildings became like a compendium of English architectural styles: Victorian, Tudor, Mediaeval, Gothic, Gothic Revival, Classical, Neoclassical, Modern and Postmodern, nearly 40 individual colleges typically sharing a common quadrangle-based layout, but detailed according to the era and depth of their benefactors' munificence.

Jane's destination turned out to be one of the newer colleges, not yet 100 years old and whose stonework resembled that of a contemporaneous high-street bank. She explained she had an appointment and was directed to the library. There she was greeted by a late middle-aged woman with long frizzy hair, home dyed and pulled back into a fraying pigtail. She wore half-moon glasses and brightly patterned leggings beneath a loose turquoise shirt. Jane decided she approved of the colour choice. She also appreciated people whose appearance seemed to match their occupation.

They were alone and the librarian introduced herself as 'Jennifer, or Jen, but not Jenny please' in a loud, enthusiastic voice that rather contradicted the stereotype. She sought Jane's ID and proffered forms to be completed and signed.

While Jane wrote, Jennifer or Jen continued the conversation.

'It's mostly theology students we get in. I've not encountered a genealogist before.'

Jane replied without looking up. 'Yes, it was kind of your head librarian to let me come over at such short notice. I think it helped that I'm working on behalf of an old student of the university. He's now a leading surgeon.'

'Our boys and girls tend to go on to great things,' replied the librarian proprietorially. 'Head clergy, top politicians, captains of industry. There may even be genealogists amongst them.' There was a thoughtful pause. 'Though only as a hobby, I suppose.'

Jane sensed a put-down but ignored it. 'I think you have some documents set aside for me?'

Jennifer or Jen nodded. 'Yes, I went down to the basement this morning. They're from a relatively recent acquisition, found in the attic of a Somerset farmhouse and donated. Plus, of course, the subject is by no means a leading figure in Baptist history, so we haven't yet done more than basic cataloguing. Nonetheless, please handle them with care. They may be of value to a serious researcher one day.'

Jane smiled. 'I was used to handling evidence when I was a police officer. Kid gloves, I promise.'

A folder was produced and Jane was shown to a table next to a sunny window overlooking a garden courtyard. The manilla envelope was labelled 'Correspondence between Rev. H Richards and Messrs Ramsbottom and Lord'. Jane didn't know who Mr Lord might be but she was hoping Mr Ramsbottom was Thomas, or at the very least, a close relative and player in the story she was trying to unravel.

The interchange of letters ran to eight individual pages. Jane quickly scanned them and was immediately disappointed. Thomas Ramsbottom had distinctly beautiful handwriting. His pen was not evident in the barely legible scrawls. She laboured through a few paragraphs and then carefully refolded the documents and returned them to their file.

She stood and walked back to the desk where the librarian was busy at her computer.

'That was quick,' she said.

'Messrs Ramsbottom and Lord appear to have manufactured church pews in Rochdale. Nothing to do with the Ramsbottom family I'm researching. It's not an uncommon name in the north of England.'

The librarian pulled a face that suggested Ramsbottom sounded decidedly common to her ears. Well, I'm sorry you may have had a wasted journey,' she said. 'C'est la vie, I suppose. Is there anything else we can do to help in your endeavours?'

'There's nothing else that pertains to a Thomas Ramsbottom, his wife or children? There's a chapter in Reverend Richards' memoirs that seems to describe them though they're not named as such.'

The librarian returned to her keyboard and began typing and then scrolling through the screen. Eventually she looked up. 'Not specifically. We do have the original printer's proof of the memoirs. There are a few corrections and annotations. Would you like to see that?'

A few minutes later, Jane was back in her window seat with a loosely bound sheaf of papers in front of her. They were open at the section she had already digested several times in its published form. A somewhat feminine hand had written 'DELETE THIS CHAPTER' across the top of the page before striking the instruction out again with a strong horizontal line. The proof had been addressed to Mrs H Richards and Jane could only assume this was indecision on behalf of a widow seeking to preserve her husband's legacy and memory.

But what had caused her doubts?

Facts

This time Jane didn't miss the entrance to 'Laynston' and turned straight through the gap in the thick hedgerows onto the gravel area below Guy and Polly Ramsbottom's house. There were two other cars parked there: Guy's black Maserati, which Jane had previously suggested was a Wartburg, and a large 4x4. That had a brand-new registration plate and was subtly different to the vehicle Polly had been driving on Jane's last visit. It was a pale silvery grey rather than white but also sleeker somehow. As ever, Jane didn't recognise it, but a quick check of the badge confirmed it was another Range Rover. It looked like Polly had upgraded to the latest model. Maybe someone had scratched the old one after all.

Jane climbed the steps and continued round to the terrace at the side of the house. Sat at the Victorian cast-iron table under the pergola of roses were Guy and Polly. Guy was cradling a large cup, presumably of coffee, and Polly was holding a glass of wine. The alcohol didn't seem to have improved her mood: she looked as sullen as ever. Polly saw Jane first and drew her husband's attention with a gesture of her head.

Guy twisted in his chair and smiled broadly. 'Jane! Thanks for coming over. Lovely to see you. And looking bright and cheerful again!'

The reference to Jane's canary-yellow shirt made Polly tut disapprovingly. It wasn't lost on Jane, but she was prepared this time and let it wash over her.

'Guy, Polly. Nice to see you again too,' she replied, mentally flagging that she was being 50% truthful at least. 'How was Spain?'

'Hot. Too bloody hot,' answered Polly.

'It's always hot this time of year, liefie. But we just turn up the air con, sit by our pool and we're fine.'

Jane wondered why Guy would refer to his wife as 'leafy', then realised it must mean something affectionate in Dutch. She briefly considered what spoilt cow might translate as, but maintained the pleasantries.

'Whereabouts in Spain is your villa?'

'It's in an upmarket golf resort on the Costa Cálida. We look out over the Med and also the Mar Menor – that translates as minor sea. It's actually a huge coastal lagoon. Nice spot,' replied Guy with his usual proud nonchalance.

'Sounds idyllic. You're golfers then?'

'Polly's much better than me.'

'You're not exactly built for sport,' observed Polly, deadpan.

'Thank goodness I'm built for eye surgery, eh liefie?' Guy gave his wife a saccharine grin and then changed the subject. 'So, Jane, you've solved the little mystery we set you? The origin of the Ramsbottoms' good fortune. Am I descended from aristocracy or bank robbers?'

'Well,' said Jane hesitantly, 'the Ramsbottoms weren't aristocrats.'

'Hah!' interjected Polly. 'I told you the sheep's arses were peasants. And it turns out they're thieves too.'

'Not thieves,' corrected Jane. 'The money was earned legitimately. In New York in the late 19th century. But the man who earned it... Let's just say the available facts suggest he wasn't the nicest, or most honest, or most decent of people.'

Polly smiled for the first time, but Guy remained impassive.

'If I can't have blue blood, then maybe a bluebeard in the family is the next best thing?' He tapped the table twice to emphasise his point. 'A bit of colour, drama, in one's ancestral make-up is all very exciting. Go on then, Jane, spill the proverbial beans. Polly and I are all ears, though I expect my wife may get more of a kick out of this than me.'

Jane pulled a folder out of her orange tote bag and laid it on the table. 'Your family tree is all documented in here, but you'll recognise a lot of it from what your cousin Betty had already put online. I've been able to take it back a bit further and wider, of course, and she did make one key mistake.'

Guy raised his hand to signal an interruption. 'Her side of the family were always a bit airy-fairy. Did you talk to her in the end?'

'I did. Nice lady. A bit... alternative, perhaps, but no fool. We spent some time together.'

'So what was her mistake?' asked Guy, clearly lacking interest in the wellbeing of his long-lost cousin.

'The man we were talking about, the man you perceptively said was a bluebeard, the villain of our piece, was your great-great-grandfather, Thomas Ramsbottom. Betty thought he died in Lancashire when he was just 37, but that turned out to be someone else. Our man swanned off to America and started a new life. He left his wife – who'd recently witnessed the violent death of one of her children – with a young baby amongst a houseful of other kids. He left the lot of them, changed his name to Ramsden, and married a new wife almost as soon as he got to New York.'

'Maybe you should change your name to Ramsden,' suggested Polly, before her comment was waived aside by Guy.

Jane's expression was hardening as she pressed on with her description of Thomas's crimes. 'That's bad enough, but it gets much, much worse, I'm afraid. He's somehow implicated in the death of his first son. There was a boiler explosion in the mill where they both worked. The engineer got the blame, but Thomas was his assistant. Within months, Thomas had run away to America. Your great-grandfather had just been born. His name was a bit confusing at first. He was called George, the same as his dead older brother. Anyway, having –

perhaps – killed his son, Thomas then kills his new wife—'

'Kills? As in murders?' Guy's veil of distant indifference had now dropped.

Jane rocked her head from side to side as she weighed up the evidence once more. 'I've been in contact with a distant cousin of yours in the States. Thomas's second wife, who was by far the most beautiful of the three, incidentally—'

'There was another one?' said Polly somewhat gleefully.

'I'll get to her soon.' Jane smiled apologetically at Guy. 'Thomas's second wife was washed ashore, drowned in the East River. I've got a copy of her death certificate. The authorities didn't seem to have any suspicions at the time, but your American cousin said there was always a family rumour that Thomas had killed her.'

'Just a rumour?' probed Guy.

'Well, we then found a memoir written by the Baptist minister of the church that Thomas attended before he ran off. There's a chapter – it's all anonymised and is very much a spiritual discussion on the nature of evil, repentance, forgiveness, that kind of thing...'

Polly scowled to signal her disdain for matters religious. Jane ignored her and kept talking as she pulled some sheets of paper from her folder.

'I've printed you off a copy and you'll see it is open to a degree of interpretation. That said, I've got little, if any, doubt it's talking about Thomas. You see, he visited England when he'd made some money, but his wife – his real wife – threw him out on his ear. She couldn't read, so he wrote to the minister asking him to intercede on his behalf. The minister dismisses the letter as full of lies. He reads into it a barely disguised confession – he says Thomas effectively admits to killing his second wife. After that he married again, this time to a shrewd businesswoman who made their fortune in a photography business. Thomas moans about her, saying she's his punishment, and seems to be trying to buy his way back into his English family's life. The minister obviously counsels against it, but there is some kind of compromise. Thomas funds his youngest son's education – he's the first in the line of doctors that leads to you – but is told to go back to America and rot. If his sins don't catch up with him in this world then they surely will in the next.'

Guy's face was pale and fixed in concentration 'Shame we don't have this incriminating letter itself.'

'Indeed. I went to an archive in Oxford, but it wasn't there. We just have to accept the minister's summary. His widow edited the memoirs after his death. She appears to have had some kind of reservation, but I suspect that was just because she didn't want Thomas's family to be dragged through the dirt. But they weren't named and I'm not sure they'd ever even know the book had been published.'

Polly was smiling again as she gave her assessment. 'This Thomas was a total, utter monster. And to think, liefie,' The endearment was laden more with sarcasm than affection, 'his genes are your genes.'

'Along with lots of others',' countered Jane. 'But interestingly, he's described as an unusually gifted child – and his education was really just limited to Sunday school. The minister actually questions whether such intelligence is a benefit or a curse for an ordinary working man. He thought he was better than those around him, wanted more than his status would allow. Perhaps that's what corrupted him. Either way, Guy has obviously inherited his brains but I'm sure not his character.'

'So what happened to the sod?' asked Guy, colour now returning to his cheeks.

'We're not 100% sure of the sequence of events. His third wife appears to have paid him off and she and her family took the business to even greater heights. We thought he was buried in upstate New York, but that was another red herring. My colleague found him back in England.'

Guy raised his eyebrows. 'So he never returned to America?'

'He definitely sailed back after that first visit. He's on a ship's manifest arriving in New York. We can't find a record of a second voyage across to England, but we've found him living here in 1911, on his own in a small terraced house in a rough part of Manchester. He was still calling himself Ramsden, but we're pretty certain it's him because in that year's census you actually see people's own handwriting. His is very distinctive, beautifully so, and he says he's a retired photographer.'

Guy jabbed his finger in the air as if driving home an idea. 'Didn't my great-grandfather – Thomas's son – set up his medical practice in Manchester?'

'Yes, albeit in a rather more affluent suburb,' confirmed Jane. 'The obvious question is whether they were in contact somehow. I've found nothing to suggest they were. It was a big city, of course, and George wouldn't have remembered his father from growing up.'

'Thomas would have been...' Guy took a breath as he did the sum. '...into his seventies by then. He couldn't have lived much longer. Hopefully he succumbed to something nasty.'

'If we were looking for final confirmation of the nature of the man, maybe this it. It made the local paper.' Jane handed over a printed facsimile of a short news article whose typeface and layout confirmed its age. 'He was found savagely beaten on a back street. Died in hospital the next day. It was an unsolved crime, but there was no sign of robbery. He could have been an innocent victim, but it's hard not to think he was keeping unpleasant company and it caught up with him. '

'And got what he deserved,' said Polly triumphantly.

'He was taken to Ancoats Hospital,' continued Jane. 'Here's his death certificate.'

Guy took the document and began reading out loud. 'Thomas Ramsden, blah, blah, blah. Depressed fracture of cranial vault – skull smashed in, basically. Signed by one Herbert Evelyn Farquharson MD. There's a name to conjure with.'

'Better than Ramsbottom,' butted in Polly

Guy ignored his wife's contribution once again. 'Jane, what can I say? It's not exactly what I was expecting, but it's quite a story. I'm sure I'll dine out on it. Rather the devil than the bland, eh?'

Jane spent 45 minutes filling in more details of Guy's family tree, but the main event had already played out. She was, however, able to offer a more positive footnote. She had found the noble blood Guy had hoped for through a DNA link on his mother's side, her ancestors having made their way into the venerable tomes of Irish landed gentry and baronetcies. Polly had wandered off, leaving Guy to express his gratitude and satisfaction at Jane's efforts.

As she made her way back to her car, a nagging sense of unease began to intrude on Jane's mood of success and closure. Had she painted a fair, objective picture of long-dead Thomas Ramsbottom, or had she let herself be swayed by her own prejudices, egged on by Polly's cynicism? Thomas had left more trace of his complicated life than most people of his era, but what sort of man was he really? How could Jane ever know? Had he wilfully charted his own course through life or drifted on the currents and tides of circumstance? Much depended on the Baptist minister's assessment. But he was intent on conveying a religious lesson, a parable. Perhaps he twisted the character of the unnamed man in his story to support the message he wanted to impart?

One thing appeared certain: Thomas had deserted his family. Jane knew that was his real crime in her heart. Was this what the psychologists call transference? Did she need to blacken his name in personal revenge? And what of her own father, the man who had walked out on her and was now eavesdropping on her life? Was there part of her that would happily see him meet a similar, violent end?

The gas lamp

It was a bitterly cold evening, but at least the rain had stopped and the tall buildings blocked the worst of the wind. Thomas Ramsden was alone, as always, walking through the poor backstreets of a wealthy city. He had turned up the black fur collar of a heavy woollen coat that was looking as tired and worn as the old man within. It had been bought to announce him as person of status and success. Now it spoke of decline and hard times. Thomas was gradually eating his way through dwindling funds.

He'd hoped to rebuild his career as a photographer, to leave a small, anonymous legacy for his grandchildren, but Kodak's Brownie camera had changed everything and Thomas was too weary to adapt. The workhouse surely beckoned and beyond that lay worse, the great uncertainty. He had long ago shrugged away the faith of his youth, like he had abandoned his own name and identity. He desperately wanted to believe there was no forever after, only sleep and dust, but the promises and threats seeded in his childhood mind still haunted him. He had sought to punish himself in life. He knew it could never be enough.

Thomas turned into a dimly lit alley. A single gas lamp hissed ineffectually halfway down its length, and shadowed beneath was a large man shouting angrily in a manner that suggested he had been fighting the cold with contents of the bottle he was waving in the air. The object of his rage was woman with a thick shawl over her head and shoulders. Suddenly the man lashed out and struck the woman, knocking her to the floor. The man stood over her, continuing his tirade of abuse.

Thomas's instinct was to retrace his steps, to walk away. Even as a young man, he would have been no match for such a drunken brute.

'You there! Stop that!' shouted a voice that was Thomas's own yet felt like it belonged to another. And he began striding down the alley with his cane raised high.

As he walked and accelerated, his life began to process through his mind, scene by scene. In truth, it was always there, constantly analysed and replayed, snapshots now sufficient to cue the detail and depth of decades.

It was a life of cowardice. That was, and always had been, his fundamental flaw. From dark bullying schoolroom, to dark bullying miners, jealous and resentful of the gifted, handsomely blond boy who was sensitive and different, he had always backed down and cowered. And they always came back for more. He had started to run and could never stop.

He saw himself trembling at the thought of Sarah's father discovering his daughter was with child. Nearly two decades later, that history repeated, with a different daughter in a different world.

And then the memories grew darker. He was in the mill engine house, a quick learner digesting the intricacies of steam and pressure, cranks and cylinders. He had escaped the mine and was desperate not to return. The engineer was a hopeless alcoholic whose hands quivered unless steadied by liquor. Thomas had seen the tendency to error and lapse, but had kept silent, fearful of reproach, afraid for his job. Had he known the consequences, the terrible explosion and the death of his first-born son, his own image in looks if not in character, he would surely have spoken out. But to his eternal shame he did not. He blamed himself, as did his only confidant, his wife, Sarah. She would never forgive him and sought solace in the affections of a gruff farm labourer, one of those who had tormented Thomas at school.

Again, a better man would have fought for his wife, but Thomas ran away, to America, vainly hoping to make his fortune and somehow buy back her respect. And there, weakened by illness, he had met an Irish girl: beautiful, sad Mary, as weak and flawed as he was, still mourning the loss of her young husband. And they had sought comfort in each others' arms and nature's chance had caught them out. Thomas the coward had lied and he continued to lie, adding bigamy to his list of misdeeds.

And God had seemed to punish him, and his poor innocent bride, by darkening her moods, making her question her own worthiness as a mother, so she passed her nights without sleep and her days in tears. And when she had finally rallied, the malaise seemingly lifted, Thomas, the craven sickening coward, had sought to ease his own guilt by offering her the truth. He had justified it to himself as an act of love, but it had been the worst of his many crimes.

Mary, the broken angel, had left in the early hours, travelled across the city and flung herself into the cold sea within sight of their first meeting. Her fragile body was dragged out by the savage currents and she was lost. And Thomas knew he had killed her, just as surely as if he had plunged her into the icy water himself.

There was one who had overheard Thomas's confession and threatened to compromise him: his daughter's Germanic nurse, hard and plain as Mary had been gentle and fair. And Thomas bought her silence through another act of bigamy. This time he had a willing, knowing partner to the sin. He did not care for the soul of his new wife and his own was already lost. He banished God from his life and sought to chastise himself through the unhappiness of a loveless union. But he also lost the one thing he had left to cherish. The daughter who had been a mirror of her mother became twisted to her step-mother's will. And Thomas had another ruined life on his conscience.

These thoughts passed through Thomas's mind in the time it took to cover a few paces in distance and were replaced by a single, simple notion: now and today he would be the coward no more.

'Leave that poor woman alone!' he shouted and aimed his stick at the man's shoulders.

It was over quickly. The man threw his bottle and it knocked Thomas off-balance and into a damp, windowless brick wall, shattering as it did so. Thomas was hauled up and hit hard with a clenched fist. And then again. His legs crumpled and he fell, his skull cracking against a stone kerb. His body lay motionless and blood flowed from his head, mingling with the rainwater still trickling down the gutter.

Thomas's assailant looked down, shocked by the outcome of his violence. The woman grabbed him by the arm and began dragging him away. Her cries had been muffled when she had been the target of his fury, now she shrieked her anguish and fear. It was her duty to protect her husband. The couple, reconciled in danger, ran.

Dr George Ramsbottom was in danger of being late. He pushed his way through the persistent drizzle and the soggy masses that crowded Mill Street, raising his umbrella high to avoid gouging the eyes of his fellow pedestrians. His day ahead would be busy enough as it was. The weather was dampening his spirits and he was beginning to think his wife was right. He should focus on his private practice, tending to ailments of the wealthy middle classes, and leave the suffering of the great unwashed to other, fresher men, physicians whose altruism had not yet been blunted by daily exposure to society's injustice.

He walked through the gothic arch of the main entrance, left his wet things with the doorman and went in search of the house surgeon. He found him cleaning his hands in one of the consulting rooms. A nurse was applying a bandage to the head of an old man lying motionless on a treatment table.

'Good morning, Evelyn. Busy night?' said George as he walked in.

'Ah, George, you're just in time to watch this fellah die,' replied his colleague as he reached for a towel. His South African accent had softened little during his years at medical school in England.

'What happened to him?' asked George, shutting the door behind him.

'Found in the street, cracked skull, rather messy. Looks like he'd been in some kind of fracas. Stank of alcohol until he was cleaned up. These people are worse than kaffirs. The sooner I get home the better. And it wouldn't rain all the time either.' Evelyn Farquharson was nearly a decade younger than George, but cynicism had found him at an early age.

George looked across at the patient. 'You don't hold out much hope, I mean for our friend here?'

'No, he's on his last legs. He drifted in and out of consciousness and rambled on at the nurse for a while, but he's getting weaker and weaker. "Totsiens" as they say in Afrikaans. Goodbye and adieu.'

George moved further into the room. 'You know, I think I recognise him. I've seen him on the streets hereabouts. He engaged me in conversation once on the tram. Took an interest in my family.'

Evelyn huffed his disapproval. 'I'd have told him to mind his own business. Not that I'd be seen dead on a tram. They ought to keep these people separate.'

George responded while studying the dying man's bearded face. 'He was surprisingly well spoken – well, there was something unusual about his accent. Oh I remember. He said he'd spent time in America. A travelled man, not uneducated. I recall thinking there was something familiar about him but couldn't place it. Do we know who he is?'

Evelyn pointed over to a desk. 'He didn't seem sure of his name, but we found that stuff in his pockets.'

George picked up the articles one by one. There was a chainless silver pocket watch inscribed, 'Thomas, with all my love, Mary.' A folded letter was addressed to a Mr Thos Ramsden and within it were two slightly battered photographs, both mounted on card. The first showed a beautiful young woman, with dark hair and pale eyes, holding an infant girl, perhaps two years old. She was equally attractive, but there was something odd about the pose and the expression of the woman, presumably the mother. She looked ill at ease, uncomfortable holding the child, almost resentful. George moved the second picture to the front and his expression slipped from contemplation to shock.

It was a picture he had grown up with.

It had lived in drawer in his childhood home, only brought out when his late mother had guests. And there she was, frozen in time before he was born, and surrounded by his own youthful brothers and sisters, a family from which he was now estranged thanks to his success and their resentment. And there was another figure in the photograph, someone George had never known, but felt he knew nonetheless, his own father.

George looked again at the hollow, barely breathing face lying in the centre of the room. He took away the unkempt whiskers and ravages of time and poverty. It was the same man.

Epilogue

It came to her in a dream.

At least she assumed that was how it had arrived into her head. The image was certainly there when she was brushing her teeth that morning. She couldn't be sure of its truth, but when she checked her horoscope over breakfast it advised taking prompt action on her intuitions. She got dressed and headed for the door.

Two hours and three buses later, Betty Ramsbottom was back in Blackwell Holme. She suspected the journey would have much quicker in the days of steam branch lines and electric tramways. But progress and economics had long ago lifted the rails, and she now stood at what had been the old tram terminus by the village school. Looking back down the winding road, there was evidence of widening and corners being rounded so that the single track could climb through the ribbon of terraces and mills. From here onwards, the contours steepened and would have halted the engineers in their advance. In this, at least, rubber tyres and diesel engines had the edge, and Betty turned to watch the brightly coloured single-decker she had arrived on disappear over a grey-green moorland crest.

The pause was brief and Betty made her way towards the old chapel at her most rapid pace, impatient to see if the expedition had been a foolish mistake. She walked past the house-like building with its oddly positioned windows towards the burial ground at its rear, and started up the cobbled, cambered path until she reached the Ramsbottom family grave with its ornate classical pediment. But it was not that memorial she had come to see, and she kept going.

Jane had emailed the final results of her investigation: the full story of Thomas and his return from America still living under his new name. And as she read it in